Longing for Home

THE MOMOPOLY SERIES
BOOK ONE

DR. KAREN S. HUTCHINS

Print ISBN-13: 978-1-737-8460-2-4

eBook ISBN-13: 978-1- 737-8460-3-1

Cover by GetCovers

Published by Walking With God

Peace Of Heaven Ranch, West Plains

Scripture taken from the New King James Version®. Copyright © 1982 by Thomas Nelson. Used by permission. All rights reserved.

This book has been produced in association with Above The Sun, LLC, which is on a mission to help authors release heaven through their authentic books. For author coaching or publishing advice, learn more at https://abovethesun.org.

This novel is a work of fiction. Names, characters, places, and incidents are either products of the author's imagination or used fictitiously. All characters are fictional, and any similarity to people living or dead is purely coincidental.

Contents

Acknowledgments

Thank you to all those who have been such an encouragement to me while writing the Momopoly Series, especially my husband and son. Special thanks go out to my beta readers:

Lyn Dickerson, Marilyn Drewlow, Harriet Kadoun, Althea Weidkamp and Jeanne Sexton-Brown.

You have helped this series become a success!

One

"Ha-ha! Go to jail! Go directly to jail! Do not pass Go. Do not collect $200.00!" Nathan cheered good-naturedly at his mother's plight.

Lindsay put on her most dramatic face as she slid her top hat token to the corner of the Monopoly board, 'behind the bars.' It was her husband's favorite game on game night, and they had made a point of honoring him by playing it often since his death, usually on Wednesday after church. Tom had been a good father. Even when she was working the night shift at the Manor, he and Nathan would play without her.

Nathan happily celebrated her incarceration, but when she finally earned her way out of jail, he slipped into a slump. The coming weekend would mark two years since the car accident that took Tom away from them. While she wanted to preserve his memory for Nathan, any game tucked away in the closet appealed to her more than Monopoly. Tonight, she was wondering if Nathan felt the same way.

He didn't act like his heart was in the game. She had just reminded him it was his turn, and then it was only after a deep breath escaped him that he finally acknowledged her. He had quickly reverted to pondering anything other than the game. What was he thinking about?

"Earth to Nathan." Lindsay wiggled her fingers playfully in front of his face, hoping to get a smile out of him. Was he thinking about his dad? Probably. And who was she kidding? It was hard for her, too, but although these weekly Monopoly games helped her, they could be making things harder for Nathan.

"Oh, sorry, Mom." After blinking a few times, he reached lazily for the dice.

"Hey, Bud, what's going on?" Lindsay leaned forward to feel his forehead. "Are you feeling okay?" she asked.

"What? Oh yeah, Mom. I'm fine," he replied and shook her hand away as he took his turn. This was not like her son. What was going on? They played in silence for another few minutes, and Lindsay surmised that neither one of them was enjoying it.

"Nathan," she said softly. "We don't have to play tonight if you don't feel like it. Do you want to play something else? Do you want to call it a night? Watch TV?"

"Mom," he said, "why do we always have to play this game?" His question surprised her as much as the crack in his voice.

Lindsay slid out of her chair and sat next to him. "Oh, Bud," she whispered, sliding her arm around the back of his chair. "We don't have to. I thought you liked Monopoly. You and your dad used to play it even while I was at work. We don't have to play this game." She slowly began sliding the pieces into a pile at one end of the table. "We don't have to play anything."

"Yeah, I know." Nathan stopped talking abruptly and glanced away.

"Hey, what was that, kiddo?" Lindsay watched her son's face closely. He shook his head but stayed silent.

A strange feeling settled in Lindsay's stomach. Was Nathan keeping something from her? That wasn't like him. Had she imagined it? Lindsay's cell phone rang, startling her. Reaching for the phone, she made a mental note to revisit this conversation with Nathan later.

"Hi, Mom." Lindsay's eyes never left Nathan as she answered her mom's call, playing with a lock of his hair. "What's up?" Nathan pulled away and put the rest of the pieces away, appearing to ignore their conversation. Lindsay interjected sarcastically, "Now? You don't think ice cream would keep him awake?"

Nathan perked up, and an eager smile painted his face, eyebrows rising. At Nathan's instant mood improvement, she replied. "Okay, we'll be there in a minute." Lindsay stood and faced Nathan.

"That is, unless you don't want Gran's homemade strawberry rhubarb ice cream," she mused playfully as she ended her call. Nathan had the Monopoly game put away and his shoes on before she tucked her phone into her pocket and pulled her keys from the rack by the front door.

Nathan was quiet on the short trip to Gran's, and Lindsay tried to shake off her concern that he could be keeping secrets. She and Tom had worked to develop a level of trust that should have prevented that from happening. Longing settled in her stomach. How she wished Tom was here now to help her raise her preteen son. He always seemed to know the right things to say.

The minute she pulled into the driveway at Gran's, Nathan's door flew open. He bolted out of the car, bounding up the stairs to the porch, where Gran waited with open arms, waving the ice cream dipper in one hand.

"I'll scoop!" Nathan swiped the scoop from Gran's hand in the midst of a hug and ran toward the kitchen as Lindsay embraced Gran. Lindsay was relieved at the change in his mood.

"I hope I'm not keeping you from your homework, young man." Gran passed three ice cream dishes to her grandson.

"Nope," Nathan said. "We were just playing Momopoly—I mean, Monopoly."

Momopoly? Where did that come from? He hadn't called it Momopoly for ages. His mood had improved so much since Gran's call, that Lindsay decided to let it go until she watched his face plummet as he mentioned the game. But now, he was immediately distant again as he slid the ice cream bowls toward her and Gran.

"How about a quick game of Dominoes?" Gran asked with a wink at Lindsay. Nathan's eyes instantly brightened, and he nodded vigorously, catching Lindsay's eye for approval. Lindsay chuckled, nodding, and Gran headed to the game cupboard. An hour later, as Nathan picked up the dominoes, Lindsay and her mom cleaned in the kitchen.

"I'm worried, Mom," Lindsay whispered. "Something

feels off with Nathan. I feel like he's hiding something from me."

Arlene comforted her. "That's not like him, sweetie. Just give him some time. He'll come around." Nathan's appearance in the doorway ended any further conversation.

Lindsay spoke. "Hey, kiddo. You 'bout ready to head home?"

"Sure." Back to the happy-go-lucky 12-year-old she knew and loved. She decided to take her mom's advice... for now.

* * *

Back at home, Lindsay listened for Nathan to turn off the shower and get his pajamas on. When she heard the familiar squeak of him jumping into bed, she walked across the hall and tapped on his door. *Lord, how do I get him to talk to me?* "Bud?"

"Come on in, Momma." He scooted toward the middle of his bed, and Lindsay sat beside him, both leaning back against the headboard.

"Ready for prayers, kiddo?" Lindsay whispered. She had been watching, or more accurately, listening, to Nathan's prayers becoming more confident and more relaxed one day at a time, but tonight his prayer wasn't as confident as she expected.

It's me, Jesus. Thank you for letting us go to Gran's for ice cream tonight. It was nice to hear Mom laugh again. Amen.

Lindsay hugged her son tightly, but the knot in her throat wouldn't allow her to say much in reply. "Thank you, Bud. I love you to the moon—"

"And back," he finished.

"Sweet dreams." Her voice cracked as she slid off his bed. She leaned over and kissed the top of his head and quickly returned to her room across the hall, leaning back against the closed door as the tears fell.

T he thunder crashed through Lindsay's thoughts like the cymbal at the end of a symphony, pulling her out of her thoughts of Nathan. Her attention was brought back to her work when Richard clapped his hands and shouted with glee, "That one hit its mark!"

As she turned around, she saw what she expected to see—her elderlies: Richard in a recliner, Margie in her wheelchair as close to him as she could get. Another dear white-haired lady, across the room in her wheelchair, was wringing her hands in fear of the storm. Her nervous murmurs touched Lindsay's heart. She walked across the sunroom and knelt beside her chair, lovingly rubbing her hand along her back.

"The storm's letting up, dear. Try not to fret." Lindsay stood and, one by one, took note of each of these cherished residents. Some of the residents enjoyed the infrequent storms. Lindsay watched as her quiet one sat in an easy chair with her walker nearby. Her eyes were closed, but her foot gently tapped to the melody that, because of her condition, others could see but only she could hear. Norman sat staring out the window, a frown deepening the lines on his weathered face. Lindsay wondered that he might be remembering the wife and two youngest daughters that he lost in the fire. She was soon proven wrong.

"If that rain doesn't stop soon, we're gonna lose that wheat." Norman's son Steven still farmed a large part of the family homestead. He came to visit every Sunday and shared the latest calamity that only lifelong farm families can truly appreciate. Lindsay was frequently tempted to ask Steven to choose happier events to share with his dad.

"You should have already had that wheat done!" Opal barked at Norman. She spun her wheelchair around and nearly ran Lindsay over in the process. Opal had farmed with her husband, Edwin, before they arrived at the Manor. Their kids weren't interested in running the farm. Edwin farmed as long as he was physically able to, then they sold the farm and moved into the Manor, putting an end to their farm life. Edwin had never recuperated emotionally from the loss of his livelihood and died the first year they moved to the Manor. Sadly, Opal's deep-seated anger was directed at Edwin often, but in her reality, Norman frequently represented Edwin.

In the relative quiet of the storm outside, Lindsay's thoughts strayed from the task at hand. As much as both Lindsay and Nathan enjoyed Gran's homemade ice cream, Lindsay was disappointed that her mom's invitation had interrupted their conversation. She couldn't bring herself to bring it up again, and she knew she needed to. But Nathan's prayer was what had burned itself into her heart. He was suffering for her, and she was hurting for him. *Lord, how do we get back to ourselves?* They used to share everything. Now she knew he was hiding something.

The antique grandfather clock in the hall chimed 1:30, signaling social hour and bringing Lindsay's thoughts back to the present. There was a subtle change in the atmosphere in the room as the residents realized snack time was approaching. Lindsay helped Norman to his feet and arranged his walker. He quietly started toward the dining room, and Richard joined him, gently pushing Margie's wheelchair. The other residents maneuvered their wheelchairs behind them. They formed their hierarchy, as this was generally the order in which their little parade rolled any time they went anywhere as a group. Once in the dining room, Lindsay helped her co-worker, Crystal, get the residents situated with their coffee and snacks.

"What are we having today, dear? Are we having scones? I do love blueberry scones." In her excitement, this normally quiet-spoken woman could be heard above the echoing noises of the dining room.

"I think it's carrot cake today. Smells good, doesn't it?" Lindsay poured her coffee and stirred in the cream as Crystal served the carrot cake.

When everyone was settled and enjoying their cake, Lindsay sat down and took a break, studying the people who had become her second family over the last two years. What stories they had to tell. It had taken nearly a year for some of the ladies to open up to Lindsay and Crystal.

With the tragedies and hard lives that had brought them here, that was understandable.

Norman was a quiet man, while Richard had been an easy talker from day one. Wherever Richard was, Margie wasn't too far away. They had known each other before their Manor lives, and he sensed what she wanted without her saying a word. That was good because she had gone silent months ago. Margie's beauty was now hidden by the years, but her clear blue eyes spoke volumes. Grace sat nearby, quietly enjoying her cake, gently swaying as if a song were playing in her head.

Social hour also marked the shift change for the Manor. Lindsay was glad to see that the storm had subsided. She clocked out and grabbed her keys, tapping her goodbye as she passed the counter on her way across the Commons to the parking lot. It was Thursday. She decided she would swing by China King for takeout after picking Nathan up from school. As Lindsay pulled out of the parking lot, she grabbed her phone to call her mom.

Arlene answered on the first ring and spoke without even a hello. "Your brother's in trouble again," Lindsay's heart twisted. Her brother, Ben, was still struggling with his divorce, although it had been two years. He had been in and out of jail, what was it, three times now? Nothing major yet, but things were escalating.

"Hello to you, too, Mom." Lindsay worked to keep her voice light. "What is it this time?"

Her mom's voice was heavy with heartbreak. "He called Janet last night after he'd been drinking again. She told him she was going to get a restraining order against him. All he wants is to see his daughter. Can't she see that?"

Lindsay bit the inside of her cheek as she flipped on the turn signal. After taking a deep breath, she spoke with as much understanding as she could muster. "I'm sure she knows that, Mom, but think about it. He never calls her when he's the calm, loving Ben you and I know. He only calls her when he's nearly three sheets to the wind and angry. I wouldn't want Nathan to have seen Tom when he was like that, would you?" Lindsay paused. "Where is he now?"

"He's here, nursing a hangover. He called Janet from his cell phone on his way out there last night to see her. He's lucky he wasn't pulled over. At least he was smart enough to turn around and come here instead of pushing it. It was too late to call last night, and I didn't want to bother you at work. There wasn't anything you could do anyway." Arlene's voice trailed off into helplessness.

Lindsay gripped the steering wheel harder than necessary as she made the right turn onto the street next to Nathan's school. Her poor mother shouldn't have to raise Ben all over again. "It might be better if he had got pulled over," Lindsay said under her breath, then hoped Mom hadn't heard it. "Anyway, Mom, I'm going to run by for Chinese food. Shall I get enough for all of us and bring it over? I can try to talk to him." Lindsay wasn't sure Ben would want to hear what she had to say, but she would drum up some compassion before she got there. Her heart truly did cry for what he was going through.

"Sure, sweetie, that sounds good. Would you mind getting me one of those California rolls I like?" Mom asked.

"Of course, Mom. I wouldn't think of bringing you

Chinese food without them." Lindsay shook her head. "See you in a bit."

Lindsay took a deep breath and released the last of her tension as she rounded the corner at the recently remodeled Madison Middle School. She reset her bad attitude, refusing to allow her own emotions to affect her son.

Three

Nathan and his friend, Alex popped out of the school doors laughing, backpacks bouncing along as they ran. She heard their voices as she rolled down her window. Nathan's smile broadened as he left his friend behind and glanced across the street to the corner where she always waited for him. His smile always brought out the best in her, and the burden in her heart lifted. Had she imagined things last night? After Tom passed away, she kept watching for signs that it affected Nathan in a bad way. But in this moment, seeing his joy, she thanked God that He had allowed them both to heal. His excitement spilled over as he jumped into the seat next to her and fastened his seat belt, chattering excitedly.

"Hi, Bud! Can you take a breath, say hello, and start over?" Lindsay considered the change in Nathan over the past couple of months. He was now a little man, nearly a teenager and growing up fast. His dad's death was still evident in his countenance, but there were more shining memories of late that revealed his old, joyful self.

"Sorry. Hi, Mom. Alex's birthday is Saturday, and they're having a whole weekend bash! Can I go, please?" As his excitement grew, he talked faster with every word.

"A weekend bash?" Lindsay queried but secretly hoped the word didn't carry the same meaning as it had in her teenage years. She wasn't looking forward to his next birthday when he would become a teenager.

"Yeah! We're s'posed to go to his house for pizza and video games tomorrow right after school, then Saturday to McDonald's for breakfast and then skating and then to the ranch to ride horses, then a bonfire and hot dogs for supper. We might even get to rope some calves. Whatya think, Mom? Can I go?"

Lindsay delayed her response as she pulled out into traffic. It could be just the thing, to keep Nathan's thoughts away from the anniversary this weekend. The second anniversary of Tom's death wasn't a date she wanted to dwell on herself, let alone watch this sweet boy struggle through it as well. So far, he hadn't mentioned it, but that didn't mean he hadn't thought about it.

"I don't see why not." She waited for the celebratory cheers to settle before she continued. "Let me call Alex's mom and work out the details. Home Saturday, right? So you'll make Sunday School?"

"Aw. Mom, can't I miss Kingdom Kidz just this once? Everybody else is staying until Sunday." Nathan's voice was nearly a whine.

"We'll see. I'll talk to Teri. How many other boys are going?" Lindsay attempted to rekindle Nathan's excitement. As she semi-listened to his answer of four, a plan formed in her mind and continued to work itself out as she pulled into the garage. She fumbled with her keys and unlocked the door while Nathan waited impatiently behind her.

"Hop up to the counter and start your homework. We're going to Gran's house for supper," Lindsay said, tapping the counter. After the joy she saw in Nathan last night, she couldn't wait to get him there tonight. Even if it may be overshadowed a bit by Ben's drama.

Nathan playfully displayed a hop and quickly pulled his books out of his backpack. He loved to spend time with Gran and would often rush through anything to be able to see her as soon as possible. It was the perfect motivator.

As Nathan studied, Lindsay made his peanut butter sandwich and automatically cut it into four pieces. She put three on the plate in front of him. Nathan eyed the sandwich and then looked up at her with a grin.

"I love you, Mom," Nathan said, and Lindsey's heart melted. "But why do you still steal one-fourth of my sandwich? That's how you helped me learn my fractions. But we're not on those anymore. Now we're doing decimals."

Lindsay chuckled. "I love you, too. So, how much would I be taking if I gave you half of this piece back?" He thought for a minute before he answered.

"But we're not in fractions anymore, Mom. I don't need to know that one." He smiled as he lowered his head deep into his math book.

"Oh, yeah, you're not getting away with that, Bud," she teased. "You could need it next week, then you'd be ahead of the class."

"I'm already ahead of the class. You would be stealing one-eighth, and you would still be hungry." He joked.

She smiled as he went back to his work. "Good job. So, if you're into decimals, what percentage is one-fourth?"

"Let me think. My teacher said a quarter is one-fourth of a dollar and that's 25%. Right?" His beaming face cheered her heart.

"You're so smart, Nathan," Lindsay said as she turned to tidy up the kitchen. The morning dishes had been rinsed, but now she put them in the dishwasher and wiped off the counter. As Nathan worked on his math, Lindsay reached for the phone and called Teri.

Two of the boys who would be attending the weekend bash were already active in Kingdom Kidz, although they missed a Sunday here and there. Teri was a member, too, but because she had missed recently, she didn't know about the festivities happening this Sunday.

When Lindsay explained that Fun Fest was a new spring outreach the church was holding, Teri was thrilled to go along with Lindsay's last-minute adjustment to the Birthday Bash. In fact, Teri told Lindsay it was the perfect way to wind up the birthday weekend. Teri took Lindsay up on her offer to call the other mothers and set it up. All they had to do was to be sure each boy brought swim trunks and a towel to the sleepover. Then she would call Pastor Stephen to alert him to the increase in numbers. She saw Nathan close his math book as she finished her last call.

"Alright, kiddo," Lindsay said. "It's all set. Now let's go to Gran's." Lindsay swallowed, praying she was making the right decision.

Four

Everything Lindsay chose from China King for their impromptu family dinner was delicious. Lindsay was glad everyone was focused on food, making it easier for her to bridle her tongue, when she wanted to chastise Benny for his continued poor choices. By the time dinner was finished, her anger had subsided into a painful position of watching her baby brother go through such heartache.

"Benny, I want you to think about a couple of things." They had filled themselves with beef and broccoli, and sweet and sour chicken, and did a quick cleanup with to-go containers. Gran and Nathan shared a glance that told everyone what they would be doing for the next hour or so. Dominoes had been a part of their lives since Lindsay's dad died and they had to move into town. She picked up an ivory domino and rubbed it between her thumb and forefinger, remembering how many conversations had taken place at this table.

Lindsay and Benny left them at the domino table and

slipped out to the backyard tree where they had played as teens. They had both been shy as kids, but Benny painfully so. They had signals that even Arlene hadn't caught on to. One of them would nod toward the crooked tree and the other would wink. Whether they would go out at the same time or not, eventually they would both arrive at the tree.

Lindsay often prayed silently as soon as she had winked at Benny, asking God to lead their conversations. She wondered if Benny did the same. Tonight, they stood shoulder to shoulder, looking at Lindsay's roughly engraved initials with Tom's inside a heart, and Benny's "Ben was here." They each took their perches in the crooked old tree, where they could talk without facing each other. They had always shared childhood secrets better that way.

"I know you're hurting, and I want to help you any way I can." She paused to gather her thoughts. "You just can't keep hurting Mom like this—or yourself." Lindsay felt a peace come over her even as the tears formed at the back of her eyes. She stopped thinking so much about her words and let the Lord lead as she had so many times in her dealings with her elderlies at the Manor.

"I know, Sis. I want to change." Benny's voice was so soft she could hardly hear him. "I really do, it's just so hard. I want to go back to having my family the way it was, and I know we can't go back."

"No, Benny," she said seriously. "You can't go back. You can only work at making a new future."

"I have to." Benny sniffed before he continued. "I miss having my family, so I'll do whatever it takes to get them back, whatever that looks like."

His words broke her heart, but she was relieved that he had already accepted that a change had to be made. "That's a good goal, Benny. And Mom and I are behind you one hundred percent." She thought carefully before she continued. "I want you to think about two things."

"I'm listening." Benny's muffled voice told Lindsay how he positioned himself. He tucked his chin in his shirt, mirroring the time when he felt guilty after getting caught breaking the neighbor's window.

She softened her tone to match his. "There is a festival going on at church on Sunday." She sensed him stiffening as he stopped swinging his legs. "I know you've got a sour taste in your mouth about church," she went on, "but these people love you. They know what you've been through, what you're going through, and they're not judging you. They want to help. They think of you as a part of the family. Besides, Sunday isn't like a regular church service; it's Fun Fest. It'll be the perfect time for you to take part in the festivities, slip back in and not feel uncomfortable." She paused to catch her breath. "Besides, they'll have great food." She tried to lighten up a bit.

"What's the second thing?" he asked. It didn't escape her notice that he never answered her first request. She took a deep breath.

"There is a man I know who has a heart for helping hurting people like you. He's the community chaplain who brought me the news about Tom's death." She hurried on. "He recommended a good Christian counselor for me after Tom died. Counseling really helped me get past the initial shock and start living again. Even just a few months with her. It happened around the same time you and Janet—well, I was so wrapped up in my own grief that I didn't reach out to you as a big sister should have. I'm sorry, but I want to help you now if you'll let me." Lindsay realized her tears were dripping onto her sweatshirt. She waited, not sure if he was listening or crying with her.

"Okay, Sis." Then he was still. He neither spoke nor moved. Nor did she. For what felt like forever, the capsule they had shared for all their lives encompassed them in peace, unconditional love, grace, patience, compassion, and mercy.

The atmosphere had changed. They were no longer on opposite sides of an issue. They were both in need of healing. They needed each other. As Lindsay slipped out of the tree, her feet hit the ground with a thud within seconds of his. Then they truly were side by side as they looked at each other's tear-streaked faces and laughed, awkwardly at first. They hugged and headed back to the house, arm-in-arm. *Thank You, Lord.* Lindsay's heart rejoiced.

"I'm sorry, too," her brother whispered. "I didn't want to add to your troubles when Janet started cheating on me. I—yeah, I could use some help." They stood, each leaning on the strength of the other, just as they had in years past. Like when Dad died, and even before that when the bullies at school were becoming too much for Benny to handle. He had always been a shy, kind boy, and the bullies took advantage of his kindness. *His deployment had changed him so much,* Lindsay thought. *Can I ever get my baby brother back?*

"The Chaplain's name is Mark Thomas. He is a community chaplain and has a counseling office. I'll give you his number," she said as they continued toward the smell of peach pie coming from the kitchen.

Arlene stood as she saw them come in. "Don't you two have perfect timing! The pie just needs to cool a bit longer and we can have dessert." She studied their faces discreetly. Seeing the peace there, she felt content as she reached for the dessert plates.

Nathan finished putting up the dominoes and joined them in the kitchen. "Sweet! Are we having ice cream or whipped cream on top?" He asked as he opened the refrigerator.

"Whichever you want, kiddo. I have both." Gran smiled at Nathan, then glanced at Benny, and her countenance fell. Lindsay's heart stung. Over the last few months, Gran had confided in her how much she missed her other grandchild, Melody. Her prayer was that Janet would eventually understand that Melody needed to see her daddy as much as Benny needed to see his daughter. Lindsay turned her attention back to the pie. For now, the only thing she could do was keep praying and remember to let God be God. Her mom had taught her that. She just had to remember it.

Five

Benny and Nathan finished doing the last few dishes while Mom and Lindsay sat with their tea on the porch swing out front. They spoke in quiet tones so 'the boys' wouldn't overhear, but by the sounds of the laughing and joking going on in the kitchen, Lindsay wasn't too concerned. She told her mom that Benny had agreed to talk to Mark Thomas, and Mom's heartfelt tremendous relief at the news. As they sat in comfortable silence, Lindsay's thoughts drifted.

It was nice to hear Nathan joking with his uncle. She knew Nathan missed his dad and she was grateful for the influence of the men in his life: Pastor Stephen, Rob, the assistant in the Children's Department at church, and his baseball coach all had taken him under their respective wings. Besides, Nathan was good for Benny, too. When they were together, Lindsay could see glimpses of her pre-army brother.

Arlene smiled inwardly. "I'm so glad Mark decided to move to this area to set up his practice." Lindsay gently shook her head. She could feel Mom's sideways glance without even looking over at her.

"Yes, Mother." She grinned as Mom looked over at her with an innocent face.

"What? What did I say?" she asked, innocently. Lindsay knew her Mom thought her period of mourning Tom's death should be coming to an end. But Lindsay wasn't ready to even think about dating, and she certainly wasn't looking forward to merging a third person into the tender relationship she and Nathan were rebuilding.

She was retraining herself to spend more time with Nathan after work, playing games. However, considering their recent conversation over Monopoly, that may have to be revisited. She had worked her way from a hovering mom to enjoying TV with him as he and Tom had done, especially the *Alaska Life* reruns.

Lindsay and her mom heard the screen door slam out back and knew that the boys were digging out the gloves to play catch. She stood and reached for Mom's teacup, and Mom stood as well. "You know, honey, no one would judge you if you started dating. Everyone in town just wants you to be happy." Lindsay heard the echo of the words she had just spoken to Benny.

"I know, Mom. I'm just not ready yet. It's not even been two years—not quite. I don't think Nathan is ready either. We're okay. No need to rush, is there?" She looked out on the porch. "Mom, don't you still miss Daddy?" Lindsay missed her dad. Was Mom thinking about him, too? Lindsay's dad had died twelve years ago, just before Nathan was born. He had been healthy right up until her wedding, and then suddenly every breath became a struggle. She was amazed that Mom had been so strong throughout his two-year illness.

"Of course, I do, dear. It isn't something you get over. You just get through it, but it does get a little easier." Mom turned to face her, smiling.

Lindsay slipped in the front door before her mom could continue the conversation. After placing the cups in the sink, Lindsay poked her head out the back door.

"Ten minutes, Nathan. We need to stop and buy a birthday gift for Alex." She watched her son playing catch with her brother and just for a moment, it was Tom throwing the ball back to Nathan. She gave herself a mental shake as she felt the teardrop slip down her cheek. Her mom came up behind her and slipped her arm around her waist.

"I know you still miss Tom, sweetie. That will never go away. It will get easier, I promise. But I won't rush you. I'm behind you one hundred percent every step of the way. You know that, right?" Mom sniffed as she finished her sentence.

"Of course, I do. Thanks, Mom. You've been great. I just need some time. It's hard to put Tom's death behind me when they haven't solved the case yet." Darkness fell over Arlene's features at Lindsay's words. It was a subject they didn't discuss much, but Lindsay prayed for often. The police suspected foul play from the beginning, but every lead brought them to a dead end. They stood in the doorway, arm-in-arm, Lindsay towering over her mom by a couple of inches yet feeling like a little girl again. Together, they could look forward to wherever God led. *Lord, give us strength.* Both women prayed silently.

Lindsay pulled into the school loading zone and got out of the car to help Nathan gather his backpack, bedroll, and duffel bag. He assured her he could pack it all himself and have everything he would need for a few days of bucking broncos. He had packed his cowboy boots, which were too big, and his cowboy hat, which was too small. Nathan insisted on wrapping Alex's gift himself and chose brown wrapping paper on which he had painted horses.

Lindsay was a bit disappointed that she wasn't going to be able to frame this artwork. Nathan had been a doodler since he was old enough to hold a marker, but his talent had really started to shine in the last few months. He frequently had a sketch pad nearby, and whenever they talked, that's usually what he was doing. It didn't bother her. She listened better when she wasn't looking at a face. She got in trouble enough in grade school for doing the same thing, so she understood.

She handed him Alex's gift, gave him a wink and a quick rub on his shoulder. She passed him the note permitting him to ride home that afternoon with Alex's Mom, Teri, so Lindsay wouldn't get her goodnight hug from her young man. They had decided that hugs were reserved for home or Gran's, behind closed doors, where they were not in view of "the guys".

"Have fun, Bud. I'll see you Sunday." She teared up as he took the initiative and fell into her arms with a quick but hearty hug. He was growing up fast, but he would always be her baby boy.

"Love ya." Nathan spoke loudly as he turned toward school. And he was off. Lindsay sighed as she got back in the car and headed for the Manor. She tuned the radio to her favorite Christian station and relaxed into the twenty-minute drive to work. *All alone, all weekend.*

How was she going to keep her mind occupied? She had a couple of chapters to finish reading in her novel, and she hadn't studied her Sunday School lesson yet. So that could take a couple of hours, and there was that movie she'd bought that she hadn't watched yet. It was one Nathan wouldn't care about, so she could watch that tonight. That took care of tonight. What about the next two days?

Her day at work was a routine Friday, and she was kept busy enough that her thoughts never strayed too far from her residents. She was still plagued by her incomplete conversation with Nathan earlier in the week. Why did he no longer want to play Monopoly? She was on her way home, envisioning an appropriate time to bring the subject up again, when her cell phone rang. She pushed the speaker on her phone and answered Benny's call.

"Hey, Sis. I need your help." Benny's voice sounded upbeat, but she held her breath and waited. As if reading her, he rushed right on. "Don't panic. It's nothing bad." She breathed as he chuckled. "I'm sorry I've been giving you and Mom so much trouble. But I called your community chaplain, Mark, and we're going to meet at Catfish Charlie's tonight, and since Nathan told me you were batching it, I was wondering—well, I'd just feel better if you'd come with me."

"Are you sure?" Lindsay wasn't sure she wanted to know all the details of what had appeared to be a nasty break-up. "I would think you would want to meet with him by yourself."

"Maybe later, but not this first time. I'm nervous about talking to a Christian Counselor about all my screw-ups." His voice trailed off. "Please?"

"Sure, Benny, I'll be there. What time?" They made plans for Benny to pick her up at 7, so she decided to stop by the gym for a short workout. She hadn't gone for a while, and as sweat dripped down the sides of her face, she was reminded how it was such therapy for her to focus on her muscles instead of her emotions.

She showered at the gym and dressed, wrapping the towel like a turban around her long, wet hair and jogged to the car. She still had plenty of time to blow it dry and style it at home and come up with an outfit to wear. Lindsay was torn. She really didn't want to have a pity party alone. It was a nice change of plans. She could watch the movie tomorrow night, order a pizza, and eat the whole thing by herself. If she could keep her mind on the movie instead of worrying about Nathan, maybe she would enjoy an evening alone!

Six

What to wear? Catfish Charlie's wasn't a fancy place, but Lindsay didn't feel like wearing jeans, in case she ate too much at the all-you-can-eat bistro. She hadn't been there since before Tom died. She chose her knee-length denim skirt and a cream-colored pullover sweater. She looked at the woman in the full-length mirror on the door, slipped the costume jewelry around her neck, and added the matching earrings.

This was one of Tom's favorite looks on her. She pulled off the necklace and the sweater and went back to the closet. She carefully folded the sweater and placed it back on the shelf, opting instead for the dusty rose lightweight cashmere set. She changed her earrings to match. She finished her hair, applied light makeup, and returned to the mirror. Not too dressy, casual, and comfortable. She didn't look like she was trying to impress anyone. The doorbell rang as she was slipping on her boots. With one boot still waiting at the stairs, she opened the door.

"New style?" Benny said awkwardly, motioning at her feet. He was more nervous than she imagined. "Just kidding, Sis. You look classy as always."

"Thanks." She sat down on the step and finished dressing her feet, watching him pace across the foyer. "Are you doing okay?"

"Sure. Why wouldn't I be?" He winked at her and motioned toward the door. She linked her arm through his, lovingly.

Lindsay comforted him. "Just breathe. Mark's meeting with you to help you through this. Let him. Don't think he's going to judge you, Benny. He just wants to be a friend and a sounding board. And if you're not comfortable with him, he can find someone else for you, like he did me. He really is a nice guy." As Lindsay finished her words, she noticed Benny's cheerful expression didn't quite reach his eyes, but he appeared to breathe a little easier.

When they pulled into the parking lot, Lindsay saw the posters advertising Karaoke night and felt a slight inside tremor. Although Tom claimed to have no singing voice, he loved to hear her sing. Lindsay's memory had already taken her to the last time she and Tom had decided to come here for a date night. She hadn't been here since that night. She stuffed her butterflies further into her insides and walked toward the entrance with Benny.

As they neared the rough-cut wood double doors, she recognized Mark's deep voice. "If I didn't know better, I'd think you two were brother and sister, maybe even twins." He teased.

Although they were nearly two years apart, people often thought Lindsay and her younger brother were twins. Both had thick brown hair and blue eyes that changed colors with their moods. Right now, Benny's eyes were gray. That told Lindsay he was scared.

They exchanged smiles, and Lindsay officially introduced them. Inside, they were escorted to the bar to wait for a table. Even with reservations, Charlie's had a reputation for being a bit slow in the service department, but the food was well worth the wait. As they waited at the bar, Lindsay ordered a glass of lemonade, while Mark and Benny ordered a pop. Lindsay was pleasantly surprised at Benny's restraint in not ordering a beer. They had taken their first sip when the hostess motioned to them and seated them at a table along one wall. *A new touch*, Lindsay thought. This side used to be filled with booths, and tables filled what was now apparently a dance floor.

They ordered, and the conversation felt stilted as they ignored the elephant in the room. "How have you been doing, Lindsay?" Mark expertly steered the conversation away from the issue, giving Ben time to relax. They were quiet while the waitress brought a basket of hush puppies with sauces.

"I'm doing pretty well." Lindsay toyed with the menu rather than meet his eyes. "You know, two steps forward and one step back. More good days than bad. I'm happy with Nathan's progress." She popped the last bite of a hushpuppy in her mouth.

"I'm glad to hear that," Mark replied, ever the counselor and friend. "But he's going to take his lead from you. If he thinks you are healing and moving forward, he'll follow suit, for the most part. What has it been, two years now?" He took a drink and leaned back in his seat, casually facing her.

"Tomorrow." She felt like her breath had been whisked away. She cleared her throat so she could speak. "Yeah, two years tomorrow."

"Oh man, I'm sorry, Sis." Benny's voice was sincere. "I didn't realize it was this weekend. If I'd have thought—"

"No, Benny, it's okay. With Nathan at this weekend's birthday bash, this works out well. I wasn't looking forward to being alone anyway." She sat back and paused as the waiter brought their salads. "I need to make a new memory here anyway." Her voice went quiet again.

"If I may ask, was this a favorite place for you and Tom?" Mark asked gently.

Lindsay shook her head. "Not really a favorite. It was just one of the places Tom liked. I haven't been here since he passed." She stopped short of sharing the karaoke part.

"Oh, that's right, I forgot." Benny broke in. "You used to sing karaoke here!" Lindsay shook her head and rolled her eyes sideways at him. "Oh, I'm sorry." Benny sunk a bit in his chair.

"I am, too, Lindsay," Mark carried the ball. "Those firsts can catch you off guard. But I promise you I won't twist your arm to sing for us. Is it Nathan's birthday?" Nice change of subject, Mark.

"No, one of his friends. They're making a whole weekend of it! Video games, pizza, horseback riding, maybe even some calf-roping, or so he tells me. The whole bunch of them are going to be at the Fun Fest at church Sunday, only Nathan doesn't know that part yet." She smirked.

Mark nodded and bit into the crisp battered, deep-fried catfish the waitress had just placed in front of them. "Hmm," Lindsay said, digging into her steaming serving, smiling to herself. It was delicious, even better than she remembered. After refills of fish were brought, they slowed their eating and resumed talking.

"Ben, how long were you married?" Mark asked. Lindsay made note of the tenderness that subtly came into Mark's voice as he gently led Benny to share his story.

"Five years." Benny took a big gulp of his pop before he continued. "And it was great. Everything was great, at least I thought so, and then I got deployed." He took another bite giving himself a minute to think. Mark gently waited for more details. Another gulp. "I found out she cheated on me. I admit, I—uh—well, I didn't handle it well. She got defensive, I got mad and walked out. She filed. I thought I would have a chance to—I don't know."

She stayed quiet, except for the few times when Benny asked her to affirm his memory of the timing of certain events. Lindsay was surprised at the details Benny shared in her presence without being asked.

She caught Mark's gentle expression a few times and wondered if he was reassessing her mental health. He had brought her the news of Tom's death. Other than that, she had only talked to him a few times when his office was in Rutledge. He had referred her to a Christian counselor named Sarah, explaining that, as a rule, he didn't counsel women. Being a single unattached man, he preferred to avoid even the appearance of anything detrimental to her or his own reputation. After a few months, she and Sarah agreed that her spiritual strength was such that she could continue healing on her own with periodic check-ins. That had been a year and a half ago, and now she was feeling much more like herself.

The evening wasn't a long one, and Lindsay felt herself relaxing more and more. She even found herself tapping her foot and laughing at some of the silliness going on behind the microphone on stage. As the waitress came and cleared the plates, the conversation turned light again.

"Horseback riding?" Mark chuckled. "Where in the world do they do that around here?"

Lindsay explained that Alex's Uncle Joe had a small farm south of town, toward Davenport, with six horses and a decent-sized herd of cattle. Tomorrow's portion would be held there. "I'm okay with horseback riding"—Lindsay laughed—"but I do hope that the calf-roping these boys are doing is with a sawhorse with a wooden steer's head on it!"

"I hear that," Mark replied. "But I haven't been horseback riding in years, so I was kind of hoping there would be a public stable."

Benny spoke up. "You know, there is one. I just realized it. I turned around at the entrance of it the other night when I changed my mind about going to Rutledge. I don't know anything about it other than where it is. Fifteen to twenty miles out, close to our old house."

Lindsay watched as Benny's sharing of his memory of that night changed the expression on his face. Benny turned and explained the episode to Mark. "I realized how stupid it would have been for me to go on out there. I wasn't really drunk, but I was close enough. It would have just made matters worse." Benny's head hung in shame.

Mark's understanding nod spoke volumes. "That turnaround sounds like a wise move, Ben."

Benny agreed whole-heartedly and downed the last of his pop.

Mark did the same and turned to Lindsay as she was finishing her lemonade. "Would you care to go for a horseback ride tomorrow, Lindsay? We can check out this stable if we can find it." Lindsay realized her heart had agreed before her mind had a chance to step in. *Had she just agreed to go on her first date since Tom died?*

Seven

I t was Lindsay's turn to cover the Saturday morning shift, so she packed her jeans and boots in the back of her Jeep before she left for work. It was hard to keep her mind on work. Lindsay was going through the motions of caring for her charges and steering them to and from where they were supposed to be. She mindlessly helped Grace sit up on the side of the bed and brushed her white hair for her. She helped her button her blouse for her and turned to get her walker.

Lindsay allowed herself to feel a slight sense of anticipation. She loved horseback riding—she hadn't gone for years, and she was going with a person whose company she thought she would enjoy. A date, for the first time in two years. Suddenly, she heard a sliding sound behind her, followed by a crash and a significant moan. Grace had fallen while trying to walk from her bed to the bathroom by herself. She crashed into her nightstand, everything on top of it falling to the floor with her. Lindsay rushed to help her.

35

After the doctor checked Grace, Lindsay helped her back to bed, adjusting it to a more upright sitting position. Luckily, she was only bruised, but she was horribly embarrassed and frightened. After a few minutes with a cup of tea, a piece of cinnamon toast, and a quiet story from Lindsay, she relaxed into the television's morning talk show. Feeling properly guilty, Lindsay told her she would check back with her before she left for the day.

Lindsay stepped into the hall to tend to the other residents and greeted those who were leaving the dining room, having finished their breakfast. Betty waved her from her chair. "Is she okay, Miss Lindsay?" Her eyes were filled with tears.

"She has some ugly bruises, Betty. But Doc says she will be okay, dear. Don't fret. I'm sure she'd want a visitor if you're up to it. But if she's dozing, it would be best not to wake her just yet." Lindsay's words cheered her, and she rolled into Grace's room quietly.

Lindsay checked the roster to learn that several of her elderlies had gone on the Saturday outing to a craft show in Batesburg, snacks, and then the trip home. Her shift would be over before they returned. She walked down the hall to see how Opal was faring. As she entered the room, Opal sat mumbling in her wheelchair, facing the window. "Good morning, Opal. How was your breakfast?"

"Who could eat?" Opal grumbled. "I can't find Edwin anywhere. He's supposed to be here with me. Where did he go? And why didn't he take me with him?"

Lindsay took a deep breath. "Don't worry, dear. Some of the folks went on an outing, but they'll be back soon. He could be with them." Lindsay changed to diversion mode. "Are you hungry? Do you want to go back to the dining room? I'm sure we could find a snack for you to eat. Or would you like to go up front and read the paper?"

Lindsay was already pushing her wheelchair into the hall when Opal shook her head in frustration and mumbled, "Up front, I s'pose." Lindsay made the left turn at the nurses' station and grabbed the *Chronicle* off the sidebar on the way by. She parked Opal near the window as she laid the newspaper on the end table nearby.

The Manor was quiet on Outing Days. Lindsay poured herself a cup of coffee and sat across the room from Opal. Opal was an amazing woman when she was like this. She was caring, kind, and completely selfless when there was a person who needed her. But when Norman returned from his outing, she would go back to thinking he was Edwin, and she would read him the riot act for not taking her with him.

When the new wing opened, she planned to suggest to the manager, Mr. Foster, that they be billeted further apart. That wouldn't make a permanent difference, because the facility was small enough that they only had one dining room, but they could stagger their meals. It wasn't Lindsay's decision to make, of course, but she was always thinking about ways to make *her* elderlies more comfortable. Besides, Norman wasn't complaining. Having lost his sweet Miriam in the fire, it appeared they were filling each other's mutual voids in companionship.

Lindsay finished her coffee and walked over to the crafts area, setting up the table for their after-lunch activity. The volunteers would be here at 1:00, but she would have been relieved by then, and she would be on her way to the stables. She let her mind wander while she set out the placemats, paints, brushes, and small cups of water.

Could she even get on a horse anymore? It had been years. Long before she and Tom had married. She loved horses as a kid, but when they moved into town, she had to give up her beloved mare, Josie. Her thoughts drifted to her daddy. She still missed him terribly. She could still picture him coming in from checking the fences. Sometimes he would take the 4-wheeler. Occasionally, in the summer, he would saddle up Josie and his young gelding, Spook, and they would ride the fence line together. "Just checkin'," her dad would say. Sometimes they would talk, and other times they would ride along for hours in companionable silence.

She often thought about buying a little ranch and a couple of horses. Nathan would like that. Most of the money from Tom's life insurance was still in the bank. They could buy a little place when she was ready to make the break from the townhouse. This was the home that Tom had shared with her—the place where Nathan had been raised. No rush; they were okay where they were.

The doors burst open, and Melissa and the rest of the staff returned from the outing, bringing the rest of her elderlies with them. Norman, always in the lead, was followed by Richard pushing Margie's wheelchair. Faces, all flushed with excitement from fresh air and junk food, turned as if attached, to the small woman who sat near Opal, outwardly checking out their new housemate.

"Hello, everybody!" Richard steered Margie toward the puzzle table. As the conversation between these friends erupted, Lindsay slipped out to check on Grace before she clocked out. She didn't wake her as she was dozing, but she checked her pulse. Not very strong, but steady. Going back to the Commons, she asked Stacy to check in on Grace later. She broke into the conversation long enough to tell everybody she was leaving and wished them a "Sunny Sunday," as was their routine.

She spent a few minutes answering the normal Saturday questions of what her weekend plans were as she headed toward the time clock. She loved sharing her life with them. She knew they vicariously lived their lives through hers, so she didn't think of their interest as being nosy or intrusive. She shared Nathan's weekend bash plans, and eyebrows went up all around when she mentioned the ride she was about to go on.

Most had been residents when Tom died. But these loving folks thought it was preposterous for a "beautiful, smart young lady" like Lindsay to be raising her son by herself. Richard had even teased her about marrying her himself, but at the very least, matching her up with his son.

She eased out of the conversation as she went to her car and grabbed boots and jeans and went back in to change. She felt her heart stepping up its pace in anticipation. Going through the front Commons, she heard chuckles from the residents, along with well-meaning quips about going for a ride with "her new cowboy". She joked with them, telling them to behave, and went about her task, noticing a song forming in her head. It had been a long time since her heart had projected songs. She felt more like herself than she had in years. *Now if this feeling of contentment would only last.*

Eight

Lindsay pulled into the parking lot of Kit's Kitchen for lunch at 11:50 AM—ten minutes earlier than she and Mark had agreed the night before. She peeked into the mirror to touch up her lipstick before she exited the vehicle. As she approached the diner's door, she sensed someone coming up alongside her.

"Mrs. Davis?"

Lindsay turned to see a man coming towards her. He was about her age or a little younger, wore jeans and a sports coat, and looked a bit unkempt.

"Do I know you?" She hesitated and stepped back a bit. The man looked vaguely familiar, but she couldn't place him.

"Not really, ma'am. I used to do jobs for your husband now and then." She relaxed a little. "But I'm sure we were never introduced."

"Ok. How can I help you?" He stepped toward her, reaching for her arm. She stepped back again and crossed her arms in front of her, unease tightening her stomach.

"There's no need to be scared, Mrs. Davis. I just want to talk to you," he said, glancing around the parking lot. Fear made her muscles tense. *Had this man known she was going to be here? Had he been waiting for her? Had he followed her?* He glanced past her and hurriedly reached into his pocket. "But maybe this isn't a good time. You call me when you're ready."

He handed her a business card, turned and hurriedly walked away. She looked at the card trembling in her hand. 'Lucky's' was splashed in gaudy print across the card with a phone number and email address. On the back, in smaller font, was a bulleted list: Casino, Pawn Shop, Gun Repair, Jewelry—New and used, Private contractor.

Mark touched her elbow, and she jumped. She hadn't seen or heard him coming alongside her. "Hey, are you okay? Who was that?" She looked up at him, shaking her head, not quite able to answer. "Lindsay?" His voice intensified. "You're white as a sheet. Who was that? What did he say to upset you so?"

She hooked her arm through his and found her voice. "Let's go in. Then we can talk. I need to sit down."

"Of course." Mark touched her back lightly and he led her into the diner to a corner booth. As he handed her a menu from the rack on the table, the waitress greeted them. They both ordered coffee, and after the waitress had left, Lindsay explained the unusual encounter with the man in the parking lot.

"I overreacted. It was probably nothing. It was probably totally innocent." Lindsay's voice was trembling. Mark watched her, concern lining his features. "If he wants a job, maybe we could—he said he used to work for Tom now and then. He used to do jobs for him," Lindsay said breathlessly, still flipping the card around in her trembling hands.

"Are you going to call him?" Mark kept his observant eyes on her face. It still had not regained its color.

"I don't know. He said, 'when I'm ready,' so I don't know how to take that. What do you think?" Lindsay's hands still trembled as she stirred the cream into her coffee.

"I guess it wouldn't hurt to call him and ask what he meant. But I certainly wouldn't meet him anywhere alone, without me... I mean without someone else there. It does seem kind of seedy," he said as he looked again at the business card. "He appears to be quite a jack of all trades. 'Private contractor' could cover landscaping, yard work, construction, just about anything." Mark paused, watching Lindsay's reaction. "You could ask him what kind of work he did for Tom. What kind of work was Tom in, Lindsay? You never said. I mean if you don't mind talking about it."

The waitress discreetly interrupted to take their orders and left quickly, recognizing they were deep in conversation.

Lindsay answered, "He was an investment properties manager with Marcus, Brand, and Shield. He was an equal partner, but when he bought into the firm six years before he died, he never wanted his name to be associated with theirs. I have kicked myself so many times. I got distracted with Nathan and never asked him why."

Mark spoke when Lindsay took a drink. "Did he suspect them of something, do you think?"

Lindsay's thoughts raced back to the conversation she remembered. She had shared her deepest thoughts with

Tom. "Tom had admitted he hadn't known the partners well enough, and he should have pushed for more answers about them before he agreed to tie his name to theirs." Lindsay felt more and more comfortable allowing this man into their lives. They stopped their conversation as the waitress brought their lunch specials and refilled their coffee.

"I did tell the police about it all," she resumed, "but it never seemed to lead anywhere. Tom managed a lot of the partners' properties. That's how we got into our townhouse without having to be on the waiting list. The firm bought the complex and offered him the vacant unit, so we jumped on it. It was perfect—close to Nathan's school and not too far from the Manor. It's even close to Mom's."

Mark nodded, taking it all in. Then, Leanne Rimes' voice filled the room from the jukebox. "How Do I Live Without You" broke the intensity of the moment.

"I love this song," she said with a distracted expression.

Mark ventured a smile. "I'd love to hear you sing it sometime."

Lindsay felt the heat climb up her neck. It was one thing singing karaoke with Tom. "That would be scary." She chuckled nervously.

"Oh, come on, you have to be better than the girl with pink hair last night!" Mark teased.

Lindsay chuckled. "I don't know. The guy with the tweed jacket and striped pants may have outdone her." They ate in companionable silence throughout the meal. As they were nearly finished, Mark took a final sip of coffee, getting ready to leave. "Well, do you want to ride out to the stables with me?"

"Well, I—sure," Lindsay stuttered. "That sounds great."

Nerves ran high through Lindsay as they left the restaurant and climbed into Mark's truck. She looked back at her car as they left the parking lot, hoping she was making the right move by going forward with this horseback riding date. She caught her eyes roaming the parking lot, looking for an unkempt young man named Lucky.

Nine

Mark and Lindsay were still chatting as he pulled out of the parking lot and turned to drive through town. The conversation lulled as they turned onto the main highway heading east of town.

"Didn't you live out here as a kid?" Mark asked with a fond smile as though he really enjoyed hearing her talk.

"Yeah, we're coming up on our old place. My folks had a farm near here, but when Daddy got sick, we moved into town. Coming out this way always feels like I'm heading home."

Lindsay watched as the houses became fewer and further between and farmhouses scattered the hillsides. As she caught a glimpse of a realtor's sign next to a mailbox near the highway, her thoughts returned to the possibility of buying a small ranch. Was God telling her it was time to move on?

Lindsay broke the silence awkwardly. "I love these old farmhouses. Where were you raised?"

"I was raised in Davenport until my folks died. Then I

moved in with my Aunt Mavis to finish high school." His short answer told Lindsay he'd rather not talk about himself. "How old were you when you moved off the farm?" Yep. He'd rather not talk about himself.

"No, we're talking about you now," she joked. "And then?" She'd rather hear his story. After all, he already knew most of hers.

Mark chuckled. "After high school, and after the homestead in Davenport sold, I went to college in Springfield, then joined the Marines, then came back and went back to school." He got quiet, and she gave him the space to continue when he was ready. She wanted to get to know this man who had come back into her life.

"I don't usually—well, I made some mistakes along the way that I don't usually share with folks." He stared at the road. "You know, stupid stuff that I'm not very proud of."

"I understand, Mark." Lindsay spoke quietly. "We all made stupid choices growing up." When he didn't say anything more, Lindsay was concerned that he had withdrawn from the closeness they had already achieved. "You know, Mark, what we have lived through, whether by choice or not, makes us who we are."

"Hmm." He hesitated. "Who's the counselor here, anyway?" He teased nervously. "You're right, of course. I am grateful that some of those bad choices led me to the best decision I ever made. Especially, because they led me to the Lord and to my passion for helping broken people."

Mark straightened his shoulders and gripped the wheel a bit tighter before he continued. "When I went to graduate school after my discharge, my tuition was partially paid by the State Highway Patrol, Community

Relations Department. I agreed to do it. I was happy to repay their generosity by serving as Community Chaplain," Mark revealed, "but that meant I had to share a lot of bad news with people. As a Community Chaplain, I frequently get called in on death notifications. That was the least favorite part of my volunteer position, but it was one of the requests from my professor. That's how I came to be at your doorstep."

"I can't imagine how hard that would be," Lindsay shared as they turned off the highway. She was surprised that he continued so easily.

"I was back for about four years when I got the call that Tom's Dodge Charger had been found at the bottom of the cliff. I remember it because I always wanted a Charger." He stopped talking and just waited, taking his eyes off the road momentarily to watch her face.

"And you came to tell me." Lindsay's voice was a whisper. Nothing more to say by Lindsay or by Mark.

"Oh look! There it is!" Lindsay yelled, pointing to the old tire suspended from a tree branch by an old rope. "There's my swing! That's where I used to wait for the school bus!" A few more miles, and she was on the edge of her seat again. The freshly painted "Happy Trails" sign over the lane looked out of place atop the worn wooden fence posts. "And that's the stables! It used to be the Donaldson place!" Lindsay's voice grew shrill with excitement.

Mark turned in and tapped the brake to slow enough to be able to read the sign on the side fence post. Prices were reasonable, but it also said: Reservations Required. They drove leisurely up the winding lane and rolled past the whitewashed barn. The "welcome" sign was tacked above the door to a tool shed that had been cleverly converted to look like a ticket booth.

Mark parked the truck, and as they walked toward the booth, the barn door slid open. A young man appropriately dressed for farm work greeted them. "Lookin' to ride today?" he yelled as he rolled a loaded wheelbarrow between the barn and the toolshed. He pushed it to the side and walked over to them.

"Well, we wanted to check it out. I just found out this place was here." The farmhand wiped his hands on his overalls as Mark extended his hand.

"We've been here for thirty-two years, but we've only been converting the place to a riding stable in the last five years or so. I'm Joe Donaldson. I run the place."

"Mark Thomas. This is Lindsay Davis," Mark said, shaking hands with him.

As Lindsay reached out to shake his hand, it all began to fall into place. "Joey? Pam's brother?"

Joe took off his hat and looked at her, straightening to his full height. "Yes, ma'am. Did you know her?"

Lindsay noticed his facial expression fell slightly. "Oh my gosh, Joey, I used to live a couple of farms over." She pointed back toward her home. "Pam and I used to ride the school bus together and go riding after school! What a small world! You were born just before we had to move into town. Where is she now? Does she still live here? What's she doing?" Lindsay sat on a tree stump decorated with colorful planters.

"I'm sorry to say she was killed a couple of years ago." The silence fell awkwardly.

"Oh, I didn't know," Lindsay stuttered. "I'm so sorry." Lindsay felt deflated. It felt like everything sad happened about the same time Tom died. *Life could be ironic.*

"You wanna ride?" Joey asked, clearing his throat. "We generally prefer reservations, but we ain't busy today. I can saddle you up a couple of mounts if ya wanna ride."

Mark looked at Lindsay questioningly. She shrugged her shoulders as she grinned. "Sure." Mark reached for her hand, and she hesitated only a moment before accepting it. They followed Joey to the barn. Lindsay felt a bit nervous holding Mark's hand, but she had to admit to herself that she liked the warm secure feeling it brought.

From the tack room, Joey grabbed three lead ropes and walked toward the corral. "You folks rode before?"

They looked at each other with revealing expressions. "It's been a while," they said together.

"We don't letcha go alone first time out, so I'll lead ya down the Creek Bed Trail. On a scale of one to 10, 10 being expert, what would you rate your horse-ridin' capabilities?" He efficiently turned from mourning brother to expert horse trainer and host.

"No more than a three." Mark laughed.

"I was an eight at one time, but it's been over 12 years! So, count me in at five and three-quarters," Lindsay replied doubtfully.

At Joey's whistle, several horses came loping into the stalls along one side of the corral. He closed the gates on three of the stalls and left the others open to let the horses return to their grazing. He dropped grain pans in front of the two mares and the gelding, brushing the gelding as he told them about each horse.

"This is Buck," Joey began. "Don't worry. He's mine, and he does not live up to his name. This little gal is Silk.

She'll be yours, Mrs. Davis." He finished brushing out the Palomino mare. "She can be energetic, but you'll have no problem with her. Just let her know who's in charge." He turned to the bay and gestured. "And this is Satin. She's a bit lazy, but these girls are both smooth as silk. That's how we named 'em. They both got long fancy names on paper, but we ain't much on fancy around here." He expertly saddled them up and brought them out of the corral. Then he tethered them to a hitching post that Lindsay had not seen on the way into the barnyard.

He brought out a mounting step and dropped it beside Silk, motioning for Lindsay to mount. As soon as Lindsay settled in the saddle, she truly felt at home. Joey adjusted the stirrups to fit her and handed her the reins. Then he stood back and watched, to be sure they were a good match. Lindsay sat nervously for a minute and then felt her whole body relax into what she used to know. It felt good.

While Mark was mounting Satin, with the same routine, Lindsay rode Silk around the barnyard. Within minutes, Joey and Mark rode up beside her, expert and beginner status being obvious. Joey trotted forward to lead, and Mark and Lindsay fell in behind, riding side by side. It was obvious that their mounts, Silk and Satin, preferred not to stray too far apart.

Mark and Lindsay talked some on the trail, following Joey, but Lindsay was at total and complete peace riding in silence. She had forgotten how riding her horse, Josie, always felt like therapy. The last time she received horse therapy was when her dad died. Shortly thereafter, they had to sell the ranch and move into town. The horses went to the new owner. She sure could have used that therapy when Tom died.

Lindsay recognized the dry creek bed where they were riding. It was part of the creek that ran behind her family farm years ago. She could feel every muscle in her body relaxing, taking her back to an easier time. It was a time of peace and security, where her world had not been shattered. It had happened not once, but twice. First, when her daddy died and again when her husband died.

Mark was getting into the swing of things, occasionally having to nudge Satin with a firm kick to keep her attention moving forward. They rode for nearly an hour, and Lindsay realized how out of shape she was. As they brought the horses back in and started to dismount, Lindsay's legs were letting her know she needed to build up those muscles. She would have to do this more often. She shook her head as Mark was presenting the same symptoms but with much more drama.

Mark and Lindsay grabbed canned pops from the cooler in the tool shed and paid the man. They were still laughing as they climbed into the truck and started back for town.

They both saw the white piece of paper on her windshield as they pulled into the parking lot. "I'll bet you got a ticket, Lindsay," Mark teased her as she climbed out of the truck. "You can't leave an unattended vehicle in a private parking lot." She chuckled as she lifted it out from behind the wiper, but her laughter immediately died as she read it. Mark was beside her before she turned around.

You may not want to talk to me, but I have information

you will want to know about. I've already waited too long. You won't be in danger as long as you talk to me. ~ Lucky

Ten

Mark caught Lindsay as she spun around, near panic, and with his free hand, he caught the note. She trembled in his arms. "It's okay, Lindsay. Breathe. Let's go back to the truck and sit down." They walked back to his truck, and he helped her into the cab. Climbing back in the driver's side, he turned in the seat to face her and took her hand in both of his. "It's okay, you're safe. Let me follow you home, and I'll sit beside you while you call this guy Lucky. Unless you want to call the police first."

She nodded and mindlessly reached for the door handle. Trembling, Lindsay pulled her keys from her pocket, left the safety of his truck, and climbed into her car. If she had lived any further away, she wouldn't have felt capable of driving. She took a deep breath and blew it away as she turned the key. She pulled out of the restaurant and, in automatic pilot, drove the few blocks to her house. Mark parked his truck in the visitor parking and then followed her to the house. As he joined her, Lindsay opened the townhouse door and gasped.

The cushions were thrown off the couch. The desk had been ransacked. The magazine rack and its contents were scattered on the couch. Books, papers, and magazines were strewn everywhere. Mark pulled out his cell phone. Numbness crept over Lindsay as she listened to Mark ask for Jim Becker. She heard him tell the police about the ransacked house. "And Jim," Mark was saying, "keep this off the radio for now, okay?" Then he told them about Lucky, the business card, and the note on her car windshield. When he hung up, he took her hand and led her from the house into the parking lot.

Before she could make sense of things, they were standing in front of Mark's truck again. He opened the door for her and helped her inside once again. She was still shaking, but the safety of his truck helped her to breathe. He climbed in beside her, put his arm around her, and just held her. Lindsay felt herself relax in the safety of his arms, but her head was still spinning. What was happening? She felt so violated. The safe little world that she had built with her son had begun to unravel in a single afternoon. A tear slid down her cheek. *Thank God Mark is here.*

"Lindsay," he said quietly, "I just talked to one of the men I know from the Police Department" Mark's eyes roamed the townhouse parking lot, the courtyard off to the side, paying particular attention to the couple sitting at the stone and brick picnic table laughing. He released his hold on Lindsay as she shifted and looked up at him.

"Am I in danger?" Lindsay couldn't stop shaking. "Is Nathan? Mark, what is going on?" Lindsay was focused now. Buying that ranch was beginning to feel more like a definite plan. But would she be safe there? Fear clawed at her belly, and she wished Mark hadn't pulled away.

"Don't think about that just now. Let's let the police go through the house. We'll talk to them and figure out a plan. And with the police also looking into Lucky," he squeezed her hand. "Just stay calm, Lindsay. You said Nathan's not coming home until tomorrow, right?"

"Yeah," she whispered. "All the boys are going to be at the church Fun Fest after service, so he won't be coming home until late afternoon." Lindsay knew she was rambling. It's what she did in times like these. The initial shock wave caused her to go mute, but as it wore off, they couldn't shut her up. Two police cars rolled into the complex, and a shiver crept through Lindsay.

"Will you be okay here for a minute?" At her nod, Mark got out of the truck and walked across the parking lot. Lindsay watched Mark as he talked to the officers for a few minutes, feeling an unexpected flood of attraction. Heat flooded her cheeks. This was so not the time for that. He was being a really good friend, and she deeply appreciated his presence here today. It was nothing more than that. Or was it? She shook her head.

The officers had begun to walk in different directions. One officer went to talk to the folks in the courtyard. Another went behind the townhouse on the other side, while another drew his weapon and cautiously slipped inside the front door of Lindsay's trashed home. A fourth officer returned with Mark to the truck. Mark climbed in while the officer walked to the passenger side of the vehicle and motioned for her to roll down the window.

"Mrs. Davis, I'm Dale Marsh, Chief of Police." The chief asked questions about the house, her regular routine, where her son was and where she had been today, how long since anyone had been at the house. While she answered the questions, the other officers determined that the culprit was no longer in the house.

Lindsay exited the truck, and she and Mark followed the chief toward her house. She inhaled sharply as she took in the scene again. Tears stung her eyes again and she exhaled slowly to calm her nerves. Her house had become a crime scene. How was this even possible? She leaned into Mark for strength. "You okay?" He whispered. Lindsay swallowed hard, nodded, and walked forward, following the chief.

Chief Marsh jotted notes as they continued through her trashed townhouse. Mark was always close by, but never intrusive. It was comforting to glance over and see him there. Ready to be at her side if given the sign. The other officer dusted different areas to find fingerprints that may have been left behind. The officer finished dusting the desk and gave the chief a nod.

"Ma'am, would you check the desk area to see if anything is missing?" Chief Marsh asked her.

Stepping toward the desk, Lindsay glanced at Mark. He came near and with a slight smile gave her shoulder a reassuring squeeze, then sat on the nearby loveseat. She sat down at the desk and started sorting through the mess, searching for anything missing.

She stacked articles, bills, papers, and old magazines, placing them in drawers that were still on the floor. Mark picked the drawer up as she finished and placed it in the desk where she indicated, and they methodically started on the next one. The middle drawer had not been taken completely out but was partly opened. She pulled it the rest of the way out, feeling along the bottom to find the envelope that had been taped there. *It was still there.* Looking up to see if anyone caught her reaction, she relaxed, replaced the drawer, and started on the top cubicles. Why should she feel guilty?

One by one, her trembling hands reached in and pulled out phone charger cords, stapler, hole punch, and other items that she used in her writing. She hadn't written for a while but felt at ease when she pulled out the manuscript she had completed in the weeks before Tom died. He loved it. He wanted her to send it to publishers, but after he died, she left it there. She never opened the pages again. She turned in the chair, facing the chief.

"I don't think anything has been taken." She glanced at Mark. He stared at her, wearing a curious expression. Could he tell that she was hiding something? Had he seen her feel for the envelope under that top drawer? She looked away, feeling her cheeks burn. The chief motioned to Lindsay and asked her to go through the same procedure on the other side of the room. She did as he instructed and put things back in order from the magazine rack. Again, things were scattered, crumpled, and slightly torn, but nothing appeared to be missing.

They did the same thing, room by room. Lindsay could not find anything missing and had no idea what the culprit was after. Lindsay and Mark followed the officers upstairs and into Nathan's room. All the air left Lindsay's lungs as her eyes took in the mess. Every drawer had been removed from Nathan's desk and dresser. Even the toy box had been emptied onto his bed.

Instead of putting things where they belonged, she filled the hamper sitting inside the door. She was not putting anything back in those drawers until she washed the filth off them. Everything had been clean when the culprit opened the drawers. They had done laundry before church on Wednesday. But she was not letting anything that evil person touched near her son. She grabbed the bedding that had been thrown from his bed and put that in the hamper, too, straightening the mattress at the same time.

Lindsay crossed the hall, walked into her room, and stood speechless. Stunned. It had not been touched. Turning around, she glanced at Mark and then at Chief Marsh, standing close behind her and Mark, the officer behind them backed up.

"He could have been interrupted or thought someone was coming, so he took off." The chief spoke expertly.

"So, do you think he'll come back?" Lindsay's voice quivered as she instinctively grabbed Mark's arm. He looked down at her with fondness in his eyes, then wove his fingers gently through hers. It felt comforting and warm. Lindsay relaxed at his touch.

"Well, that's hard to say. More than likely not right away, but he could if he didn't find what he was after," the chief replied. "We'll station an officer in the parking lot for tonight. But there was no sign of forced entry, so you'll want to get the locks changed right away."

Mark pulled his hand free and reached for his cell phone. She slowly stepped away from him and went into her bedroom. It didn't look like they had even come in here. Maybe she could breathe in here and feel less violated. She noticed that she was suddenly thinking of the culprit in the plural as being more than one now. She sat down on her bed, trying to keep it all together.

Mark stood in the doorway watching her. "I called a locksmith that I know. He's on his way. I called Ben. He'll be here shortly."

"Oh, no, he'll tell Mom! I have to get to her first." She jumped up and started toward the door. Mark stepped in front of her and took her gently by the shoulders.

"Lindsay," Mark said in a pseudo-calm voice. "Try to stay calm. I told him not to tell her yet, but you need to. He's on his way over here to help you put things in order. But I'd rather you not stay here tonight."

"It might be a good idea, Mrs. Davis," Chief Marsh said. "We'll have our man out front, but there's no need to take a chance if you've got somewhere else you can stay for the night. I do have a few more questions if you would come back downstairs." She nodded in agreement, though she could feel the panic setting in again. The chief quietly turned and left the room.

"Mark, what is going on?" She searched his gaze. She could see the same question in his eyes. He pulled her into his arms and whispered a prayer that God would keep her safe as they tried to find answers.

Eleven

Mark and Lindsay joined Chief Marsh in the kitchen. Nervously, Lindsay busied herself loading the dishwasher with dishes that had been removed from cabinets by the culprits. She grabbed the skillets from the floor in frustration. They had been in the warming drawer of her stove until the culprits dumped them out onto the floor. She ran water in the sink, adding knives and silverware, then she poured enough dishwashing liquid to clean all the neighbors' dishes, too.

Mark sat on the sidelines, watching her, praying under his breath. Lindsay stopped at the sink, took a deep breath, and exhaled. She turned and sat down at the table, facing the police chief.

"Mrs. Davis, we're going to need your help to catch this guy, Lucky," Chief Marsh said bluntly.

Mark stepped closer to the table and stood beside Lindsay as the chief continued. "There is no address on his card for us to check out, just Brookings, South Dakota. There's no casino named Lucky's on record anywhere in the tri-state area, so it's probably a private club. Obviously, he wants to talk to you, but I advise against meeting him alone. We're running a check on the phone number on the card he gave you. But if you want to call him, we'd be here. Set up a place to talk in public. My men will be there in plain clothes. You can even tell him off about ransacking your house if you want to. We're assuming he's the one that did this, but it could help us to learn what they were after."

"I—I don't know if I can do that right now." Lindsay was exhausted, mentally and physically. She just wanted to curl up and go to sleep, but she knew she would never sleep. The doorbell shattered the silence, and everyone in the kitchen jumped. They all stood and nearly walked as a unit to the living room, stepping aside only when she reached out to answer the door. Benny looked around sheepishly. As she was closing the door, a voice from outside called her name.

"Mrs. Davis, Mark Thomas called me." She let the locksmith in, and he and Mark stepped aside to talk about changing all the locks. Benny hugged Lindsay and stood with his protective arm around her.

"You doing okay, Sis?" Benny's voice trembled.

By now she was feeling much better and told him so. "You didn't say anything to Mom, did you?" That was all Lindsay needed to make this night even worse. For anyone to tell her mom. She didn't want to burden her with this, unless and until she had to.

"No, of course not. I came straight from home. That's

why it took me so long to get here. What can I do?" he asked as Mark walked back in. Lindsay took a breath intending to send him home, but decided she wasn't sure she wanted him to. As she began to ask him to stay, Mark answered for her.

"If I know Lindsay, she'll want to stay here tonight. Chief Marsh and I both told her she should go spend the night at her mother's house or yours, or anywhere else." Mark smiled at her as she faced him.

"Apparently, you know me better than I thought you did. But I won't sleep, no matter where I am, so I might as well get some cleaning and laundry done around here."

"And that's why I called in your brother." He turned to Ben. "Can you crash here tonight so she's not alone?"

Lindsay went through the motions of protesting, but didn't sincerely try to convince her brother to go home. He could either sleep on the couch or in her bed. She certainly didn't plan on using it.

Chief Marsh agreed that it was a good plan. He released the other officers and then turned to face Lindsay. "If you change your mind about making that call–"

"Yes, let's do it." Lindsay decided to get it over with as quickly as possible. He exchanged a concerned look with Mark then handed her back the business card. They followed her to the desk, so she could call from the landline. Not surprisingly, Mark stayed close to her side, Benny right beside him.

She dialed the number and put it on speaker. Lucky answered right away. "Hello, Lucky. It's Lindsay Davis."

He was silent for a few beats. "I thought I'd hear from you tonight."

"Was it because you ransacked my house?" she asked before thinking better of it.

"What? No! I was nowhere near your house today." Lucky said emphatically. She looked up at the three men. Their expressions were skeptical.

"But listen." Lucky reined in his tone. "If they're pulling that kind of stuff, it's more important than ever that we talk." He was silent for a few moments. Lindsay's throat was too dry to respond. Mark squeezed Lindsay's shoulder and gave her an encouraging nod. "Did you hear what I said?" Lucky's tone raised again. "Please."

"Yes," she choked out. "Let's meet at Kit's Kitchen at 4 tomorrow afternoon." She tried to speak calmly, but she sounded nervous even to herself.

After he agreed, a cold, empty feeling settled over her as she hung up the phone. It would be okay, she told herself. Chief Marsh would have a team in place both to protect her and to listen to the conversation.

"Good work, Lindsay. Now please get some rest. My man is in the parking lot." The chief wrapped up his investigation in her house and left. His words sounded simple enough, but Lindsay couldn't imagine her getting any rest as being a possibility, and she doubted that he thought so either.

Mark and Benny watched in silence and followed as Lindsay went to the kitchen and walked directly to the refrigerator. She pulled out a large rectangular pewter tray from the cabinet above the fridge and placed it in the center of the table. Mark and Benny glanced at each other; brows furled in curiosity.

She opened the refrigerator, pulled out a pitcher of iced tea, and offered them a glass. Puzzled and curious, they both accepted. The three of them sat down at the table, and Mark and Benny watched her curiously as she flipped the tray over.

There, taped securely to the back of the tray with duct tape, was a large manilla document envelope similar to the one taped under the desk drawer. Lindsay pulled the envelope off and opened one end with a paring knife. She didn't look at the contents; she slid the paperwork across the table where both Mark and Benny could see it.

"I don't know what these envelopes are." Her voice was soft as she continued. "This is the only thing I can think of that they could have been looking for. Tom put this up there and told me to forget about it. I did. He told me these papers might come in handy someday." Clipped on the top, the stack of papers revealed documents that Tom had been saving. She had truly forgotten them, until tonight—until she saw that the cabinet had been opened but none of its contents disturbed, not even the tray.

She unclipped the pages and, not having any clue what she was looking at, passed them on to Mark. "If that's the reason they invaded my home, I'll give everything to Lucky tomorrow night. If that's what it takes to keep Nathan out of danger!"

Mark started looking at the pages, then one by one passing them on to Benny, his facial expression eventually revealing concern. For several minutes they sat, sipping their drinks, Lindsay not really seeing the patio she was staring at out the back window, Mark and Benny occasionally looking at each other with raised eyebrows.

Finally, Mark passed the last loose page to Ben. It was a handwritten account delineating a timeline of events and the documents referred to. It showed a lengthy and detailed plan that Tom believed was being put in place by his firm. It indicated an in-depth plot to swindle both private and corporate investors on a wide scale and long-term basis. Benny passed the page to his sister. What was Tom uncovering here? What had he gotten into? And was his sister in danger?

Twelve

Lindsay pressed her fingers against her temples, head pounding as she listened to Mark tell her the horrifying details revealed in the documents. She only summarily understood what she was hearing, but there were a few words that jumped out at her—extortion, murder, blackmail, kidnapping.

She presumed if the theories presented in this paperwork were true, and if the firm even suspected the existence of this evidence, she and Nathan were definitely in danger. The figures in the documents indicated a multimillion-dollar scam. It would more than likely land the partners of the firm in deep trouble with the locals. If Tom had turned this paperwork in, the federal government, including the IRS, would also be interested. The documents even referred to investors from South America and Saudi Arabia. The final item that had been under the clip was a small sealed envelope addressed to Lindsay. Mark tapped it on the table, thoughtfully.

When Lindsay looked at him, Mark spoke in a near

whisper and gave Ben a sidelong glance. "Lindsay, didn't you tell me you and Tom purchased this townhouse from Tom's partners—Marcus, Brand, and Shield?" Benny's head popped up at about the same time Lindsay's did.

"Yes, why?" Lindsay reached for the envelope, and Mark released it. Mark reached for the written document in front of Benny and slid it over to her.

"Is this Tom's handwriting?" Mark asked. The document had not been signed.

"Yes, it looks like it." She put the envelope aside and read the document. Mark and Benny looked at each other. Benny stood and turned the kitchen light on, then walked into the living room, looking out the front window. From the corner of her eye, she could see him looking for the police car sitting in the corner of the parking lot. Lindsay couldn't blame him. This whole thing was a bit much. He turned on the living room lamp and stepped back into the kitchen.

"You can go ahead and open it, if you want." Mark told Lindsay. She picked up the knife and shakily slit the envelope's flap open. She read it aloud.

My dear sweet Linds—

If you're reading this, I waited too long, and I have left you with a terrible mess. I am so sorry. The paperwork you just looked at may not make much sense to you, but it is important that you follow these instructions very carefully. First, go to the library, run copies of everything, and take them to the police. It'll be best to keep a copy, too. Then take all of these documents to David Harrell at the Attorney General's office. Don't tell anyone about this, Linds, especially not anyone from the firm. I am so sorry to put you and Nat in danger. I just need a little more proof before I do that myself. I love you more than life itself.

Lindsay looked at Mark through her tears and handed him the first page of the note. There was a business card in the envelope with the Attorney General's name and address, and a key. She flipped it around in her hand, contemplating how her life felt like it was spiraling. She had a sense of foreboding that everything was about to change. She continued reading.

You need to go to the bank—the one where we opened that CD, not our regular bank. The key opens a safety deposit box that has some cash in it. I'll keep adding to it as much as I can. There's also a life insurance policy that I took out when all of this started happening. I got scared, Linds, and wanted so badly to tell you, but I was afraid you'd panic. I get panicky myself at times. There are some other papers in the safety deposit box you'll need. You'll need to grab the deed envelope from the desk, too. There are more instructions in there. I am so sorry, baby. I don't know what else to say. I'm hoping to provide you with everything you need to start over. I just don't know what else to do. I'm in too deep to drop it all. I love you and Nat. I am so sorry.

Lindsay sat stunned as she took both pages, folded them, and replaced the letter in the envelope. Mark reached across the table for Lindsay's hand, and then with his right hand, reached for Benny's. "If you don't mind, I think we need to pray. I think we should have prayed before now, but especially now."

Lindsay nodded and blinked back tears as she reached toward Benny, and Mark grabbed both of their hands. They all lowered their heads, but no eyes were closed, they each studied their own pattern on the tablecloth as Mark began to pray, while Lindsay's tears splashed.

Our Gracious Lord, we thank You for keeping Lindsay safe today. It's been a long day, Lord, and we are tired, but we need You, we need to feel Your presence and power, we need to hear Your voice. Help us to know how to go forward. If Tom's instructions are correct, help us to follow them and go with us and keep us safe as we do so. Whatever Tom got into, we ask that You guide us to either finish it or stop it as You see fit. I lift Lindsay and Nathan to You and ask that You guard them with Your angels. I ask that You keep her mom and Ben safe, Lord, and all her family. Thank You, Lord. Amen.

Lindsay looked up at Mark with pleading in her eyes. "What do I do now?" Mark looked into those eyes and kept her hand in his. Benny pulled his hands back and clasped them on the table in front of him. Lindsay wiped her tears with her free hand.

"First and foremost, you breathe," Mark began, wrapping his hands around both of hers, "and you let God be God. Then, well, you could get the deed envelope so you can see what's next."

She nodded and crossed the room. She went straight to the desk and pulled out the middle drawer for the second time that day. She worked the tape loose and brought the envelope to the table. "I don't know if I can do this tonight. I'm just completely—" Her voice failed her.

"Lindsay, if you are in danger—and it sounds like you are—it may be important that you do this tonight." She gave him the large envelope and the knife. One by one, he pulled out documents, each in their envelopes.

They found a deed to a place in Rutledge, another to a place in Davenport, the deed to Lindsay's mother's house, and another to a place in Washington State. There were stock certificates, certificates of deposits. All were in her name alone. Strange, she thought, that in a separate envelope she found the deed to the townhouse, upon which Tom's name was still on as co-owner. An envelope from the brokerage firm of Whitley, Morris, and Cruz in Davenport. Mark straightened. "These are yours, Lindsay, and could be personal, I don't want to intrude—"

"Please, Mark. I trust you to read them. I really can't, and I probably wouldn't know what they are anyway." Lindsay got up, poured more tea, and put the pitcher on the table. "I've got a casserole in the freezer. I'll warm it so you guys can eat." Lindsay's default was to fall back on mundane service tasks, like putting a casserole in the oven.

Lindsay went to work doing anything she felt she had control over. She realized she was defaulting to her norm. When she felt life was going to overwhelm her, she withdrew and put on what she called her "pseudo-calm" demeanor. Then she deferred the issue to someone she knew she could trust, but she was listening. Ben and Mark started perusing the paperwork from the deed envelope that had been on the desk, comparing it to what they had just scoured.

The men paused in their studies and looked at her. Mark spoke intently. "Lindsay, it appears that John Morris has been paying the taxes on the properties. He's also been investing for Tom. Looks like he's jumping through financial hoops and real estate loopholes to obtain the properties for Tom."

Benny looked up from a sheet he was studying. "Sis,

Tom's been setting up an entirely separate life for you, but with a Plan B in place if Tom were taken out of the picture." Benny sat back in his chair gazing at her with raised eyebrows.

Lindsay had always called Tom's death "the accident," but now, she wasn't so sure. But why would Tom's firm wait for two years after his death to do anything about her living in the townhouse... unless they didn't know about the evidence Tom had been compiling, until recently.

"Lindsay, I think we need to call Chief Marsh back." Benny nodded at Mark's suggestion, and Lindsay partly turned to him.

"Okay, Mark, whatever you think." She went back to regular, calming mundane kitchen duties, tossing a salad, as Mark called the police chief from his cell phone.

Thirteen

olice Chief Marsh arrived just as Lindsay was taking the chicken and rice casserole out of the oven. She placed it in the center of the table and turned to retrieve the plates. Placing four settings on the kitchen table, she looked up. "Come on, guys, please sit and eat. I need some normalcy and you need some food." She brought out another glass for Chief Marsh, and they all sat down. "Mark, would you bless the food, please."

He did, and they ate in relative silence while Chief Marsh skimmed the paperwork they were stacking near his plate. Chief Marsh ate heartily, but no one else had much of an appetite. They started talking about the paperwork before they had finished eating. Lindsay listened while pushing grains of rice around her plate, occasionally putting a bite in her mouth.

She slipped into the laundry room and transferred a load from the washer to the dryer, then threw Nathan's linen and some towels in the washer. She still hoped to get it all done and put away before she brought Nathan home tomorrow after church. When she returned, Chief Marsh had pushed his plate aside to better view the pile of documents in front of him, making notes in his pocket notebook. Lindsay was pleased to see that he was respectful of all of it, even to the point of replacing each document in its envelope after he searched through them for the details.

"Well." Chief Marsh offered. "I'll be honest. This is a lot for a small-town police chief to decipher. But I agree that for your own safety and that of your son, you need to leave this house. From what I see, your husband has given you some options. It looks like the house in Washington has been under lease for several years. The rents go through a management company, with net proceeds going to an account in your name. They act as executors, so they can pay expenses out of the same account. It looks like your husband did an amazing job. The house doesn't have a mortgage on it, so it's clear. It looks like there is correspondence from caretakers to Marcus, Brand, and Shield; looks like more on the firm in Davenport. I don't see anything about the one in Rutledge, and I don't see any leases on the other properties; of course, I see your mother lives in one of them."

"What? The firm owns Mom's house?" Fear re-entered Lindsay's heart even as she spoke.

"No, no, Mrs. Davis, you do," Chief Marsh said quickly. "You own all of these properties. You can move to any one of them, except the one in Washington. If that's where you want to go, I'm sure you could give the tenants the proper notice, depending on what the laws are there. And like I said, you own the one your mom lives in. This really is above my pay grade."

They were all thoughtful, waiting for a plan to hit one of them. Finally, the chief spoke: "Let's do this. Meet with Lucky as planned tomorrow. Let him do the talking. See what information he has. Figure out what he wants from you, without volunteering anything about these latest developments. Let's see if we can figure out what his story is, just whose side he's on."

Lindsay stood, nodding, and began clearing the table and loading the dishwasher. "You'll be there, right?" She turned back around, waiting for his answer nervously.

"Absolutely. Yes, ma'am. My men will be stationed around the restaurant just as we talked about earlier. You will not be alone." Chief Marsh poured himself another glass of tea.

"And I'll be there." Mark and Benny spoke simultaneously. Mark went on, "We'll sit in the booth right behind the one where we sat today, okay?" Benny nodded.

The chief continued, "Then Monday, we'll take a little drive up to the capital. We'll meet with the attorney general or his deputy, David Harrell. In the meantime, I'll get in touch with a friend I know from Securities and Exchange. If she's available, we'll meet with her, too, while we're up there. Mrs. Davis, are you up to calling this broker in Davenport and setting up an appointment?"

Lindsay looked at Mark, and he answered. "We can take care of that. For Tuesday?" Mark looked at Lindsay then back at Chief Marsh.

Lindsay interjected. "I work all this week, every day until 2:00." I don't want to take off work. Nathan can walk to Mom's after school, and I can pick him up there later." She was going to have to let Mom in on this, but she wanted to wait until she had a handle on it herself and could talk about it without having a panic attack.

"That's fine," Chief Marsh said. "Mark, if you'll give me your cell phone number, I'll call you when I know what we can line up for Monday. You can set that up for Tuesday after we know more."

Lindsay felt like she could at least rest, now that a plan of action of some sort was in place. As Mark walked the chief to the door, Lindsay heard Chief Marsh suggest that Mark do some research on the other properties. She had some choices as to where she could move. She heard the chief reiterate that moving was not a decision that should be put off.

Mark agreed and went back into the kitchen. Lindsay and Benny set to work vacuuming the living room, even rearranging all the furniture. Lindsay said she wanted a totally different arrangement, so she would feign being bored in Nathan's absence, when she explained it to him. She had no intention at this point of telling Nathan anything more than necessary, but she might mention the ranch for sale that she and Mark saw on the way to the stables Saturday.

"After all," Lindsay told them, "I have been thinking about buying a little ranch somewhere. I just thought it would be later, whenever *I* was ready." She sat back down feeling deflated.

Mark sat across from her, leaning forward with his elbows on his knees as he spoke. "One of those properties may be suitable. They only had legal descriptions on the deeds, no addresses. Is it okay if I take a picture on my phone? I can do some research from home to see what these properties are if you want me to."

"Sure, Mark. Thank you so much for everything." She felt numb. Having so many choices really didn't make her feel better. She felt like she was being forced out of her home.

Mark went back to the kitchen, picked up the packet of deeds, and sat back down. "If they aren't what you want to move into, you can sell them and go wherever you want. Do you know a realtor? If you don't, I think Cass Stewart is still doing that. It doesn't look like there is a mortgage on anything. Course, you could use her to sell this place, too, if you want to." He watched her for a moment, regretting he had gone so far as to suggest a realtor.

"I think I'm crashing. If you don't mind—" Lindsay felt lightheaded.

"I'm sure you are. Give me a minute, and I'll finish these pictures." Mark opened each deed, taking pictures of the legal descriptions on each one and carefully replacing them. "I'll head on out, but call me if you need me. Deputy Stevens is out in the parking lot, and Benny will be here. Okay?"

She nodded wearily.

He put his hands on her shoulders as they stood at the door. "You're going to be okay, Lindsay, and so will Nathan. There are two sets of keys on the desk, and each key fits all three doors." He gave her a quick hug. "Lock this." He smiled and slipped out the door and closed it securely behind him, waiting to hear the deadbolt click.

Lindsay locked the door obediently and leaned back on it, closing her eyes. "Hey, Sis. I know you said you won't sleep, but why don't you go up anyway? You look whipped," Benny observed.

"Thanks, bro—you don't look like spring sunshine, yourself." She fell into her brother's embrace, clinging to his strength. The tenderness brought tears to her eyes once more.

When Lindsay stepped away, she had a determined look on her face. "I'm going to go put Nathan's sheets back on his bed. You can sleep there if you want. Then I'm gonna have a soak in the tub and do my Sunday School lesson." She turned around and headed to the dryer to grab the sheets for Nathan's bed, then toward the stairs. "By the way, church starts at 9:00!"

Fourteen

Lindsay walked upstairs, made Nathan's bed, and then dragged herself into her bathroom, turning on the water to fill the tub. It took most of her strength to get undressed. She laid her head back, letting the hot water soak into her tired muscles. She nearly fell asleep before she dried her hands and reached for her Bible. She read some of the Psalms and then turned to her lesson for the next day.

The Prayer of Jesus—Lindsay read the title and closed her eyes. "Our Father, who art in heaven..." *Oh, God, how I need You to be right here with me right now. I need so much more strength than I have, to be able to get through even tomorrow.* She opened her eyes and blinked back the tears, trying to focus again on her Sunday School lesson again.

"Matthew 6:9-10: In this manner, therefore, pray: Our Father in heaven, hallowed be Your name. Your kingdom come, Your will be done on earth as it is in heaven."

Yes, Lord, she prayed in her heart. *I can exalt and praise Your Name, because I know You are God. You are all-powerful. All-knowing. I gave You reign in my heart when I was a kid, and I have never faltered, Lord. Tom and I were married according to Your plan for us, and we raised Nathan from the minute he was born to know who You are and how to live for You, and he invited You to reign in his life, too. So why is this...? No, I don't want to question. I want to trust You. Just as Mark prayed earlier, we thank You for Your peace, Your protection. I trust You have a plan for us, and You are in this!*

Lindsay put the book on the antique oak stand near the tub and closed her eyes, convincing herself yet again. Of course, she trusted God. He had never let her down. He had strengthened her when her dad got sick, guiding them to the perfect buyer for their farm. Keeping costs down, even to the point where they didn't have to pay commission. Lindsay hadn't understood it then, but that sale went through within a week of putting the 'for sale by owner' sign where their lane met the highway. The "first-time buyer" program limited the costs the buyer could pay but selling without getting a realtor involved more than made up for it.

God had stepped in and allowed Arlene to find the house she was living in now, with a low price because of so much work that needed to be done. Tom and Benny were able to step in and do most of the updates themselves. They had so much fun choosing colors. When did Tom buy her mom's house? Lord, so many questions. Would she ever have the answers?

Lindsay picked up her Sunday School book again and kept reading:

"Matthew 6:11-13: Give us this day our daily bread, and forgive us our debts as we forgive our debtors. Lead us not into temptation but deliver us from the evil one, for Yours is the kingdom and the power and the glory forever. Amen."

Lindsay followed her lesson guide to the commentary:

When we pattern our prayers after this one, we acknowledge who God is. God is our Father, and worthy of praise. The word hallowed does this! "Thy Kingdom come, Thy will be done," tells God that we agree with His plan. Our daily bread is our petition - our request. It refers to physical food, of course, but also to spiritual food and "food for thought." It tells God we trust Him for tomorrow's bread without praying for it today! This perfect prayer asks God to forgive us, but also to help us to forgive those who sin against us. This model prayer asks God to protect us from the temptations we meet in life, but also from our enemy. Lastly, it declares that we accept by faith, that God's kingdom and power and glory will last forever!

Lindsay realized afresh that this model prayer asks God to protect us from the temptations we meet in life but also from our enemy. Lindsay closed her eyes and focused her thoughts:

Deliver us from evil. Lord, I feel like we are right smack dab in the middle of danger. I pray for You to deliver us from this!

Lindsay put the book back on the table, soaking up the hope and life that the words brought to her exhausted soul. She slid down into the tub until the water reached her chin. Every muscle in her body screamed at her, but she repeated the prayer, letting the peace of God pour over her like the warm water she was soaking in.

Lord, I trust You to give me what I need, when I need it. I trust that I don't need to panic if I don't have what I need a day early, or even an hour early. I will have it when I need it. I don't know what Your plan is for us, but I trust You to keep Your promises that Your plan for us is for peace and not evil, for a future and a hope. Thank You. I love You, Lord. Amen.

Lindsay took a deep breath and reached for the shampoo. As she scrubbed away the day, she truly felt God's peace. She thought of all the trouble Tom had gone to to be sure that she and Nathan had a future. Tomorrow, she would finish "the cleansing" and put the last of Nathan's things away before she left for church, and when they came home, they would start their new life, knowing God was going before them, orchestrating it all.

She climbed out of the tub and dried off before heading into her room. Searching through the closet, she found her favorite pajamas and slipped them on.

Bringing the book from the bathroom, Lindsay put it on the nightstand, checked the alarm, and turned off the light. She was excited to see her son. She had seen Ben's dress shirt lying across his duffel bag downstairs. Under the circumstances, she was sure Ben would go to church with her. She was still thinking of how coming to church could be a huge step in her brother's life when sleep finally overcame her.

Fifteen

The smell of coffee woke Lindsay from a deep sleep before the alarm did. She looked at the clock. 6:25. She was surprised she had slept so long. Benny sat at the kitchen table with the newspaper spread out, both hands cradling a cup of the steaming brew when she walked into the kitchen. He had pulled the funnies out, leaving the rest of the paper a mess, just like he used to do when they were kids.

"Smells good. Thanks for making the coffee." Lindsay opened the dishwasher for a cup, only to find it had already been emptied. "What time did you get up?" She found her favorite mug in the cabinet.

"Not long, 6:00. How did you sleep?" He handed her the front page as she sat across the table, stirring cream into her cup.

"Better than I expected to, that's for sure. You?" Lindsay pulled one foot up in the chair with her and sipped her coffee.

"Not bad. A little bit of a stiff neck, but it'll loosen up.

Do you want some breakfast? I make a mean waffle." Benny laughed at her crinkled-up nose. She was the cook in the family, certainly not him!

"I'll make breakfast for you since you made the coffee." She toasted him with her cup. "What'll it be? I can do waffles. Or I have ham or bacon, eggs, hash browns, or pancakes. Your wish is my command. I can even do oatmeal."

"Looks like I'm getting the better end of the deal. I don't know, how about cocoa puffs?" Benny joked. He got up and opened the refrigerator, viewing its contents. "You didn't eat much supper; how about bacon, eggs, and fried potatoes? I'll peel the potatoes."

"You're on. Toast or biscuits?" She asked and he handed her the box of Bisquick from the top cabinet. She turned on the oven and started mixing the dough. Before long, the house smelled like a country farmhouse, with all the breakfast fixings underway. They ate without talking much.

While Lindsay was putting the dishes in the dishwasher, Benny poured them both another cup of coffee and walked to the front window with his.

"Looks like Deputy Steve was relieved by another officer. Can't see him well enough to see who it is." Lindsay joined him at the window.

"I'm not telling Nathan anything about yesterday," she whispered. "I'll tell him I saw that 'for sale' sign, feel him out, and see what he thinks about moving. I'm sticking to my story. I rearranged the living room out of boredom. It's the same reason I cleaned out all his drawers. I don't know what to tell him—yet, anyway."

"I know, Sis. I think you're on the right track." He

squeezed her shoulder. "You'll be able to tell him more after the meeting with Lucky tonight, and then you'll know even more after you go to the capital for those meetings. I wish I could go with you, but I've got to work." Benny took his cup to the sink.

"I know, Benny. Thanks for staying here last night. I don't think I could have slept nearly as well as I did if you hadn't been here."

"Hey, what are brothers for?" He smacked her on the shoulder. "Okay if I take a shower?"

"Sure. You can use Nathan's bathroom or the guest bath, whichever you want. You're coming to church with me then?" She asked with hope in her heart. "And the Fun Fest, too?"

"Yes, ma'am." Benny acquiesced. "I'm going to tag along with you all day. Nothin' better to do; besides, those church women are good cooks!"

As her brother went upstairs, Lindsay looked at the deed packets on the living room coffee table. She gathered them up, along with the paperwork that had been stashed above the refrigerator, and put them all in the desk drawer. Then she took them out again and headed upstairs to the roll-top desk in her room. No need to take a chance on Nathan finding anything.

She went to her closet and pulled out the ensemble she had chosen for the day. Then she decided it was too dressy to wear to Fun Fest, so she pulled out khaki slacks and a print tunic top instead. It was still early, so she made her bed and then took her time with her hair and makeup. Then she rummaged through her jewelry box for just the right splash of color. As she came down the stairs, Ben was on his cell phone, talking in a voice near a whisper.

From the pantry, she pulled out the slow cooker and the ingredients for the cheese dip she had committed to making for the Fun Fest. The kitchen committee made it so easy. All she had to do was leave all the ingredients in the kitchen and they'd take it from there. They were busy during a lot of the service, so everything was done at noon-ish when the Fun Fest was scheduled to begin.

"That was Janet." Benny said with a sheepish smile. "She's going to bring Mel to church. Then I can take her home after the Fun Fest."

"Aw, Benny, I'm so glad. I know you miss her." He beamed. He casually threw his arm around Lindsay's shoulders. "And she's going to let me have regular visitation like the papers say I should. I told her I was getting counseling. I think that's why she changed her mind." Lindsay looked up at him and noticed his eyes were filling.

"You like Mark?" she asked as she was loading up the tote. She could have kicked herself for bringing up his name.

"What's not to like? He sure came through yesterday, when the sky was falling, didn't he?" She nodded, and he went on. "Do you like him?"

"Oh, sure." She turned so he couldn't see her face. She could feel herself blushing. She wasn't ready to talk about him yet as anything other than the champion he had been. "I would have been a mess if you both hadn't been here yesterday."

Benny simply smiled. Her face warmed even more at his expression. Shaking it off, she went upstairs and gathered her book bag, laden with her Bible and Nathan's, and her Sunday School quarterly and notebook. She snatched her purse off the doorknob and slung it over her shoulder as she slipped on her flats.

Benny grabbed the bag on the table. "Got everything?"

"Let's see," Lindsay started taking a quick inventory. "Chips, cheese, Rotel tomatoes, mushroom soup. Yep, I think that's everything. I'll meet you there, or shall we ride together?"

"My truck's a mess; why don't I ride with you?" They loaded everything in the back seat of Lindsay's jeep, then waved at the deputy.

Ben spoke again. "Come to think of it, I'll meet you there. It's a good time to get the truck washed. What time does church start?"

"Sunday School's at 9:00. 10:15 for fellowship, 10:30 for worship." She cheered inwardly as she closed her door and rolled her window partially down. "See you there!" The fact that Benny was on a positive track with his healing and Mark's counseling made her hopeful that she would see him at church. If only Janet would come through with bringing Mel to church, it would be such a good start at that new beginning,

Sixteen

Lindsay was surprised that she was able to pay attention during Sunday School. She was so hoping Benny would come to church and that Janet would live up to her promise to bring Melody. As they walked out of the Sunday School classroom, cars were streaming into the parking lot. So many people were cheating themselves, she thought, by skipping Sunday School, but at least they came to church.

The parking lot was partly blocked off with game booths and a bouncy house for the little ones, and the rest was nearly full even before fellowship time. She saw Teri's suburban pull in the back entrance to let out the boys. Taking a deep breath, she whispered a prayer. *Lord, don't let Nathan see anything in me that upsets him. Let him not even notice anything unusual. I'm not ready to tell him about the break-in just yet.*

As she rounded the corner of the building toward where the boys were unloading, she waved to Nathan and pointed to her Jeep. They met there, and as Nathan threw his gear in the back, he wrapped his arms around her waist in a bear hug.

"Hey, Mom. Did ya miss me? I'll bet you had fun without me, didn't ya?" Nathan's smile could always make her feel higher than a kite.

"I did miss you lots, and I only had a little bit of fun without ya!" She smiled. It was so good to have her boy back beside her. "So, did you rope some calves?"

"Sure did, and I won first place!" Nathan's excitement couldn't be contained.

"Really? With real calves?" Lindsay was surprised.

"Well, just one." He hung his head nearly to her shoulder briefly. "But we took turns trying to catch him and I'm the only one that did!" He pulled open his jeans jacket, and sure enough, there, pinned to his shirt, was a brown construction paper badge that looked like leather, proudly stating he was a #1 CALF ROPER. She handed him his Bible, and they turned to go into the church.

"Good job, Bud," she said as she took his hand in hers for the moment. Lindsay noticed Mark coming toward them. She hadn't thought about this. Was he expecting to sit with them? She, Nathan, and Arlene always sat together, and of course, Benny, and Mel would be here. She took a deep breath. She'd just tell Nathan the truth—*he was a friend, and they went horseback riding. She'd tell him it was a date. Maybe.*

Mark stopped to talk to Benny, as he arrived at the same time. They all gathered at the front and went inside, where Arlene was waiting. Nathan got big hugs from Gran, and everyone talked at the same time when Janet drove up. She and Melody both got out of the Jeep. Mel immediately ran toward them, embraced Gran, then acted a little shy with Benny. Lindsay watched the interaction with sadness. Mel had seen way more between her mom and dad than a 7-year-old should have. *Divorce can be so horrid.*

Lindsay watched as Nathan slipped in and took Mel's hand. It had been nearly a year since they had seen each other, and Mel's eyes sparkled. As the overhead lights started blinking, everyone started toward the sanctuary to find their seats for the worship service. Arlene beamed every step of the way as she entered and greeted her friends with her two grandchildren. Arlene found two rows with empty seats near the aisle. She, Nathan, Janet and Mel took the front row, leaving Lindsay in the row behind them with Mark and Benny. Finding herself between Mark and Benny, just as she had been most of yesterday, Lindsay felt safe and protected, but also very natural.

She whispered introductions between them as the singers began. As awkward as it seemed for the first few minutes, everything faded as she focused on the worship of her King. She found herself basking in the joy that Arlene was near tears just to have her entire family with her this morning. Lindsay was equally as sure that her mom was happy that Mark was sitting next to Lindsay. She allowed herself to be swept up in both the sweet old hymns as well as the contemporary songs and the harmonies that floated up to heaven.

They sat down as the announcements began, telling of all the community things going on this week, but then focusing on Fun Fest and the way things were set up for after service. The sermon was, as usual, a balance of Scripture and examples, peppered with the pastor's delightful sense of humor. They were truly a blessed congregation to have Pastor Billings and his family.

He and his wife, Carol, were in their mid-fifties. Their daughter, Alicia, was in her twenties, a college student who came home nearly every weekend and played the piano. Their adopted son, Chan, was Nathan's age. He and Nathan had hit it off instantly, but Alex and the other boys had taken a firm stance against Chan. Nathan had frequently found himself in the middle of their disagreements.

Pastor Stephen stood at the end of the last song and gave some last-minute instructions before he closed the service in prayer and blessed the food. Kingdom Kidz were to go out the back door while the adults and the littlest children were excused through the side door.

They all met up again outside at the table and served themselves from different sides of the potluck tables before finding a place on the grounds to eat. The folding tables had all been set up with napkins, plastic cups, and pitchers of lemonade. Lindsay thought that the chatter and laughter warmed hearts for blocks around.

Pastor Stephen, Carol, Alicia, and Chan came around with the trash bags as people were finishing their dessert of brownies and homemade ice cream, and the Fun Fest began. There were games for adults as well as the kids and the two hours passed quickly. Mel had finally warmed up to her dad, and they were holding hands walking between the ring-toss and bottle-throwing games. Lindsay was sitting on one of the benches with her lemonade when Mark sat down beside her.

"Is it okay if I sit with you?" he asked nonchalantly.

"Of course; why wouldn't it be?" Lindsay hadn't meant to sound sharp.

He looked around and said, "I don't know. I wouldn't want anyone to get the wrong impression." His semi-smile aroused her curiosity.

"What do you mean?" She felt herself blush again.

"Lindsay, I like you, and I think you like me. We're not a thing—yet. We're just friends right now, right? I mean, I don't want you to be upset. I know people. You know people. And people talk. Are you okay with that?"

Lindsay felt herself relax and chuckled. "Yes, Mark. I think I am okay with that. Like you say, people are going to talk. That's okay. We're just friends." *Why didn't she tell him she liked him, too?*

They talked about the Fun Fest and how successful it appeared to be. Nearly all the town had turned out. Benny was getting to visit with his daughter, and he was renewing some acquaintances of his Sunday School days. Nathan was laughing with Chan and some of the other boys. Arlene was in hog heaven talking with her friends about both of her grandkids being here. Life was good. Lindsay avoided thinking about the meeting with Lucky scheduled for later this afternoon. Or the stuff with Tom and the firm. No, she wouldn't think about that now. She would focus on the moment. On the answered prayers.

They decided the kids would go home with Arlene. That way, she and Benny could keep their 4:00 appointment with Lucky, assuring her they would be back no later than six. No one needed to know anything more than that. Janet had agreed that Benny could keep Mel until eight.

Mark and Benny would be her champions again

tonight while the policemen would be scattered throughout the diner. As Lindsay's thoughts began to prepare questions and comments, she felt herself tensing up. *Lord, I trust You. Go before me, please. Give me wisdom and discernment to learn the truth. Help me, please.*

She took a deep breath and looked at her watch. 3:10 pm. She stood, reminding Mark of her plans to meet Lucky at 4:00, and went to find Nathan.

"I'll be there." Mark stood and went in the opposite direction toward the parking lot.

Nathan came running up behind Lindsay, laughing when she jumped as he grabbed her. "Hey, Mom, what's up?"

"Hey, Bud. Your Uncle Benny and I have an appointment, so you and Mel are going to Gran's. We'll be there later. You leave here when Gran is ready, okay?" Lindsay chucked him on the chin at his grin.

"Aw, Mom. We'll be good to Gran. She plays dominoes and lets me win. We'll be fine!" They laughed and headed off together to find Benny and Mel. With everyone on board, Benny and Lindsay walked confidently toward the parking lot, their solid steps presenting a powerful team to be reckoned with. They came to Benny's truck first and separated with a fist bump. She could hear his truck start as she opened her car door.

Lindsay went home and changed into jeans and tennis shoes to feel more relaxed. They had planned to walk into the diner separately, so as not to arouse suspicion. Benny and Mark would be there before she got there right at 4:00. She took a deep breath as she locked the front door and got back in the car.

Seventeen

Kit's Kitchen's parking lot was relatively empty as Lindsey pulled in. Her eyes were drawn to Mark's truck, and a tender warmth filled her. She knew he would be here, but having him close put her at ease in a way that surprised her. As she exited her Jeep, she spotted Benny's vehicle as well. She crossed the parking lot, walked into Kit's, and asked the hostess for the corner booth.

Lindsay didn't recognize the police officers seated randomly around the diner. She hoped to sit in the corner booth where she and Mark had sat. The booth behind that one was where Mark was sitting. Benny would be joining him so they could hear what was being said when she met Lucky.

"Yes. Right this way." The waitress picked up a menu and led Lindsay to the booth. She sat down and ordered a sweet tea. Slipping off her jacket, she laid it beside her on the seat, covering her purse.

As she muted her cell phone and set it beside her, the

text screen popped up. It was from Mark. "I'm right beside you."

Instinctively, she looked to the left and chided herself inwardly at the partition that kept him hidden from her. Although hidden from sight, the latticework woven with greenery and coarse fabric would allow him to hear their conversation. She glanced around at other patrons of the diner. In her mind, she was deciding who was a policeman and who wasn't. She did see Chief Marsh in the back corner, talking with other people. Lindsay couldn't tell from his back who the man was. Two women were laughing over their drinks a few booths away from them.

The waitress brought her iced tea, and Lindsay told her she wasn't eating. A glance at her cell phone told her it was 4:05. She was slightly surprised that Lucky would be late after stressing the importance of this meeting. The door opened and Lindsay watched as a slightly scruffy man walked up to the counter and sat with his back to her. She sipped her tea, waiting as patiently as possible.

Minutes dragged before the door opened again and Benny walked in. He threw her a wink before heading behind the partition and sitting down with Mark. Another sip of tea, another peek at the cell phone, another deep breath. A group of teenagers came in laughing and headed to the game room in the back. The door opened again, and a couple came in and went to the booth beside the chief of police. They slipped in, both on the same side, his arm around her.

When the waitress came by to refill her tea, Lindsay ordered French fries. Munching on them would help pass the time. It was already 4:20. She wasn't sure how long she should wait. A cell phone rang from the booth where

Mark and Benny were seated. Mark spoke, and she realized he was giving her instructions.

"If you can hear me, cough," he said.

Lindsay faked a cough.

"Chief says you can wait as long as you want to. He will stay here with you and so will we. I heard you order fries; if you want to leave after you finish them, I'll meet you at your house. Chief says if this guy doesn't show by 4:45, he probably won't. But if you have his number with you, feel free to call him." He paused. "You've got this, Linds."

Lindsay picked up her phone and pulled Lucky's business card out of her pocket. She was hesitant but finally decided to call the number on the card. Ironically, a phone rang in the game room at the same time her call rang. A second ring, a second ring from the game room. She started to hang up. Nervousness prickled at her senses, causing her stomach to tighten. A click through the phone. Had it been answered? It was completely silent, except for shallow breaths. No more rings from the game room, either.

She trembled as the waitress brought her the fries. The waitress tapped the table until Lindsay looked up at her. She handed Lindsay the check, turning it over to show her the note written on the back of the check:

I'm not stupid. I don't know why you think you need police here. You're not in danger. You might be, though, if you won't talk to me. Privately. Some other time and place.

The phone in the game room did not ring again. Quickly, she texted Benny, and within seconds he said, "Hey, Mark, let's say we go in the back and check out the games."

Benny and Mark hurried across the room to the chief's table and laid what appeared to be Benny's cell phone in front of the chief. Then they turned and went into the game room. She couldn't hear what was said. The chief stood and walked to the counter and spoke to the couple sitting there. The couple got up and left rather quickly. Then, without looking at her, he quietly went to his table and sat back down.

Her phone chirped. She picked it up with shaky hands and read the text from Mark:

No one here but some kids. He must have gotten away.

Mark and Benny returned at the same time as the couple that the chief had spoken to. The couple went to the chief's booth while Benny and Mark went back to their booth next to Lindsay. She breathed easier at their nearness. After a quick conversation with Chief Marsh, the couple left. The chief and his partner started toward the door but stopped at Mark and Benny's table.

The chief spoke in a whisper but made sure she could hear. "A man was hanging around the back door. We took him in for questioning. I want to talk to this guy. We checked his phone, and found the townhouse address on it.. His ID says he is Donald Brand. Of course, Lucky could be his nickname.. We don't know if it's the man you saw in the parking lot yesterday or not. And he may not be working alone. Mark, you said you saw him briefly. Do you think you'd recognize him enough to identify him at the station?"

Lindsay's head swam. Yet she felt some relief. If they did have him in custody, they would get some answers, and she wouldn't have to face him alone.

"I think so. I'm willing to look." Mark stood and

followed the chief outside. Within seconds there was another text on her phone:

Chief says you're done here. Finish your fries and head on back to your house. I'll text Benny, and then I'll see you there.

Lindsay pushed her fries away, confusion making her brain feel foggy. If "Lucky" was still sitting here, that would leave just her and Benny. The sight of the fries made her sick. Couldn't she just leave and go home? This situation was making her skin crawl. She was about to text Benny back when he came out from behind the partition and slid into the booth across from her. He nonchalantly plucked a French fry from the basket in front of her, dipped it in the ketchup, and popped it in his mouth, never taking his eyes off hers.

Eighteen

"Hey, Sis, I didn't know you were here." Benny winked at his stressed sister. "Not much of a supper. Why don't we go to your house, and I'll fix us a real meal?" He slapped a $10 bill on the table, grabbed the check with the note on the back of it, and bowed toward her, motioning for her to head for the door. On the way to her car, he said, "Chief says we need to let Mom in on this situation. He and Mark are heading to her house now and they want us to meet them there."

"Benny, I'm getting scared. What is going on?" Lindsay's voice was low and shaky. He hugged her, took her keys, and opened the car door for her.

"I don't know, Sis, but it sounds serious. The chief has some answers already. Let's wait till we get to Mom's. I'm right behind you, Sis." She slipped into her car, and he turned around. He had parked his truck right next to her car, so he got in it, started it, and looked over at her, waiting for her to leave the parking lot first. Shaking her head, she started the car, took a deep breath, and drove out of the parking lot. *Lord, please, I don't know what's going on, but please keep my family safe and help us get to the bottom of all of this.*

When Lindsay pulled into Arlene's driveway, she parked near the garage so that Benny would have room behind her. Mark's truck was parked on the street out front, but he wasn't in it. As she opened her door and stepped out, the police car pulled in behind Mark's truck. Mark and the chief both got out and walked toward them.

"Mrs. Davis, why don't you and your brother go in first? We're right behind you," the chief suggested.

"I wish you hadn't involved Mom yet!" Lindsay barked. "I wanted to keep this quiet until I knew what was going on."

"I understand that," the chief answered. "Believe me, I do. But I don't think we can wait. Please, let's go in, and I will explain it to everyone all at once." Reluctantly, Lindsay and Benny stepped forward. He knocked on the door, as he opened it. Arlene sat at the table, dominos around her, as both kids jumped up and greeted their parents. They stopped short when they saw strangers come in the door also.

"Hi, guys," Lindsay said in her best cheerful voice. "We need to talk to Gran. Can you guys go out back and play for a while?"

"Sure, Mom. Come on, Melody. I'll show you what I found in one of Gran's trees." Nathan took Mel by the hand, and they were racing out the back door, letting it slam in their wake.

"Mom, this is Police Chief Marsh, and you know Mark. I don't even know what is happening, but Chief Marsh wants to bring us all up to speed at the same time.

Shall we sit down?" Lindsay sat on the couch as her mother joined her, concern showing in Gran's eyes.

The chief and Mark took side chairs while Benny pulled the chair over from the desk. The chief explained what had happened so far. Arlene sank back into the couch, reaching for Lindsay's hand when he got to the part about the break-in at her townhouse.

"This afternoon we took a guy in for questioning. We thought he was the man who confronted you, Mrs. Davis, in the parking lot yesterday. Mark says he was not the same man. We're not completely sure what part he has in all this yet, but we do know he is the rogue grandson of one of the partners where Tom worked. We have learned that Tom had some inside information that could put all of those partners away for years. It also appears that the partners were not aware that Tom had that information until just a few weeks ago." Chief Marsh shifted in his chair and took a deep breath. "This guy named "Lucky" told you he used to do jobs for your husband now and then, so it's my thinking that he is running scared, not from us so much as the partners. We think he helped Tom compile all this information, and when this grandson came into the picture, somehow, the word got out. The partners found out about Tom's evidence against them and hired the grandson to break into your house to find the evidence." He paused to let everyone catch their breath.

What kind of trouble had Tom left them with? Her mom squeezed her hand harder, and she met her gaze. Lindsay looked around the room with what she hoped was a comforting smile. She saw the same questions and fears buried deep in their eyes. *Lord, give us strength to endure whatever is ahead of us.* She returned her attention to the chief as he continued his not so terrific report.

"As I stated earlier, we also found the townhouse address in his phone," the chief declared. "And that's why we think he's the one who ransacked your house—by himself or with an accomplice, we don't know yet. But based on what you found, Mrs. Davis, we're assuming that he didn't find what the partners wanted." Lindsay felt her mom squeeze her hand when he mentioned the ransacking.

"Where does that leave us? What do we do now?" Lindsay whispered. Mark moved to sit on the arm of the couch nearest her.

The chief stood. "Well, as I advised earlier, I strongly urge you to move out of the townhouse. Even if just around the corner to your house, ma'am," he addressed Gran. "Lock your houses tight. My cars will make extra patrols around your house and the townhouse. I don't have your address, Ben." He pulled out his notebook as Benny stood and gave him the address of his apartment in Rutledge. "We'll continue questioning this kid. He seems to be on the outs with his family, and this may have been his way of getting back on good terms. We'll take all the evidence to the capital tomorrow and see what the Deputy Attorney General wants to do; then, we'll know how to proceed. We'll know a lot more by this time tomorrow."

Arlene stood first, followed by Lindsay. "You and Nathan can move right in over here tonight, dear. Don't you work tomorrow?" She faced Lindsay.

"Yes, I do, Mom. Can you keep Nathan after school?"

"Of course, sweetie. I'll fix supper and make sure he

gets his homework done. But, Lindsay, dear, if the chief thinks it wise to move out of the townhouse—"

Good old Mom. Lindsay could tell she was afraid of what was going on, but she was always the practical one. The chief turned back to her.

"My man will be close by, ma'am. No need to be concerned." As Lindsay walked the chief to the door, he continued. "Mrs. Davis, I'd like to pick you up after work so we can get going right away; will that work for you?"

"Sure, I get off at 2:00." She gave him the address of the Manor and closed the door behind him. She turned back to the room just as Nathan's head peeked in from the back door. "Yes, you can come in." She joked. Mel walked sheepishly to Benny, who swept her up in his arms.

"Whatya say, Munchkin, are you ready to head home or are you hungry?" Benny's eyes sparkled as he resumed his role of her dad—carefully, so as not to scare her away again.

Melody's lower lip stuck out. "No, Gran gave us sandwiches and mac-and-cheese. I'm not hungry. But we didn't get ice cream."

"Uh-oh, my bad." Gran was already going to the kitchen. "We still have time, don't we?" She looked at Benny. She already had dishes out. "Who wants a sundae? Strawberry? Pineapple or chocolate?" Everyone swarmed into her kitchen and sat around her table. Arlene was at her best when serving.

Toppings were placed in the center of the table and sundae dishes of vanilla ice cream in front of everyone. Mark joined them, sitting between Melody and Nathan, like another one of the kids. Lindsay stood back, leaning on the door frame, observing while eating her treat quietly.

What did she know about Mark Thomas? Obviously, he fit into her tight little family with ease, and he had played a huge part in her protection over the last two days. He had already won Mom's heart. Benny trusted him enough to begin counseling with him next week. When he had come to her house that horrible night of Tom's death, he was so caring and kind. He had recommended the Christian counselor, Sarah, an older woman. Lindsay reminisced what a help she had been, and appreciated Mark Thomas' concern counseling a woman.

Melody stuck her chocolate-covered spoon into Mark's strawberry sundae. Lindsay watched Mark as he pretended to be angry, returning the favor by smearing strawberry topping off his spoon into her dish. Melody giggled and finished the last bite of her crazy concoction of vanilla, chocolate syrup, and strawberry topping, along with the dab of pineapple she'd already swiped from Gran. *Mark is fitting right into this crazy bunch.*

"Okay, I'll take that, thank you," Gran said as she grabbed Mel's dish before a full food fight broke out. "Come let me clean you up a bit, little one." Melody slid off her chair and stuck her face out as she got near Gran. "Hands, too, please." Lindsay could tell how much her mom savored every moment of having both her grandkids with her. She expertly washed and dried Melody's hands and wrapped her in a tender hug before releasing her to her waiting father.

Melody jumped up into Benny's outstretched arms, laughing. Janet might not appreciate the sugar rush, but it was still early, so hopefully, Mel would wind down before bedtime. As they grabbed Mel's stuffed animals and the Bible character puppet she won as door prize at the Fun Fest, hugs were shared all around, and Benny and Melody left Gran's to take her home.

Sadness fell over Gran's features as she walked over to Nathan and lounged against his shoulder. Nathan finished his ice cream with a slurp. He took his dish to the sink and turned around. "Mom," he said quietly, "I have homework."

Everyone laughed. It had been a crazy, emotional weekend, but Lindsay was glad for the call back to normalcy, if only for the evening. *The kid has homework.*

Nineteen

After Nathan got in the car, Mark and Lindsay made plans. Mark was going to pick her up the next morning and take her to work, leaving her car at the townhouse. Then he would leave his truck at the station, and they would both ride with Chief Marsh after work to go to the Capitol; there wouldn't be such a vehicle shuffle when they returned.

As Lindsay got in the car, she could tell Nathan was waiting for an explanation. He did this every time he was asked to leave the room so the adults could talk. He always drilled her like an NCIS investigator to find out what it was all about.

"How much homework do you have, Bud?" She avoided the topic, knowing her tactic wouldn't work for long.

"I just have a couple of pages of math problems. It won't take me too long. I have this really cool mom who taught me all about fractions and stuff." Even as dusk was transitioning to dark outside the car, she could see his wonderful silly expression—the one he always wore when he was trying to pull something over on her.

"Okay, you work on your homework and then we'll talk." Nathan's eyebrows shot up. This was different. No interrogation? Hmm. He was at the counter with his math book before Lindsay had completely unloaded the car. She grabbed an apple and went upstairs to put away the last of the laundry while he finished his homework.

She poured herself a glass of iced tea and went into the living room. Peeking between the blinds, she could still see the police car in the parking lot. She went upstairs and put the "evidence" in a book bag and went downstairs. She'd run copies at work tomorrow before turning it all over to the Deputy Attorney General. She was crashing. She still had to decide how much to tell Nathan. She was thinking it through when he appeared.

"I like the living room, Mom." Nathan smiled. "I think it looks bigger. Get bored while I was gone?" He threw himself across the couch, eyes sparkling at her.

"Well, that's what I was going to tell you, but you'll be happier with the whole story." He flipped over so he was sitting up facing her, all ears. "While I was gone Saturday, the house was broken into and ransacked. I decided it was just easier to move the furniture while I was cleaning it all up."

"Did they find the—uh—anything?" Nathan's face was serious.

"Like what, Nathan?" She was interested in what Nathan knew or what he suspected.

"Oh, come on, Mom." He covered well. "On TV, whenever the house gets ransacked, the bad guys are looking for the loot, money or diamonds, or anything valuable."

She breathed a bit easier, but she still felt he was hiding something. "Well, you're right. They were looking, but we don't think they found it. The police came and—"

"The police were here?" Nathan interrupted. "And I missed it? Aw, man, that stinks. Wait 'til I tell Alex!"

"Nathan, wait. Please don't say anything to anyone just yet, okay?" Lindsay waited until he settled down and looked at her, puzzled. "This is serious, Bud. Until we know more about what's going on, you can't tell Alex or anyone else, okay?"

"Yes, ma'am." He was still focused on her and frowning, so she continued, still not sure how much she should share.

"You've kept Melody occupied a lot today while we've been talking, and I thank you and love you for it. But I need to let you in on what it is you've been missing out on." She studied his face. "Your dad hid some paperwork here that would implicate some people in some wrongdoing."

"Implicate?" Nathan asked.

"Implicate. It means—well, the paperwork could make some people look guilty of committing a crime."

"Okay." He looked directly at her, giving her his full attention.

"There were a lot of papers—" She began.

"You mean Dad's real estate project?" he asked, eyes wide like he may have given away too much information.

Lindsay's heart sped up. Did Nathan know about the paperwork? "Nathan, what do you know about this?" Lindsay asked cautiously.

"Well, um, Dad had a real estate project that he worked on sometimes while we were watching the games." Nathan hesitated and then continued. "He didn't tell me a lot, just now and then. Like one time, he said Gran's house was a safe house. He said it was like a game, and he called it Momopoly, like I used to call Monopoly, only it was real. But we don't get to play it until later on."

"Did your dad talk to you about this house?" Lindsay held her breath.

"Yeah." Nathan began studying his feet. "He said he didn't like this house much. He didn't want us to live here anymore, and he was going to find us a better place so we could have a better life."

"Did he talk about any other houses?" Lindsay was really intrigued now but didn't want to pump her son.

"Sure. Lots of 'em." Nathan talked more freely. "A place called Sunny Side Up—that was the place on a hill. He said when the sun came up, the lake looked like an egg in a skillet. And Lucky Dog—that was a secret game room. And there was a place called the Presidential Palace, and Old McDonaldson's Farm, and—um, oh, Happy Trails. Then he'd always sing some dumb old song he knew. It was fun, Mom." He paused. "I sure do miss him." Lindsay's heart was sputtering. *Happy Trails? Old Mc Donaldson's farm? These were places she knew.*

"I know you do, Bud." Lindsay took a deep breath to slow her pulse. "I miss him, too." Lindsay decided to postpone further discussion until some other time. "Did you finish your homework?" At his nod, she moved to the couch beside him.

"I want you to walk to Gran's house after your haircut

tomorrow and stay there until I pick you up, okay? I have an appointment after work. Then we'll have supper with Gran.. I don't know for sure how long I'll be, so do your homework when you get there. Okay? But it's important that you not tell anyone about this, okay? And nothing about Dad's real estate game, okay? Or Momopoly. That's just for family."

"Sure, Mom. I promised Dad that, too. I never said anything to anyone, not even you!" His features flashed regret, and he studied his lap.

What did he just say? Lindsay replayed the conversation they started but never finished. Nathan had been keeping a secret for his dad. Sadness struck her heart. How in the world was this happening? "But I—" Nathan broke into her thoughts.

"But what, Bud?" Lindsay asked, noticing Nathan's gaze was glued to the floor.

"I didn't like not telling you about it. But I promised Dad, and I can keep a secret." His voice quivered. He glanced up at her and immediately looked away, wrinkling his sweet young face into a sad frown.

"Aw, Bud." Lindsay slipped her arm around him on the back of the couch. "Of course, you can. I'm so sorry you feel bad. I understand it because we're not supposed to keep secrets, are we? I'm sorry Daddy told you to not tell me." Lindsay was determined to turn her anger toward Tom into some compassionate way of salvaging the situation for his son. "But maybe Dad thought I would be worried or upset if you told me about it."

"Yeah, maybe that's why." Nathan looked up at her hopefully, and she saw a glint of a tear. Adding a squeeze to her hug before she moved away from the couch, she spoke gently while every muscle in her body was tensing as if ready for a fight.

"Why don't you go hop in the shower and get your pj's on, and then we'll pray. Okay?" Lindsay felt like her heart was plummeting, as she watched her son—who had carried such a burden for so long—walk slowly up the stairs. *How could Tom have put Nathan in this position?* She put her hands on each side of her head and spun around. *Poor Nathan. Oh, Lord, help me to help my son. Take this burden from him!*

She felt totally overwhelmed by all that her husband had orchestrated before his death. When she first started finding things, she thought it was all for her and Nathan. And part of it was, for sure. But how much did they really need? He had amassed so much more than they would ever need, and she was sure they hadn't discovered it all.

"Oh, Tom." She felt a tear slip down her cheek as the words escaped her trembling lips. How could Tom put such a burden on their son? How much did Nathan know? Old doubts came rushing back to her—was Tom's death an accident? Was she being naïve? Or was she being paranoid? No, she needed Chief Marsh to check into it.

Twenty

earing the shower in Nathan's bathroom, Lindsay went upstairs to her bedroom window and looked out across the parking lot. The unmarked police SUV was still there. Lindsay was surprised that she didn't feel at peace as she expected to. After Nathan was in bed, she would call Mark and let him know what Tom had confided in their son. Was there more? How much should she "drill" Nathan? She wanted to protect his nice calm life, but she wasn't sure she could do that anymore. She undressed, slipped into her pajamas, and started out the door to get a snack from the kitchen when she heard Nathan calling her.

"Right here, Bud." She stood behind him quietly. He was at the top of the steps, all ready for bed, with his hair dripping water everywhere. "You can be such a goof," she said, steering him back to the bathroom and grabbing the towel from the side of the tub. Both of them were laughing as she towel-dried his thick curls like she did when he was a toddler.

"Ready to hear my prayers?" he asked.

"Of course," she said, throwing the towel into the bathroom hamper. "Hey, Bud, do you know where Dad kept his Momopoly papers?"

"Sure. The first level is above the refrigerator. The second level is under your bed. The third level is in the trunk of his hide-and-seek den. The last one is in his gun safe in the garage." Lindsay had to sit down. A thick fog rolled over her mind. This couldn't be right. They had only found the first level.

She forced herself to breathe as she grabbed hold of Nathan's hand, she tugged him forward into his bedroom "Okay, sweet boy. Let's pray."

He nodded and took her hand before kneeling beside his bed. Tears welled in Lindsay's eyes, and she joined her son on the floor. "You start tonight, okay?" she asked, throat tight.

Dear Lord, Nathan prayed, *I'm sorry for making fun of Chan today. Thank you for having him 'cept my apology. I'll do better with that. I'm sorry I missed all the 'citement when the police came, but I thank you for keeping Mom safe. Thank you for bringing Mel back to Gran. She was real happy 'bout that. I think I'm sorry I didn't tell Mom 'bout Dad's game, even if Dad asked me not to. Help her to not hurt anymore. Amen.*

Lindsay let the tears fall and sniffed before she shifted into automatic pilot and added her prayer, falling back on the acronym for help: A-adoration, C-confession, T-thanks, and S-supplication.

Oh, Lord, we love you. You are such an amazing God. We adore You. I ask that you forgive us both for our wrongdoings, even those we forget. I thank you for my son. You know what it feels like to watch a child who is hurting. I ask You to lift this burden from him and continue to guide us to the truth and protect us in our quest for that truth. I ask You for a good night's sleep for both of us, and a good day at school for Nathan and for me at work in the morning. We do love you, Lord. Amen.

"Nathan," she said, "you didn't have to apologize for keeping Dad's secret. It's kind of a hard call because by not telling me, you were obeying your dad. I think..." Lindsay faltered. "I think your dad was wrong to ask you to keep that secret, but I think he meant well. I understand why he did it. Please don't feel bad about it, okay?"

Their hug was especially poignant for Lindsay that night. Thoughts of how dangerous things could really be tainted her usually sappy good-night with her son. Lindsay found herself at a loss. As soon as she reached her room, she went first under her bed. As quietly as possible, so she wouldn't disturb Nathan, she pulled the storage tub out from under the bed and opened it. There, as she had expected, were Bible study guides. She and Tom had attended these together. A blue notebook held those that they had facilitated together before Tom got too busy at work. There on the bottom were all the notebooks with his notes, nothing out of the ordinary.

She pulled out one of the notebooks, *Gripped by the Grace of God* by James McDonald. Opening it, she methodically thumbed through the loose-leaf pages. Nothing unusual. As she pulled out another binder, loose papers fell out of the back. She straightened them, trying to keep them in the order they had been placed inside their hiding place. After pulling out all the remaining binders, she stacked the papers that Tom had stashed in the back of each of the remaining notebooks. They weren't a a part of the Bible Studies. When she finished, the stack of evidence was nearly seven inches tall. She gathered all the loose papers and put them in a boot box from her closet. She couldn't focus on the content of the papers yet. She didn't want to know. Working diligently, she closed the storage bin and shoved it back under the bed, less the overflowing boot box. She moved to the door partially hidden by the chaise lounge in her bedroom. She hesitated as she looked at the door, willing herself to open it, praying for the strength to attack the trunk inside.

It was the only thing Tom had left after losing his parents. It was old and musty when he had brought it here, and Lindsay had paid dearly to have an expert restore it. That's when he placed it up here, beneath the window in the hide-and-seek den—his man cave. She hadn't been in there since he died. She heard her heart pounding in her ears, as she slowly unlocked the door, turned on the light, and released the breath she was holding when she saw nothing amiss.

The stuffy smell irritated Lindsay's nose as she slowly stepped into Tom's sanctuary. She realized that she had forgotten all about this room when the police were there. Tom had hired contractors to seal off the hall entrance and rebuild one from the master bedroom. That must have stopped the intruders. She went to the trunk, carefully removed the heavy wool army blanket on top, and opened the lid. The lid opened easily, and Lindsay was surprised it didn't creek with its age.

She turned on the lamp near Tom's recliner to better see inside. Tears were starting to slip down her cheeks as she smelled the leather of his chair. How many times had she crawled into his lap to kiss him goodnight before she went to bed, leaving him to whatever project he was engrossed in?

The college letter jacket was on top of the trunk's contents, followed by some pictures, pennants, programs, and other memorabilia that had been on the wall in their previous house. She blinked back the tears and took a deep breath. *Focus, Lindsay.*

Moving all these treasures—the mementos of the night they met, their dating and courtship—all these memories could have set her back any other time. But she was on a mission. Her determination paid off. Finally, she found the stash of folders and boxes.

On top of the folders was a copy of the handwritten letter that Tom had written. The original had been found in the folder above the refrigerator. She opened the folder lying on top. *Had Tom realized the extent of the crimes that had been committed?* She couldn't imagine that. But the evidence lying before her was too much to deny. Level 1—2—3—4... to her, each level indicated worse crimes.

As Tom discovered another "level" or depth to the criminal activities that his firm was involved in, he must have felt he had to find another hiding place for the evidence he was amassing. Lindsay wasn't sure what she was looking at. A draft of a deed that had handwritten changes in dollar amounts. There were carbon copies of papers that showed the changes had been typed into new documents. She saw scraps of papers that had the signatures of the parties to the documents written repeatedly. Practicing to forge a signature? Her heart was beating wildly as she realized he had been getting in deeper and deeper. *No wonder he was afraid. How could she not be afraid? Maybe she should consider moving in with Mom.*

✦ *Twenty-One* ✦

Lindsay pulled out the boxes holding level 3 and put them directly into the back of her Jeep. Then she hurried to the garage, found an empty box, placed the folders in it, and stashed that in her car as well. After making sure the Jeep was securely locked, she went upstairs to collect the book bag that contained Level 1. The boot box holding level 2 and the stack of papers and boxes was in her Jeep with level 3. That left level 4 —the gun safe in the garage.

Lindsay focused her steps to the gun safe and examined the lock. Staring at the safe, she racked her brain. No matter how she tried, she couldn't remember the combination. At some point, way back when, Tom had told her the combination. Or had he told her where he had written it down? She pinched the bridge of her nose, trying to fend off a tension headache. *Think, think, think.* She ran her hands along the back and sides of the safe. How ridiculous. Tom was too smart to leave the combination near the gun safe. She was too tired to figure it out.

She turned off the garage light and went back up to Tom's man cave, slipped quietly back into the door, and sat down in his recliner. Closing her eyes and taking in a deep breath, she could practically smell Tom sitting here with her. She looked around the room at his bookshelves. Her thoughts betrayed her. No longer could she focus on the here and now. All she could remember was a snippet of a conversation—about his birth parents. It was probably the only thing he had ever told her about them, and she couldn't remember what he said. The trunk had sent her memory into overdrive.

She left the room, closing and locking the door. A glance at the clock on her nightstand told her it was 10:15. She sank into the chaise lounge. Reaching in her robe pocket for her phone, she searched for Mark's name and hit send. As it rang, she drew the throw around her shoulders.

"Everything okay?" He answered quickly. She could sense the concern in his voice and took a deep breath.

"Sorry to call so late. Nathan and I had an enlightening conversation tonight." She whispered so as not to awaken Nathan. "It seems his father confided in him some interesting information." She stopped to regain her composure. She was so angry with Tom at this moment, she didn't want that anger to flood onto Mark. "There are a lot more properties involved. It looks like we only uncovered level 1 of Tom's 'real estate game'. He called it Momopoly, because that's how Nathan used to pronounce Monopoly." She went on to explain where Tom had hidden the other levels and what she had found. "I can't remember the combination to the gun safe, and that's where Nathan said the last level is supposed to be."

"Wow." Mark sounded as tired as she was. She heard his sigh. "Well, you can get the combination from the manufacturer, so don't lose sleep over that for now. I'm beginning to think this went a lot deeper than Tom originally thought it would. No wonder he got scared."

"Yeah." Lindsay just wanted to breathe.

"Linds, that's a lot. I can't imagine why Tom would have told Nathan these things." Mark was at a loss as to how to comfort her, other than just letting her talk.

"I know. I don't know what to make of it." Lindsay bit her bottom lip to hold back the emotion threatening to overtake her. The whole view of the life she had with Tom was crumbling. She wanted to believe the best of him, but none of this made sense.

"I am so sorry, Lindsay. It looks like the more he tried to wrap it up, the more he found. I wonder why he only locked up the last level. That's the one that got him—" He cut his sentence short, but it was too late. Lindsay finished the sentence in her mind. That was the one that got him killed. A sharp gasp escaped her lips.

"Tom's death wasn't an accident, was it, Mark?" she whispered. She waited for a few beats. Mark's silence confirmed everything she'd been afraid of. "How long have you known?"

"Well, Chief Marsh and I have been throwing around some what-ifs. We're not sure, but—"

"But you're sure," Lindsay said, the back of her eyes burning. "In your heart."

"I was going to say, he's checking into it. He's pulling

the old investigation reports. Lindsay, I'm so sorry," Mark said sincerely.

Lindsay sat in stunned silence, unsure how to respond. "Thanks, Mark. Me, too. I'm so tired. My brain is just fried."

"I can understand that. Is Nathan asleep? How is he doing?"

Lindsay smiled slightly. It touched her heart that the counselor in him would be concerned about the welfare of her son. Or was he showing his care for her on a more personal level?

"He's feeling pretty bad that his dad asked him to keep a secret from me. He apologized to God for that, so I think he's feeling guilty. I think he's asleep. He had a very busy weekend. Anyway, I loaded everything in the car and locked it in the garage, so if you want to come early to pick me up, we can transfer it to your truck and then give it all to Chief Marsh. If—"

"If what?" Mark asked.

"I'm scared, Mark. I don't know who to trust. Can we trust Chief Marsh?" Her voice faded away as she finished the thought.

"Lindsay, I don't want you to think like that." Mark's counselor training against paranoia kicked in. "I know it looks bleak, but Chief Marsh wasn't in on any of this before now, so I think he's safe."

"Oh, of course, you're right." Lindsay felt like she was convincing herself.

"I'm going to call the chief tonight. He might want to come and get it directly in the morning. But either way, we'll take care of it in the morning. Can you try to get some sleep?"

"Yeah, right." She yawned as exhaustion tugged at every muscle in her body. "You, too." She ended the call and leaned back on the chaise, feeling too tired to make it to her bed. She closed her eyes to shut down her mind, but it kept spinning around the day's discoveries. *Lord, I'm not sure how to face these things. Give me strength and wisdom. But mostly keep me and my loved ones safe.*

In her mind's eye, she saw a picture of the shadow of the Almighty hovering over her and Nathan. Peace washed over her as she felt the truth of Psalm 91 envelop her. It was He who guarded her. She would once again put her trust in Him, believing deep down, it would be enough.

Twenty-Two

Five AM came way too early. Lindsay stumbled from the chaise lounge to the nightstand near the bed. She slapped the snooze button on the alarm. She lay across the bed to get a few more winks, but the alarm insisted that it was indeed time to get out of bed.

She slipped groggily into the shower, hoping it would pour some life into her stressed body. She wished she had skipped her excursion through Tom's records and gone to bed and read her Bible for a while instead. Going through the motions, she pulled her wet hair into a bun at the base of her neck and put on her scrubs. She glanced at the clock as she sat on the bed to dress her feet. *Wow, it's already 5:45.* Chiding herself for not setting her alarm earlier so she had time to read her Bible this morning, she dragged herself toward the stairs.

Starting the coffee pot, she pulled out the griddle and turned it on to heat. She whisked the pancake batter and poured four perfectly matched pancakes onto the griddle. Nathan stumbled down the steps and into the kitchen.

"Hey, Bud. You're down early." She went to the fridge, poured a glass of milk, and set it down in front of him. She flipped the pancakes and set the butter and silverware on the table. She put the syrup in the microwave to heat, and grabbed two plates from the cupboard, setting them on the warmer next to the griddle. She poured herself a cup of coffee and added cream, taking a sip before setting it on the table at her place. She turned and plated the pancakes and placed them on the table. She sat down across from Nathan. After grace, the butter and syrup were passed, and they bit into the perfect pancakes. "Mm-mm," Lindsay said, finally starting to wake up.

"Mm mm-hmm," Nathan replied. It was their normal morning conversation. Until he had finished his first pancake and until she had a good start on her coffee, their words were mostly monosyllabic. She shooed Nathan back upstairs to get dressed as she rinsed their plates. Lindsay was pouring her coffee-to-go when she heard the light tap at the door. She poked her head out and told Chief Marsh she'd raise the garage door. Nathan came out to the garage as they were busy transferring the "evidence" to the chief's unmarked car. Lindsay noticed Nathan was watching intently. After realizing what she saw, she again wondered who she could trust. Apparently, Tom had trusted someone he shouldn't have. Who might that be? Surely, she could trust the chief of police.

Chief Marsh shook his head and raised his eyebrows as he looked at her. "I'll take a good look at all of this before we get together. Mark will be here to pick you up pretty shortly, I just wanted to get a head start on this."

"Chief, this is my son, Nathan. Nathan, Chief Marsh. I'm sorry you weren't properly introduced yesterday. I was a little distracted." She closed the hatch as they shook hands. "Chief, Nathan and his dad watched a lot of football games, and this paperwork represents the levels of a "real estate game" called Momopoly that Tom was working on during those games. There are a lot more properties here, like a monopoly game, Nathan said. But this appears to be more than a game. Nathan was instrumental in leading me to all of this."

"Nice to meet you, Nathan. It sounds like your dad knew his stuff. It's great that you were able to tell your mom where to find all of it. This is really important stuff." She watched as Nathan beamed. "Can I give you a ride to school or is it too early?"

"Wow, Mom, can I?" Nathan's eyes lit up.

"Grab your book bag, but remember—" Nathan took off before she had a chance to finish her thought. "Hey! Wait!" She followed after him. He stopped mid-stride and turned toward her. "You say nothing to anyone, just yet— not even Chief Marsh," she said quietly and peeked to see if the chief noticed their exchange. He seemed to be busy inspecting the new items she'd given him.

"Yes ma'am," he whined as he screwed up his mouth and tipped his head to the side for a moment, but then turned and headed into the house.

"Mrs. Davis, I'll need you to sign this please." Chief Marsh held out a yellow pad on which he had written brief general descriptions of the contents of the boxes as evidence. He made an "X" under a handwritten statement that declared that she had given him files and all the paperwork—and that no one else had tampered with them since she had found them. She signed it, and then he signed it below her signature and dated it. "I'll have copies made for you before we turn it all over to the Deputy Attorney General," the Chief said as he started toward his car.

"Thank you, Chief." Lindsay decided not to tell Chief Marsh that there were more files in the gun safe. They were locked up, so no one needed to know about them yet anyway. Nathan returned from the house and stood beside her sheepishly, his book bag hooked over one shoulder.

"I'll see you at Gran's tonight," Lindsay said. Nathan hesitated for a second to hug her, then continued on his way to Chief Marsh's car. Waving, she lowered the garage door and stepped back into the kitchen, turning off the coffee pot.

Gathering her things, she took another sip of her coffee and walked to the front door just as Mark pulled up. She locked the door behind her and slid into the passenger seat of his truck.

"Mornin'," he said. "How'd you sleep?"

"I was really surprised. I slept better than I expected to, but it was a short night. You?" She fastened her seat belt and settled in the seat.

"Pretty well. Why a short night?" Mark asked.

"Well," she began, "I didn't go to bed after I talked to you. I kept exploring and found some interesting things."

"Like what?" he asked as he turned out of the parking lot.

"Like what looks like a practice sheet for copying a signature. Like legal papers that look to me like the numbers have been changed after they were signed. But I don't really know what I'm looking for, so I finally quit and went to bed."

"Wow," Mark said. "That is certainly another big layer. Did you tell the chief about it?"

Lindsay shook her head. "Not yet." *Should she tell him about this sudden unease about confiding in him? She wasn't sure.* "With everything spinning, I'm just not sure who to trust anymore."

Mark swallowed hard. "Understandable." He paused for a beat. "But I hope you know you can trust me."

"I do," she said quietly, and another few minutes of comfortable silence engulfed them.

"You have a busy day planned at work today?" he said as he turned onto the highway, breaking the silence.

"Not too busy," she answered. "Mondays the nursing students come from Rutledge and do a lot of the work for us, and all the CNAs get to play Supervisor. We like that. We usually have our staff meetings mid-morning while the students are covering for us." She smiled at the thought of such normalcy. It would be nice not to think about the insanity for a few hours. She could just slip into her normal routine and forget that her whole world had been turned upside down. "How about you?"

"I have two sessions this morning," he answered. "I cleared this afternoon so I could go with you and the chief. By the way, I never did thank you for referring Ben. I appreciate it."

"Oh, Mark, you did so much to help me with Tom's acci—with his death. Benny really needs to get his head straight, and I was hoping you had time to take him on."

"No problem. I'll do what I can. You get off at 2?" He pulled up to the front entrance of the Manor.

She nodded. "I'll be right here."

"Thanks. I shouldn't be late." She gathered her things

and slipped out of the truck. As she strode up the walkway, she noticed Crystal grinning at her from the window.

Lindsay stepped through the door and turned toward Crystal. "Girl, don't even think about what you're thinking about." Lindsay walked right past her and down the hall toward the time clock. Crystal was right behind her. Lindsay's mind raced. How would she ever explain this weekend's events? Was there a simplified version that would even make sense? None of it made sense to Lindsay. She would be at a loss to relay the information to anyone else.

"Oh, come on, you haven't even had so much as a date since Tom died, and Mr. Twin Peaks Family Counseling himself brings you to work? You can't for one second think you're going to get past me without explaining!" She chuckled at Lindsay's look of surrender. "Spill it!"

"It's not a short story, and it isn't anything like what you're thinking." Lindsay hung her jacket on the hook and punched the time clock, then turned to face Crystal. "My brother Benny is having trouble getting past his divorce. Mark is meeting with him." Lindsay attempted to slip past her, and Crystal side-stepped in front of her.

"Not even close." Crystal's smile broadened.

"Okay, my house was ransacked Saturday while we were—okay, Mark and I went horseback riding on Saturday and while we were gone, my house was trashed. Since Mark was with me at the time, he stayed to be sure I was okay."

"All weekend?!" Crystal squealed.

"No! Come on, Crystal, you know me better than that! Mark and the chief of police are picking me up after work today so we can go see the DA. He picked me up at home this morning to bring me to work to avoid having to shuffle vehicles later. That's it, plain and simple."

"Not quite!" Crystal was nearly hugging Lindsay's side as she walked beside her. "Who ransacked your house? What's that all about?"

Lindsay took in a breath ragged with frustration. She wished she knew, but it seemed like the deeper she dug, the scarier things became. Much like what happened to Tom.

Twenty-Three

"Oh, Crystal," Lindsay said, "I've already said too much. We don't know much yet other than my house was completely ransacked. The police are involved, and more questions are popping up than answers. Please don't say anything to anyone. This is serious stuff," Lindsay whispered.

Crystal made the motion of a zipper across her mouth. "My lips are sealed. Just keep me posted. I need some excitement in my life." Crystal playfully slapped her on the shoulder as Lindsay ducked into the laundry storage room for clean linen. Crystal turned and went into the dining room to prepare for breakfast. Six nursing students came through the side door into the dining room and headed straight to the kitchen.

The routine for Mondays simplified what had once been a complicated day-long fiasco. Because the nursing students came for the entire day, the staff took advantage of the extra hands. After all, their presence doubled the workforce. Crystal took the first group of the students and

Lindsay took the last group. Mondays were laundry day, so all the beds were stripped and made up with fresh linen.

Lindsay felt free to let her thoughts show on her face as she worked alone for the next hour. Her feelings had been all over the board these past few days, and she relished in the peace of the laundry. Her son had kept a difficult secret from her. As hard as that was to accept, it was even more difficult to see how much it hurt him to betray his dad by telling her. Tom never should have put this sweet boy in that position. Lindsay tried to fold up her emotions and organize them as she did the sheets, to fit into a nice little package that she could put aside and deal with later.

Crystal's team went to each room in the West Wing, bringing the residents to the dining room, making sure everyone had breakfast. The soiled linen was in the washers before the residents finished their breakfast. Then the process was repeated for the East wing residents. Every bed in the entire manor had clean sheets by mid-morning every Monday. The laundry staff could handle the washing, drying, folding, and storing, so the nursing staff was performing actual nursing duties for the rest of the day.

Lindsay's team had the East Wing residents in the Commons by the time the regular staff walked toward the Conference room. Lindsay took the time to touch base with each of her elderlies. She was happy to see Betty and Opal had settled nicely in the TV area watching *Dr. Phil*. Margie and Richard, always together, were pondering over a puzzle near the window. The lid stood propped up against the lamp, revealing a magnificent painting of a hillside of snow with a waterfall cascading into a frozen lake. Norman was reading a newspaper at the same table. Grace sat off to the side, a near-smile on her face, with her frail hand keeping beat on the arm of the recliner.

The staff meeting went well with the normal cinnamon buns and coffee helping the mood. Each department gave its weekly reports. Gripes were addressed and many resolved; others were tabled, to be addressed at some future date. Mr. Foster announced the date and plans for the Annual Safety Awards Banquet and happily declared that financing for the renovation had finally passed and the plans were at the architect's office. This brought a cheer from the staff. The main building had been built in 1947, with the West Wing being added in 1969. Since that time, the maintenance had been diligently addressed, but there was nothing more done. He also announced that budgeting had been approved for another CNA, so they would be taking applications immediately. Everyone chatted enthusiastically as they came out of the meeting.

Lindsay slipped through the Commons and walked down the hall to the dining room. She pulled her lunch out of the fridge and sat down at a table in the corner near the drink machine to take her break. Her mind wandered to what the new wing would look like, and her excitement began to grow in anticipation.

After the break, Lindsay pushed Betty's wheelchair out to the front porch. Richard came out the door with Margie. When Lindsay went back inside to get Grace, she met Norman pushing Opal's chair. The sun peeked through the trees, so the porch would soon be in the shade. It wouldn't be too warm, and none of the residents would need sunscreen.

Most of the residents loved to be outside when the weather permitted. They always gathered at the tables, with their backs to the building, facing the driveway. However, Grace always stayed close to the door, sometimes even blocking it. Lindsay maneuvered Grace's chair to one side of the front doors and sat in the patio swing near her.

Everyone appeared to be at peace, some chatting, some just enjoying the singing of the birds perched in the bushes along the sidewalk. The high school shop class had donated several birdhouses last year, and the maintenance crew had placed them on poles at varying heights. It appeared to Lindsay that there were no vacancies, and the residents thought it a delightful pastime. Lindsay looked up happily when Melissa came up the walk. She didn't want to be late, and Melissa was her replacement today for the second shift.

Crystal came out bringing warm apple crisp, fresh out of the oven. Lindsay helped them serve and went inside to clock out. As she stepped back outside, she saw Chief Marsh's car pull into the drive and stop. Mark got out of the car and stood beside the front passenger door, handing her a McDonalds iced tea. Thanking him for the unexpected treat, Lindsay climbed in. Mark closed the door, opened the back, and slid into the seat behind her. Lindsay could only imagine what the comments were going to be tomorrow, not just from Crystal, but from this elderly family of hers as well.

Chief Marsh began to speak as he pulled away from the curb. "Hello, Mrs. Davis. I talked to Deputy Attorney

General David Harrell this morning. He and your husband had been working on this for three years before Tom just suddenly stopped contacting him. That appears to be a couple of months before your husband died."

"Chief, please call me Lindsay, and exactly what is the *this* we're talking about?" Lindsay fastened her seat belt and took a long drink of the refreshing iced tea, thinking how thoughtful Mark was. Then she held her breath, dreading hearing the answer, yet knowing she had to know the truth.

Twenty-Four

Mark spoke from the back seat. "That's not completely clear yet, Lindsay. But we'll find out a lot more at this meeting."

'For sure," Captain Marsh chimed in. "We're meeting with David Harrell—he's the Deputy Attorney General—and a woman from the Securities and Exchange Commission, and a man from the FBI."

Suddenly, the atmosphere in the car changed. Lindsay felt like the air was sucked right out of her lungs. "The FBI?"

"That's right, Mrs.—I mean, Lindsay. There apparently are a lot of laws that Tom felt were being broken by the firm's partners. We're guessing he didn't know who he could trust. Not to mention what agency would be best to handle it. We'll have a lot more answers in just about twenty minutes."

"Have a good day?" Mark asked. Mark tried to lighten the mood. Lindsay appreciated that his efforts seemed to put her at ease again.

"Sure." Her reply was automatic until she shifted gears in her brain. "We got the good news that we finally got approved for funding to do a full upgrade on the Manor. I'm sure you can see what needs to be done to the outside, and the inside needs it even more. The plans are with the architect now, so we should be able to start work next spring." Lindsay knew she was rambling. It's what she did when she was nervous.

"That sounds great," Mark replied.

"It sure does," Captain Marsh commented. "My aunt was there for the last several years of her life. She died in —oh, I guess it's been about 10-12 years now, and it looks exactly the same as it was when we brought her in!"

"I'm sure it is!" Lindsay shared with them when it was last renovated, and they made small talk the rest of the trip, making the time pass quickly. As they reached the edge of town, she felt her stomach get a little queasy. Mark seemed to notice everything.

"You okay, Lindsay?" he asked gently.

"I guess so. I should be looking forward to this, so we can get some answers, but I just wish the whole thing was already over." She took a deep breath as Captain Marsh pulled into the underground parking lot of the capitol building. Lindsay felt a little bit better when he had to show his badge at the security booth.

They parked, and Mark and the chief unloaded boxes from the chief's car. Another security guard met them at the door and led them to a conveyor belt where they set the boxes to be x-rayed. The guard carefully studied the security screen, and once he was satisfied that the boxes contained nothing but paperwork, he hailed the elevator for them. He also wheeled out a small dolly and helped them stack the boxes onto it.

"I'm going to ask you both to remain quiet unless someone particularly asks a question, "Captain Marsh said with a half-smile. "Sorry, but I already told them everything we know, and they know a lot more than we do, so let's just let them do most of the talking, ok?

"I'm great with that." Lindsay nodded as she stepped into the elevator. They were greeted by a uniformed bailiff who signaled for them to go through security, then they followed the officer down a hall that appeared to go to the complete opposite side of the building.

They went through another metal detector further down the hall to an unoccupied desk, where Lindsay disposed of her iced tea. The bailiff reached across the desk and pushed a button to an intercom, announcing his name. "Majors plus three." The door buzzer surprised Lindsay, and she jumped.

"Sorry, ma'am." The young officer looked up at her as he motioned them toward the door he had opened. "I forget how loud that can be. I 'bout jumped out of my skin the first time I heard it!" Lindsay thought how kind he was to try to put her at ease, but his efforts were in vain. They walked into a well-lit room where a man and a middle-aged woman sat around an oval table.

Mr. Harrell appeared to be in his early fifties, obviously in charge as he introduced himself and Mrs. Coleman. Captain Marsh introduced himself. "This is Lindsay Davis and her advisor, Mark Thomas." Everyone shook hands and sat down, leaving the dolly piled high with the boxes near the Captain's chair. Captain Marsh handed David Harrell the yellow pad she had signed that morning, and he signed for possession of the evidence and cleared his throat before he began.

"I'm sorry, but Agent Whittier got detained. He will be here shortly. He already knows most of the story, anyway, so I'll bring you up to speed before he gets here if that's alright with you."

Lindsay's head was in a whirl. She was so glad that the chief had asked them to be observers because she didn't think she could form two coherent thoughts at the moment. The story Mr. Harrell was sharing with them was something out of a Detective Show—only this was real life and there could be, according to him, real danger. They had been concerned when Tom stopped contacting him, and when they sent a messenger to check on him, Tom said he was finished with the intrigue, had gone as far as he was going to go, and was done with it all. Mr. Harrell was concerned about his safety and offered to relocate all of them, but he said Tom had declined his offer, reiterating that he was done playing spy so the danger should be over.

It was about six weeks later that Tom had called him and said he thought he'd better get some protection after all. But Tom had said that he didn't want to go into protective custody. He only wanted his family to be safe. According to the Deputy Attorney General, Tom said he had waited too long. David Harrell apologized, telling her that he blamed himself. After all, Tom was innocent in this. He had come to the Attorney General's office with amazing information, and they had assured him safety if he would keep digging until they had enough to put this bunch away for a long time.

Twenty-Five

Mr. Harrell repeated how much he regretted not stressing the danger. Tom and David Harrell had been working on this for three years before Tom suddenly stopped contacting him. "That appears to be a couple of months before your husband died." The words still echoed in Lindsay's brain. Tom had waited too long. Mr. Harrell apologized, telling her again that he blamed himself for Tom's death.

"After all, Tom was innocent in this," Mr. Harrell repeated.

Then Mrs. Coleman stepped in. She began explaining the details of the crimes the firm had been getting away with—for 15 years, that they knew of. Most of it was above Lindsay's head; after all, she didn't know anything about real estate or RICO.

She sat and listened as Chief Marsh had asked her to, but the whirling in her head was giving her a horrible headache. Despite her efforts, Lindsay couldn't pay very close attention. It felt like this conversation was beginning to echo. She heard Chief Marsh's voice asking about the accident.

"We have done some further investigation into that," Mr. Harrell was saying. "But it has been inconclusive so far. Some questions were not answered during the original investigation, so we're going to keep digging."

The buzzer went off and was answered, and another man walked in. Suddenly Lindsay was on alert as introductions were being made.

Alan Whittier, FBI Agent, shook her hand. He held it a little longer than she was comfortable with, and then she realized he was concerned about her. "Are you alright, ma'am? You look like you're not well." Mr. Whittier asked as she replaced her hand in her lap. Mark looked at her from across the table.

"Lindsay, do you want to take a break?" Mark was standing next to her, and she didn't remember seeing him move.

"Good idea," she mumbled.

"Mrs. Davis, there really isn't a need for you to be here for all of this," Mr. Harrell said. "If you'd like, we have a nice staff lounge down the hall; you could rest there till we're finished. I'm sure Chief Marsh and Mr. Thomas can fill you in. There really isn't much more to go over."

"No, please," Lindsay said, standing. "Just let me take a short break, and I'll be fine. If there is a ladies' room nearby?"

Mrs. Coleman stood. "Of course, I could use a break myself. Right this way." The men stood as Lindsay and Mrs. Coleman walked out of the room, followed by the bailiff, who buzzed doors open for them all the way to the other end of the corridor. As he stood aside and let Mrs.

Coleman take the lead, Lindsay already felt like she was regaining her composure. Mrs. Coleman wasn't as tall as Lindsay, hair neatly cropped close to her business attire collar. Up to this point, she had been nothing but all business, but when she looked at Lindsay and smiled, she was a very pretty woman and younger than Lindsay had originally presumed.

"Don't let them get you all tied up, Lindsay. May I call you Lindsay?" At Lindsay's nod, she continued. "I'm sure this is overwhelming to you, but this is what we do every day. Some of the terminology may seem extreme, but it's just our code. Don't let it frighten you. To be sure you know, Tom was a true hero, civic-minded to a fault. I'm so sorry for your loss. He truly was doing what he felt was his duty."

Lindsay held a paper towel under the cool running water and folded it, placing it against her forehead, then her cheeks and the back of her neck. "I know very well, he was a hero, Mrs. Coleman, but he had a wife and a son to consider, too. I don't think Tom would have gone so far with his investigation if he hadn't been assured that we would be safe." Lindsay hadn't meant to sound harsh, but she hadn't had time to process what Mr. Harrell had said. Tom had made several attempts to turn in his information and end it, but they had convinced him to dig deeper, not warning him that it was his own grave he was digging. Mr. Harrell had as much as said so. "I'm sorry, I—" Lindsay stuttered.

"No, please. I'm sorry for speaking so boldly." Mrs. Coleman's voice had softened considerably. "I'm just realizing you didn't know about Tom's working with us.

Did you? We thought you knew about it all along." Mrs. Coleman's face was gentle and sincere.

"No, I just found out about it yesterday, or was it the day before?" Lindsay's voice trailed off as they left the ladies' room. The bailiff joined them again, escorting them back to the conference room. Yesterday. Was it only yesterday? The day before? It felt like she'd been on this roller coaster forever. *Lord, please help me get through the rest of this.*

They all stood as she walked back into the room. With a bravado that even surprised herself, Lindsay said, "Thank you, gentlemen; I'm much better now. Please continue." She took her chair, and Mrs. Coleman took hers, nodding to Agent Whittier.

"Mrs. Davis, while you were out, we've just been reviewing what you already know, and at this point, we'd like to know what you want." Mr. Harrell stopped talking and rested his eyes on her face. "Understanding that you have family, and you will, of course, want them to be safe, we can offer you protection." That meant little to her now. Lindsay felt him studying her. Lindsay sensed this man and his concern for her was less than genuine. "We don't believe protective custody will be necessary, but there are other safeguards we can put in place. We are prepared to go forward in the case. Now that we have Tom's evidence, we can prosecute successfully, we believe, without having his direct testimony." Mr. Harrell motioned to the boxes still sitting on the dolly as the room sat in silence as everyone seemed to process his words.

Agent Whittier spoke intentionally. "It is our opinion that you will not be in danger once the trial is over. In truth, we don't believe you are in danger now. But there is a possible window when the arraignment comes up, that we would want to put an agent or two on the scene."

Lord, who can I trust?

Agent Whittier continued. "As we've been talking, I agree with Chief Marsh, that it would be best for you to remove yourself from the townhouse immediately. We talked a bit about the other properties, and we believe that there are some advantages to be considered. Mr. Thomas can review those with you."

Mr. Harrell leafed through the papers in front of him. Then he picked up the conversation again. "And please, if there is anything we can do to make the move easier, we would be more than happy to assist you."

Lindsay's brow furled. "I do have a question." Agent Whittier and Mr. Harrell both leaned slightly forward. "If I am not in any danger, why do I have to move?" The men looked at each other for a long moment.

Mrs. Coleman spoke first. "Lindsay, the firm still holds an interest in the townhouse."

"You mean, I don't own it?" Lindsay was puzzled.

"Not completely. When Tom bought it, it appeared to be a totally innocent clause that has to do with his employment." Mrs. Coleman said to her. "We're not exactly sure why they haven't enforced it, but you are living there on what we call an "at-will" basis. Tom's cessation of employment happened two years ago. They can exercise the clause any time within 90 days of the termination of his employment, whether by him or the firm. But now, as the clause reads, they can evict you without cause, or they can give you notice. They can let you sell it and get your equity out of it if they choose to, but you can't put it on the market without their written approval. If you do that, they can demand you sell it. Then, they are not required to give you any equity at all. They have written it in very detailed language."

"What—how—" Lindsay stammered.

Mr. Harrell explained further. "It's a very unusual clause, Mrs. Davis, and we're not sure it is completely legal. It would be up to individual court interpretation. We believe that's how the firm has acquired many of its properties across the state. No one ever fought the clause, so they got away with it. Tom had just uncovered properties across the state line, and that's what we needed to make the charges federal. We feel it would be best if you moved out and then approached the firm with your request to sell."

Lindsay sat in shock. Mark spoke up. "What kind of time frame are we looking at here?"

Agent Whittier replied, "We've got some details to work out here, but I would say the latest would be May or the first of June, don't you agree, David?"

Lindsay looked at Mr. Harrell just in time to see his nod.

"Then I could stay until school's out." At least that would keep Nathan's world from totally flipping upside down.

"But the sooner the better, Lindsay," Mrs. Coleman interjected sternly. At Lindsay's puzzled expression, she went on. "I know I told you not to let these events frighten you, but there is one detail these fine gentlemen have not found it in themselves to share with you." She seemed to search for words.

Agent Whittier cleared his throat. "The file on your husband's death has not been closed. When the FBI picked up the investigation, we learned that the sheriff in Richards County was never convinced it was an accident, so he didn't close the case. We are still investigating, but our research is only being met with more questions. Having said that, Mrs. Davis, we highly suspect that both your husband and the woman with him were murdered."

Finally, her fears were put into words—they were murdered. Wait! *The woman with him?*

"The woman? There was someone with him?" Lindsey couldn't breathe. She never would have dreamed that Tom would have been with another woman. But then she would never have dreamed that he would have kept secrets from her like he had. She began to steel her heart against whatever she was about to hear. Again, she bit the side of her cheek to keep from crying as the room started spinning.

Twenty-Six

Lindsay opened her eyes, meeting Mark's gaze, his eyes studying hers intently. He handed her his handkerchief, dampened from his bottled water and helped her to sit up. The room had emptied except for the two of them, Chief Marsh and the bailiff leaning against the wall. A wave of exhaustion spread over her. She searched for words to speak but found none.

"Let's head for home, Chief," Mark said, holding her gaze. At her nod, he took hold of her hand, giving her strength. It probably would have felt nice if she weren't so numb. The bailiff stepped forward, the nice young man who had attempted so sweetly to put her at ease. Her mouth wouldn't form a smile. Quietly, he went to the door and opened it for them. He escorted them back down the long hallway, bypassing the security checkpoint this time.

As they pulled out of the parking garage into the waning sunlight, Chief Marsh watched her closely. "You are mighty quiet, Lindsay, are you alright?"

"Yes, Chief, I'm fine." She looked out the car window. "I didn't know he was with a woman."

"I'm so sorry you found out like that. But it's not what you're thinking." Chief Marsh's voice was a whisper.

Mark spoke from the back seat. "Lindsay, listen. It doesn't appear that they were together. Tom was alone in the car. There was no sign of anyone with him. He was thrown from the car when it went over the cliff."

"Alone?" Lindsay met his gaze. "He was alone?"

"Yes, Linds." Mark continued. "The woman's body was found nearby, so it was assumed she was the driver. They realized their mistake when they checked the driver's seat. It was pushed all the way back. Your husband was tall, wasn't he?"

"Yes, six-foot four." She took a breath, preparing to ask a question that she thought she already knew the answer to. "Who was the woman?"

Mark scooted up to the edge of the back seat and leaned over the front seat. "Pam Donaldson."

How could she not have known? *I'm sorry to say she was killed a couple of years ago.* Lindsay could hear Pam's brother, Joey's, words as clearly in her mind as if he had just told her. She remembered thinking at the time that it was about the same time Tom had been killed, but she was shocked to learn that it was exactly the same time. And the same accident? *How could she not have figured this out?*

"How did it happen?" Lindsay asked.

"That's the part that they are having trouble figuring out. She might have been walking along the road or hiking along the cliff." Mark gave her a minute to let it soak in before he continued. "There were some folks at the bottom of the cliff having a picnic. They're the ones who called it in. They didn't know her, but they saw the car hit the guardrail. They saw Tom being thrown before it went over, so they knew it was a man who had been in the car. And they saw no one else in the car with him. But when they found her body, the police assumed she was driving."

"So, they don't know where she was or what she was doing?" Lindsay was trying to sort out the pieces.

"No, her brother said that she worked nights, and he thought she was at work. Her boss said she didn't show up that night, and her car was never found."

"Oh my gosh, they murdered both of them?" Lindsay was near panic. "Mark, tell me about the properties we can move into. Do I own them? I need answers, Mark, please!"

"Wait a minute, Lindsay, there's no evidence that says they were both murdered. It may have been a freak accident. She may have just been in the wrong place at the wrong time." At her pleading expression, he continued. "About the properties, okay."

Chief Marsh had kept quiet during this exchange. "We're almost back to the station. I have copies of everything for you in my office."

Mark and Lindsay loaded the copies into the back seat of Mark's truck and climbed in the front. "You want to go over to your mom's, or I can take you home."

"Do you have time to stay around a while?" Lindsay asked. "You understand all this so much better than I do. I don't want to alarm either one of them, though. I want them to just think it's what I've been wanting to do, and that it'll be fun. Oh, Mark, I'm so scared."

He put his arm around her shoulders and let her cry.

"I'll stay as long as you need me, Lindsay. I'll help in

any way I can." Mark said softly. She nodded into his shirt collar.

"Then let's go to Mom's and have supper. Then we'll tell them about at least some of the paperwork." Lindsay wanted to have his undivided attention to look over those deeds. There were so many properties, her mind was in a whirlwind. "Can you tell me which property you think would be best? We should move, right? Which one?" Lindsay's mind was still spinning.

He was quiet, appearing deep in thought. "I'm honestly not sure. How about I tell you some things about each one? You own your mother's place. That might be the easiest one to move into for the time being." He smiled as he continued. "One thing you don't know is that you own Happy Trails. They make payments to the brokerage firm of Whitley, Morris, and Cruz in Davenport. You also own the farm you were raised on, Lindsay. It was labeled Old McDonaldson's Farm in the Momopoly paperwork, so that threw me. The Happy Trails is actually the former Donaldson farm." He stopped for a breath. Lindsay's eyes grew wide. How was this even possible? How was this her life? Her excitement began to overshadow some of her fear.

"There is a place on the outskirts of Rutledge—a place on Lake Juniper. It was labeled 'Sunny Side Up'." Mark continued. "You also own the place where my aunt used to live in Davenport. It looks like it's had some renovation. All the others—at least those that are vacant,—appear to have had building permits, so they may already be at least partly renovated or updated. I can't remember off the top of my head which ones have leases, but some do. They all pay rent to Whitley, Morris, and Cruz. There's a four-plex in Florida that is fully occupied. Rents for that one go to Martin Johnson, CPA. You also own a 20-acre ranch called Heavenly Acres in Washington State. Looks like that place has two houses on it. At last count, one is rented out. It doesn't look like the other one is. You also own a Casino in South Dakota called the Lucky Dog."

"The Lucky Dog?" Lindsay wanted to laugh at the absolute insanity of the situation, but instead, shook her head. "I assumed all the deeds were in Tom's deed packet from the desk drawer. You found more?"

"Yep. I haven't had the time to research the last ones that we found. The bottom line, Lindsay, is you never have to work another day in your life if you don't want to. And most of these places are big enough that your mom, Benny, and two-thirds of this town could move in with you. I suggest you go to Davenport to see Whitley, Morris, and Cruz. They can better explain what you have and what it's all worth. Then you can decide if you want to keep them all, sell some, whatever you want. You have a lot of options."

A lot of options. Lindsay was thrilled that Tom had loved her enough to set her up with so many options, but she was so angry that he had put her in this position in the first place! What was she supposed to do with all these properties? How was she to get back to some sort of normal life? Immediately, she felt guilty. Christians aren't supposed to get angry, are they? And she was definitely angry. Scripture says "be angry, but don't sin." And how was she supposed to get rid of this anger, before the sun went down? Lindsay took a deep breath. *God, please help me with all of this.*

She forced herself to take a deep relaxing breath and

look at Mark. Thank God he was beside her. She was beginning to realize that she wanted him to be beside her often. She reached over and took his free hand in hers as he gave her a tender smile in return, squeezing her hand. She felt another deep breath further calming her spirit. By the time they pulled into Arlene's driveway, Lindsay had regained her peace and felt ready to have at least some of her ducks in a row, ready to talk to Nathan and Arlene.

"Mark, are you free Saturday to take me on a tour of some of the places that are close by?" Lindsay asked as they got out of his truck. They clasped hands again as they walked up the front walk.

"I am at your service," Mark said, bowing. Nathan heard the remark as he met them at the door. When Gran joined him, they both witnessed Mark's slight bow and looked mischievously at each other. Out of Lindsay's peripheral vision, she caught the look and smiled. She'd let them enjoy their mutual secret for now.

Twenty-Seven

Lindsay hadn't said much to her mother about what her meeting entailed. She didn't want her to be as frightened as she was. But she knew she had to share with her at least part of what she knew.

Her mother filled the table with all the comfort foods that would help Lindsay through the rest of the night. She had prepared her specialty fried chicken, mashed potatoes and gravy, scalloped corn, homemade applesauce, and garden salad. A pineapple-cherry dump cake was still warm enough to melt the vanilla ice cream. Everyone ate their fill and dutifully pitched in for cleanup. Lindsay asked everyone to come into the living room and sit down so they could talk.

"Hey, Bud," she whispered on the way to the sofa, slipping her arm around Nathan's shoulders. "Did you have a lot of homework?

"Naw, just some math and some history reading. I already got it all done." He beamed at her, and she snuck in a hug.

"I'm so proud of you!" They sat down on the couch together, and Arlene and Mark took the side chairs. She took a deep breath and spoke. "No need to beat around the bush. I've been thinking about finding us a little ranch and selling the townhouse."

"A ranch? Really, Mom? Like Alex's Uncle Joe? Cool!" Okay, she got Nathan on board easily enough, if they took one of the country places. "Somewhere around here?"

"Could be. Mark has offered to take us to look at a few that are around here on Saturday. Mom, you wanna come?" Lindsay so wanted to have her mom close to them, but she wanted her to maintain her independence, too. "And, Mom, I'd like for you to come to live with us, too, if you want to." Lindsay watched as her mom's eyebrows went up in surprise. Then Lindsay squirmed a bit in her seat.

"Wow!" Nathan jumped off the couch. "Gran, that would be so cool!" He sat on the arm of Gran's chair and draped himself across the back of it, hugging her.

"I—uh—I don't know, Lindsay. Isn't this a bit sudden?" Of course, Arlene would be studying her daughter's face instead of just going along with the excitement.

"Not really," Lindsay said, innocently looking into her mother's semi-suspicious gaze. "I've been thinking about it off and on for a while, but our trip today revealed that Tom left us in pretty good shape. So, I'm able to live my dream sooner than I expected, and I really want you to be in on it with us... that is, if you want to be."

"Well, I—" Arlene crossed and uncrossed her arms,

looking at Nathan and then back at Lindsay. "If you're sure you want your old mother tagging along, it wouldn't hurt to go for the ride and see what's out there."

Nathan whooped and hollered as he escaped the living room for the backyard. Lindsay relaxed as she felt the weight of today's secrets falling away. Rusty in his house on the other side of the complex probably heard Nathan's shouts of joy.

Lindsay and Mark exchanged a glance, then Mark left to join Nathan. Lindsay's gaze fell on Arlene. "Mom, of course, I want you with us. I never would have suggested you come along if I hadn't already thought it through." She moved closer to her mom. "I'm struggling with all of this, Mom. It just seems that every day I learn more about what Tom did—the great lengths he went to for us. But everything he was doing left us in a rather complicated position, too. So I think it's wise to go ahead and do this now rather than later." She blinked back the tears as Arlene draped her arm across her daughter's lap. "I have always counted on your wisdom, and I sure need it now." She took a deep breath before she continued the thought: "I need your help in sorting out some of what Tom left us. And—I—uh—especially need your wisdom in—uh—if —how I go forward with Mark."

Lindsay's conversations with Mark became more frequent over the next few days. She called Whitley, Morris, and Cruz and scheduled an appointment for later in the week.

Benny called Wednesday afternoon and gave her a

happy update on his counseling with Mark. Lindsay was encouraged that her baby brother was excited about the progress after just two sessions. She was also excited that when she told Benny about her weekend plans, he asked if he could tag along. He also asked if he could come along to their mid-week service.

She began to think about the possibility of having her entire family living under one roof. Of course, she assumed Benny would eventually want to strike out on his own again. For now, the idea intrigued her, and she allowed herself to engage in some excitement. Arlene called, and Lindsay was excited to hear that her mom's enthusiasm over moving with them was growing.

Thursday afternoon, Chief Marsh called. "Lindsay, hello. I hope you are doing well." He sounded cordial and upbeat.

"Thanks, Chief, we're doing very well. I hope you are too." She tapped on Nathan's book as she passed him and went into the living room to retrain his attention on his homework. She sat down at the desk.

"Not bad, not bad." He seemed at odds with what to say, so Lindsay suspected there had been a development. "I, uh—is this a good time to talk?"

Lindsay put down her pen and focused on the call. "It's a great time. What's up?"

"We had to release Donald Brand. He's the one we took in for questioning Sunday night outside Kit's Diner. He is the grandson of one of the partners. I wanted you to know so you would be sure and lock your doors and windows. Just, you know, be extra smart, be alert." He stopped to catch his breath. "I can send Deputy Stevens out to patrol your neighborhood a little more. Tonight and tomorrow, I can post one of my cars then see how it goes."

"Okay," Lindsay said. Her heart rate sped up as she was mentally anticipating the possible trouble this young man could cause. "Thanks. He wasn't a part of what the FBI has been investigating?" she asked, fear threatening once more.

"Doesn't appear so. But, well, between you and me, we're keeping an eye on him, just in case." They said their goodbyes and Lindsay peeked in to see how Nathan was doing. Satisfied that he had moved on from math to history, she went upstairs and grabbed her Bible. The week had been such that she had missed her quiet time twice, so she decided to get caught up tonight. She read the two daily readings in her "Through the Bible in a Year" schedule.

Then she read the 5th Chapter of James, reviewing her notes from Pastor Billing's sermon of last night. Patience—Lindsay felt convicted. She had not been exercising her patience well lately, but everyone around her seemed to be pushing her into some quick decisions. She knew they meant well and were looking out for her safety.

Lord, please help me to be wise, but not in a hurry, Lindsay prayed. "*I trust You to guide me to the perfect place that You have already chosen for all of us. Help me to hear Your voice and to move forward with patience. I count myself blessed that Tom left us with so many options. I trust that he was listening to Your voice as he made the decisions he did, and Lord—help me to forgive him for leaving me.*

Lindsay's mind drifted to an easier time in her life. As a child, growing up on that farm, life was simple. Fun. She had a story-book childhood, right up until Dad died. How would Mom feel about moving back there, where she had lived with Dad all their married lives? For that matter, how would she feel about moving back to where there were so many memories—of her dad, her childhood, her horse, Josie, and Dad's horse, Spook? A hobby ranch would be a lot of work, but she felt they could handle it. How many acres was her childhood farm?

The ring of her cell phone interrupted her memories. It was Mark.

"Hey, there," she answered. "What are you up to?"

"Just planning our trip Saturday. Are you getting excited?" he ventured.

"You know what? I am. Thank you for taking on the planning of it! Oh, by the way, Benny wants to go. I told him it was okay. Think we'll have room for all of us?" Lindsay asked, laughing.

"Sure, Benny told me. I think it's great. We should take your Jeep. Are you thinking about him moving with you, too?" Mark joked.

"Why not?" She asked. "We've always been a close family. I'm sure he wouldn't stay forever, but I'd love to have my whole family under one roof while I can. Especially if they're in danger, too."

Lindsay would have loved for this to have happened before Tom died. Her anger toward him was subsiding, but it stung to be planning this without him. She had to face her feelings for Mark. Deep in her heart, considering what Tom had gone through to ensure her safety, she just felt he would want her to move on with a man just like Mark.

"I found out some news," Mark said. "The property you own in Davenport isn't just my aunt's place. It's the whole block. Apparently, Tom hired out some renovating on some of the buildings and tore down the condemned ones to make room for a nice little gated community. Your man missed his calling. He should have been an architect." He chuckled, trying to keep her in this good mood. "Some of the units are rented out, some aren't. We'll look at those on Saturday. Did you meet with the management company?"

"I have an appointment there after work tomorrow. Wanna come along?" she asked hopefully.

"I don't want to wear out my welcome, but if you want me to come, I'm there," he replied, equally as hopeful.

"I really do appreciate your knowledge. And I enjoy your company as well." Lindsay felt her cheeks warm and hurried back to safer ground. "You know a lot about areas that I am clueless in. The appointment is at 3:00. Can you come?"

"My last appointment is at 1:00, so I should be able to. Want me to pick you up from work?" Mark's face seemed to light up.

"That's perfect, Mark. Thank you." She sensed his smile on the other end of their conversation, and she smiled in return. "I'll bet Mom would even buy you dinner when we get back; 'course it's at her house, and it's homecooked," she teased.

"Sounds good to me. She's a great cook," Mark replied.

"She's always been an amazing cook. I think she believes that's why I want her to move in with us, so she can do all the cooking." Lindsay laughed.

He paused and then took a playful jab. "Is it?"

"Do you really think I would do that?" She decided to play along. "Besides, are you so sure I can't cook? What makes you think my amazingly good cooking Momma didn't teach me everything she knows? Who do you—?" She couldn't contain her laughter.

"Okay, okay, sorry. I was just kidding. I'd be willing to bet you are just as good a cook as your mother." Mark chided.

She answered so quietly he caught himself leaning forward to hear her. "Well, you'd lose that bet, so don't bet the farm." He could hear her chuckling. "I'm decent, but not quite in Mom's league," she whispered.

Nathan came in, plopped his book bag in the chair, and turned on the TV. He sat on the couch with his legs reaching across the entire coffee table. *When did he get so long-legged?* "Listen, I'm going to run. I'll see you tomorrow." She reluctantly ended the call, and squeezed in on the end of the couch, snuggling up with her son. "What are we watching, Bud?" she asked.

"*Alaska Life*. It was Dad's favorite," he said without taking his eyes off the set.

"I remember. Would you want to live in Alaska?" Why not ask, see what he truly thought about moving so far away from his friends?

"Hmm. I don't know. I think I'd like the adventure, living off the land. Kinda like being a pioneer, ya know? That could be cool." Nathan was still thinking.

Lindsay smiled. Just like his dad. He loved adventure and had no fear of how much energy or work was involved. But it gave her new insight into where they might want to move. They watched the rest of the show, then she sent him up to take his shower and get ready for bed. She wandered through the house, turning off lights and checking doors, but it was a mundane task and her mind wandered to the upcoming meeting. Would she get more answers or more questions? *Oh Lord, go with me, please. I need your strength to get through this.*

Twenty-Eight

Lindsay's sleep had been interrupted frequently with thoughts of the meeting with the attorneys after work. Her brain felt foggy, and she wasn't mentally equipped for irritable residents. They were usually all easy to get along with. She noticed that every one of them had 'technical' difficulties that she had to deal with. Even Grace's internal sound system appeared to have shut down.

She wasn't superstitious, but the full moon was a different matter. The day could not end quickly enough as far as she was concerned. It was so gloomy, she went to the kitchen and pushed for early afternoon snacks and a movie. By the time Mark pulled into the drive, everyone was eating puff popcorn and laughing at the craziness of Jerry Lewis. She grabbed two bags of popcorn and slipped out the front door, determined to leave the stress in the front courtyard as she walked through. Mark had to dash to get around the truck in time to open the door for her.

"Hi, Mark. How was your day?" She felt giddy as he

made sure she was settled, passing the seat belt buckle to her while she held onto the popcorn. A quiver of attraction flickered inside her as she watched him stroll around the front of the truck to get in on his side of the truck.

"Good. How about yours?" He buckled his seat belt, reached for one of the bags of popcorn, and handed her a bottle of sweet tea before he pulled into traffic.

"Thanks. My day was crazy." She laughed, opening her tea. "I've never seen so many grouchy people in one room in all my life." They shared the popcorn and talked easily all the way to Davenport. After working through the maze of one-way streets, they finally found the storefront sign declaring Whitley, Morris, and Cruz: Investments, Properties, and Management. As he turned into the parking lot, she asked him, "Do you remember how many acres were on the farm where I grew up?"

"Not offhand, why?" Mark parked the car and turned to look at her.

"I'm just wondering. If we move to one of the ranches—I remember Dad working from morning to zero-dark-thirty. With us working, I'm not sure I'm up to that."

"Lindsay, I'm not sure you realize it, but you can hire people to help. In fact, you can hire people to do it all if you want. You could keep some of the caretakers that are already in place. Let's go talk to them; you might have a better idea." She nodded, already deep in thought as they went in and were greeted very happily by a young lady sitting at a round modular desk unit.

"Good afternoon." She extended her hand. "I'm Marci; how can I help you?" Lindsay introduced herself and explained that she had a 3:00 appointment. "Let me see who you are scheduled with." As Marci flipped open the monitor on her laptop and tapped a few keys, she found the appointment. "Oh, wonderful. You are with Mr. Morris. You'll like him. Let me show you into one of our conference rooms, and I'll let him know you're here." She showed them around the reception area to a nicely decorated room that felt more like a den than a conference room. As she motioned them through the door, she offered coffee or hot tea. When neither accepted her offer, she pointed out the lemonade bar near the window. "Please, help yourselves. Mr. Morris will be in shortly." She backed out the door and closed it behind her.

"I'm a bit nervous, Mark," Lindsay whispered as she sat down on the gray leather tufted sofa.

"Aw, relax, Lindsay; they're just regular folks." He poured them both some lemonade and brought it over to her. She stood and walked to the round table and sat down. He sat with her and reached across the table, placing his hand over hers, instantly putting her at ease.

"Can you do the talking for me?" she whispered.

"If you want," he answered gently, "but sooner or later, you're going to need to know what your assets are. 'Course, you should have a good idea by the time we leave here today." Mark pulled his hand back awkwardly and sipped the lemonade. Lindsay's hand immediately felt cold. She wished she was forward enough to take it back.

The door opened quietly, interrupting her thoughts, and a man with slightly long hair, graying at the temples, entered the room. He wore dress jeans and a neatly ironed light blue button-down shirt with a light-weight sports coat over it. Lindsay noticed he wore cowboy boots and no tie.

"Good afternoon; I'm John Morris. You are Mrs. Davis?" He held out his hand, and she took hold of it for a good shake. Then he reached for Mark's hand.

"Lindsay, please. This is my friend, Mark Thomas. He already knows about much of what my husband, Tom, purchased before his death, so he is acting as my advisor." Lindsay was impressed with herself for not stuttering over the introduction.

"Nice to meet you both. Shall we sit down?" Mr. Morris sat down at the table, opening a leather portfolio that he had brought into the room with him, and slipped the first several pages aside. "I must say, I was surprised you hadn't contacted us sooner. I was sorry to hear of your husband's passing and put together a summary report for you as soon as I heard. After we got your call, I updated that report to give you the most current information available."

"Thank you. I was unaware of your—" Lindsay hesitated. She was rather tired of telling the story. She was tired of thinking about the story. Mark picked up where she stopped.

"We were only just recently informed of your agreement with Mr. Davis. Otherwise, I'm sure Mrs. Davis would have contacted you sooner."

"Of course, Mr. Thomas. No matter. We had instructions to carry on business under the specified guidelines, indefinitely if anything—unforeseen— happened, as it, unfortunately has." He flipped a stack of papers around so that they could both read the columns of figures.

To Lindsay, Mr. Morris appeared to be a bit of a snob. As he pointed at columns and guided them through the report, Mark asked questions that made no sense to her and received answers that made even less sense. After a few moments, the paper was turned over and laid beside the stack, and the process was repeated. Page after page, comments were made, questions asked and answered.

<h1 style="text-align:center">Twenty-Nine</h1>

It appeared to Lindsay that Mr. Morris had changed his opinion of Mark's ability to read financial reports as he slowed down and started using more technical terms that Mark followed completely. Lindsay was pleasantly surprised at Mark's financial savvy.

Finally, Mr. Morris collected the papers and placed them back in the portfolio. Then he picked up the top pages that he had originally placed off to the side. "And lastly, Mrs. Davis, Mr. Thomas, this is a copy of the fiduciary agreement that your husband made with our firm." He slid it closer to Mark, who picked it up and read it carefully. "I believe you'll find everything in order," Mr. Morris continued. "Of course, I'll be happy to answer any questions. Mr. Davis didn't pull a salary or allowance, but there is a stipulation for you to do so if you decide."

Mark carefully perused the second and third pages as carefully as he had page one, taking what appeared to Lindsay an unusual amount of time in doing so. Lindsay was becoming concerned when he finally pushed them back across the table.

"They appear to be just fine. Are these copies for Mrs. Davis?" Mark leaned forward in his chair, his forearms resting on the table, keeping eye contact with Mr. Morris.

"Well, no, uh, but I can have a set made for you to take with you." He pushed the remaining papers back into the portfolio and slid them across the table toward Lindsay. "These are yours, of course. You will find there is a listing of all properties and Mr. Davis's—I'm sorry, I mean *your*—holdings, Mrs. Davis, in the back of the portfolio." He stood and pushed a small buzzer near the lemonade bar and Marci came bouncing back into the room. "I'll also need a copy of our agreement, please." Marci took the pages and appeared to do a bit of a curtsey as she left the room. Mr. Morris turned back toward them.

"Do you expect to be making any changes, Mrs. Davis?" He looked at Mark as he asked the question, but Lindsay answered.

"Not at the moment." She met and kept his eye. "I'm looking to relocate soon, so when I determine where I will live, that will be a distinct possibility." Mark nearly choked, suppressing his laughter at her spunk.

Mr. Morris smiled uneasily. "Oh, yes, well, of course, you'll want to have everything close to you. However"—he cleared his throat and continued—"with the internet, everything is at your fingertips, no matter where the office is physically situated."

Marci returned with copies that were still warm, and everyone got up from the table. Handshakes were extended.

"I'm sure we can recommend a firm that will honor

our agreement should you decide to move your account, Mrs. Davis."

"Thank you, Mr. Morris; it's been a pleasure." Mark opened the door for her, and they left. They were in the car and pulling out of the parking lot when Lindsay reopened the portfolio and stared again at the figures. She looked at Mark and then back at the papers in her lap, speechless.

"Quite a sum, isn't it?" Mark smiled as he backed out of the parking space and drove to the exit. "And you told me last night that you hadn't gone to the bank yet, right? That safety deposit box will more than likely have the actual stock certificates."

"Oh, yes! That bank is here in Davenport," she said, reaching for her purse. "Would you mind? I have the key in my purse." At his nod, Lindsay gave him the name and address of the bank. The bank was open until 4:30 PM on Friday, and it wasn't too far away, so they should be able to make it. She was glad that he knew his way around town. Mark made a few easy turns and pulled into the bank parking lot. She opened her door and turned back to see him still sitting in the truck. "Please?"

"If you're sure," he said quietly.

"Of course, I may need you to pick me up when I open that box. At this point, I'm expecting the unexpected!" He got out and caught up with her, and they went inside together, asking for the safe deposit box manager.

A tall thin man came up to them, smiling. "Hello, I'm Joshua Jacobs. How may I be of help?"

Somehow, Lindsay thought of Ichabod Crane and coughed to keep from laughing.

"I need to get into my late husband's box, please." She let herself smile.

"Of course. Do you have his key?" She held it out to him, and he looked at the number on it. "You hang on to that one and I'll go get ours." He made a slight bow as he passed the key back to her, and he left them, returning only a moment later. "I will need some identification, please." Lindsay pulled out her wallet and handed him her license. "This way, please." He took her license with him and ran it through a scanner, punched a few numbers, and the heavy metal door unlocked.

He turned to Mark and asked if he was planning to join her. When she said yes, he asked to see Mark's license as well and ran it through the same process, then handed it back to him. Again, a slight bow, just the head, but Lindsay found such an archaic expression of respect to be quite refreshing.

He led them inside the vault and toward an entire wall full of long narrow metal boxes. He placed his key in one lock and pointed to the other lock for her to do the same with hers. They turned the keys and the box lid popped slightly ajar, then he stepped aside and motioned for them to remove the box.

"I'll give you some privacy." Ichabod walked over to a tall desk in the corner of the room near the entrance and sat on the stool beside it, pretending to study a folder on the desk. "We close in precisely fourteen minutes," he said sternly.

Mark moved the metal box to a nearby table, and he and Lindsay flipped through papers. Some appeared to be originals of deeds, mortgages, and leases, some sealed envelopes, way too much to go through so quickly.

"Can I take them home and go over them this weekend?" Lindsay asked Mark.

"I'm sure." He turned to Ichabod. "Excuse me, sir, do you have some large envelopes that we can have? Mrs. Davis would like to remove some of these items."

"Of course, would three be sufficient?"

Mark looked at the envelopes he was pulling out of the desk drawer. "I think we'll need at least six if it's possible," he answered.

"Of course." Ichabod pulled out a stack without counting them, and walked across the room, laying them on the table beside the metal box. Just as quietly, he returned to his desk. Lindsay noticed he made a note of the time before he sat down.

Mark flipped through the papers, passing to Lindsay the ones he thought they should take home. Ten minutes later, when they left the bank, they carried with them a disposable shopping bag with seven stuffed legal-size manilla envelopes.

As tempted as Lindsay was to view the paperwork in at least one of the envelopes on the way to her mother's house, she knew she wouldn't understand any of it anyway. She called her mom from her cell phone when they left Davenport to tell her they would stop at the Manor to get her car and they would be on their way.

"Perfect! The roast has been smelling so good, it's hard to keep Nathan out of it!" Arlene teased. "See you soon, sweetie."

Thirty

Gran turned to Nathan. "You'd better step it up, kiddo, and finish that homework. Mr. Thomas and your mom are only about twenty minutes away."

Nathan pushed his math book aside and opened his science book. "Almost done, Gran." He made the notes in his lab notebook that he would need in order to do the experiment in class. Then he sat tapping his pencil eraser on the table, staring off into space.

"Gran?"

"You need some help?" She turned and sat down at the table with him.

"No, I just want to know somethin'." He didn't look at her. His gaze was fixed on the magnets on her refrigerator door. "Who is Mr. Thomas?"

Arlene took a deep breath. She knew what he was really asking her. "Well, when your dad died, your mom had a hard time getting through it. She was struggling to get back to just being herself, remember?"

"Yeah, I remember she cried all the time, and I couldn't get her attention sometimes. Is that what you're talking about?" Nathan flipped the corners of the pages in his textbook. Gran pulled out the stool beside him at the counter and swiveled to face him.

"That's it. And she was having trouble sleeping, and that's not good. Anyway, Mr. Thomas is a counselor, and he set your mom up with a lady he knew who was also a counselor. Remember Sarah?" At his nod, she continued. "She helped your mom get through all that so she could be your mom again." She took a breath and watched his face to see how he received her explanation.

"Is she having trouble again, Gran?" His sweet little face was screwed up into a ball of pain and compassion for his mom.

"Oh, no, sweetie. He and your mom have become friends now, and he's helping your Uncle Benny to get better."

"From his divorce." Gran thought it sad for Nathan to know, but he was a very sensitive and intuitive 12-year-old.

"That's right," Gran replied.

"Good. I think that's good—isn't it, Gran?"

She nodded and hugged him and turned back to the crockpot on the counter. Nathan flipped his science book and lab notebook closed and put them in his backpack with his math book. Then he tossed the backpack across the floor toward the door. He misjudged though, and the backpack slid to a stop forlornly in the middle of the floor. He snarled as he got up and positioned it next to the door. He came over and stood next to her at the counter.

"You think it's good that they are friends?" she asked as she placed the roast on the platter to carve it.

"Sure. He's cool. Dad used to say you can never have too many friends." He grabbed a piece of the tender meat that fell from the plate and cocked his head as he looked at her. "Do you think it's a good thing, Gran?"

Gran decided against telling Nathan at this point, that she had been praying for God's choice in a man to come along to fill the void that Tom's death had caused.

"I do, Nathan. Mr. Thomas did such a good job finding help for her that I think he's kind of a hero. You know what I mean?" Gran took plates from the cupboard and passed them to Nathan to set the table.

"You mean, he kinda saved her. Yeah, I remember. Yeah, he's a hero." He took the plates from her and placed them on the placemats she had already put around the table. Without a word, she began to hand him the silverware, the butter, and the rolls, and he meticulously placed them where he thought they should go.

By the time they were finished setting the table, they heard Mark's truck and Lindsay's Jeep in the driveway. Mark and Lindsay walked into the kitchen as Nathan started putting ice in the glasses.

As soon as Gran finished saying grace, the chatter around the table began. The momentum increased to loud and silly laughter while all the food was passed. There was tender juicy roast beef, browned potatoes and carrots, and Nathan's favorite: apple salad with walnuts. The conversation was suddenly so quiet you could have heard the proverbial pin drop. It was a sign of good food, Mark commented.

"Everyone is so busy enjoying the food that no one wants to talk."

Gran sat quietly biting back tears of joy at the scene. It just felt right. The meal was finished, and the table was cleared when Gran and Nathan shared a smile.

"Now?" Nathan asked.

"Perfect timing," Gran replied. Gran poured the coffee, while Nathan placed Gran's white T-towel across his left arm. He brought the creamer and sugar containers to the table, placing them just so on the table. Then he turned and one at a time brought their coffees.

Grinning, he turned toward Gran, and when he faced them again, he held two slices of blueberry cheesecake with a peak of whipped cream. He placed one in front of his mom and said, "Your dessert, ma'am." He bowed slightly. He placed the other carefully in front of Mark and bowed again, "Your dessert, sir. Enjoy."

They praised his regal serving capabilities and he giggled cheerfully, then he placed another plate, just as meticulously, in front of Gran. Another bow. More thanks, more laughing, and then he plopped the last plate at his chair and dived in, all manners forgotten.

The dishes were done quickly and put away. Hugs were given all around, and Lindsay, Nathan, and Mark walked out the front door. "You're coming by to look those papers over?" she asked.

"I'm right behind you."

When they got home and Mark went inside with them, Nathan asked what was going on. Lindsay explained that they were going over some paperwork having to do with the houses they were going to go see tomorrow.

"Cool!" Nathan said excitedly. "I've been working forever on homework and don't want to look at any more papers!" They all laughed, watching Nathan go into the living room. He snuggled into his dad's favorite chair and found a rerun of *Alaska Life*. Lindsay considered Nathan's disinterest. His dad had already previewed the properties in the game that she and Mark were now discerning the truth about. She decided to disregard Nathan's foreknowledge at the hand of his father. Maybe he should be allowed to just enjoy being left out of the loop for the time being.

Mark joined them momentarily, and he and Lindsay sat at the kitchen table. Lindsay deposited the contents of the safe deposit box and Chief Marsh's copies on the table, and they both began sorting through them. As they found some duplicates, they organized those with the originals found in the safe deposit box. They reached simultaneously for four envelopes that were alike. They each unsealed one and found it full of $100 bills. Exchanging glances, Lindsay counted one, and Mark counted the other. Both envelopes held $50,000.

"Mark?" Lindsay whispered, leaving the question incomplete.

"His note said he left some cash," Mark answered with a shrug. "I think I would hang on to it." The other two looked to be the same, so they didn't take time to count them. $200,000 in cash. "If Tom thought it best not to put it into an account, there must have been a reason."

There were two more deeds in the paperwork. One of the properties appeared to lie between Lindsay's family farm and the Happy Trails Riding Stables. They started organizing everything by how far away they were. Using her townhouse as the hub, they estimated the distance. Their paperwork showed seven properties within the circle. Eliminating the townhouse and Gran's house, that left five. Since they had already been to Happy Trails, Mark laid out a route to go see the other four.

With Gran, Mark, Lindsay, Benny, and Nathan, they decided it would be more comfortable to take Lindsay's Jeep. They called Benny and arranged it. He would pick Gran up and they would all meet at Lindsay's townhouse. They planned to have breakfast at Kit's Kitchen at 8:00, then get started.

Lindsay sent Nathan to the shower, and she and Mark sat outside in the courtyard in the cool evening air. "Mark, I can't thank you enough for being my 'advisor'." She made quotation marks with her fingers in the air and laughed. "I don't know what I'd do without you."

"Please, stop thanking me. You would do fine, a little slower, maybe, because I'm so efficient," he teased. "Seriously, I'm intrigued by the mystery of all of this. I'm having fun, and I'm totally enamored by the company, especially yours." He hesitated. "'Course, your son is an amazing young man. Your mother is the county's best cook, and with your referral of your brother, I'm making money on this adventure." He threw her a playful wink.

Lindsay's face grew warm, and she took a deep breath. She was much more comfortable when the tone of the conversation stayed light. She liked Mark. He was the kind of solid Christian man who would be a good mentor for Nathan. Her mother was obviously in favor of him. She had told Lindsay of her brief conversation with Nathan and his approval of "Mr. Thomas." If she was ready to seriously consider... If...When...Maybe.

Thirty-One

Lindsay and Nathan were ready and waiting at 7:30 A.M. for their road trip. They sat at the kitchen table with orange juice and coffee reading Nathan's Sunday School lesson together after Lindsay had gently reminded him, "Tomorrow is Sunday, Bud, and we'll be gone most of today."

In his excitement over this family outing, Nathan didn't balk. Lindsay smiled, realizing Nathan knew nothing about why they were exploring properties. Come to think of it, neither did Benny, and her mom knew very little. *All in due time. Tell me when, Lord.*

They were into one of Lindsay's favorite Old Testament stories—Jonah. Lindsay read from his lesson book and noticed the word 'whale,' but wanted to wait and see where the lesson went with it. Then they looked at Scripture. Nathan was reading out loud and stopped.

Jonah 1:17 Now the LORD had prepared a great fish to swallow Jonah. And Jonah was in the belly of the fish for three days and three nights.

Nathan looked at her with a puzzled face. "What are you thinking, Bud?" she asked.

"So, was it a 'great fish' or a 'whale'?" Nathan asked. Lindsay looked up at her son as he continued. "My Sunday School book says whale and the Bible says great fish. What's the difference anyway?"

Lindsay took a deep breath before she answered, mentally gathering everything she'd ever learned about the story.

"Well, a lot of times people call it a whale, but you're right, the Bible does call it a 'great fish'." she began. "The people who have studied it a lot more than you or I have think that it was a great fish that God specifically designed so that Jonah could live inside of it where he could breathe." Lindsay waited a bit to let her words settle in, "Think about what you learned in health class. When you eat food, there are juices in your stomach that start attacking the food to digest it."

"Enzymes!" he cried.

"Bingo!" Lindsay said. "Well, the same thing happens when a horse eats, or a dog, or even a whale."

Nathan was getting excited. "So if a whale had swallowed Jonah," he said, "those enzymes would have attacked Jonah and started to digest him!"

"Right! But that didn't happen, did it? Jonah was in there for three whole days." Lindsay stopped for breath. "You're right, your book says, 'Jonah was in the belly of the whale three days and three nights.' If that had been a regular whale or fish, Jonah wouldn't have been alive after that long!"

"Cool!" Nathan replied. Lindsay loved watching Nathan get excited about God's Word. "But what's the difference between a great fish and a whale?" he asked as the doorbell rang, and Lindsay chuckled to herself when the thought hit her. Literally, saved by the bell!

When Lindsay opened the door, Benny and Gran stood with their backs to the door, watching Mark drive up in his truck. He parked right behind Benny's truck in the driveway.

Lindsay grabbed the cooler of bottled water, juice, and sweet tea, and they all headed toward her Jeep. Lindsay noticed that Deputy Stevens was in his parking place in the corner under the live oak tree. She gave him a quick nod, noticing the thud in her heart. It still bothered her that they hadn't found the person or persons who broke in, so there was no logical explanation. Chief Marsh had practically closed the case because they had no leads. She tried to shake it off and join everyone at her Jeep. But it kept haunting her—*was it dangerous for them to not have this culprit exposed and arrested?*

She playfully tossed her keys to Mark with no heads-up and chuckled when they hit him in the chest. His quick reflexes enabled him to enclose them in both hands. Laughing, he handed her the map he had printed out with their route and did a perfect "to-the-rear march", never skipping a step. Benny, Gran, and Nathan were in the back seat. Nathan propped up his feet on the cooler on the floor in the middle in front of the back seat. He lay back as if it were his recliner. Benny teased him about being too big for his car seat, and thus the jovial tone of the day was established.

The first stop was breakfast, and it didn't take but a minute to get there. Lindsay's mood had lightened, and they were all laughing as they walked in the door of Kit's.

The waitress filled her arms with menus and led them to a round booth in the back. As they sat, she handed each one a menu. Nathan dived for the middle, with Benny next to him and Gran on the outside. Lindsay sat between Nathan and Mark on the other side. The waitress took drink orders as they opened their menus.

"I hope it's okay with you, Lindsay; I mapped us to go to Davenport first," Mark said. He leaned back when the waitress passed Nathan's chocolate milk and Lindsay's coffee before setting his coffee down in front of him. "I haven't been back to Aunt Mavis' house for years."

"Hey!" Benny said jokingly. "Why do you get to choose which one we go to see first?" Everyone agreed in jest.

"Several reasons," Mark said, straining to maintain the serious expression on his face. "Number one—it's the only in-town site that Lindsay wanted to take a look at so technically she's the one that chose." He winked at her. "Second—my aunt used to live there. Third—I printed the map of properties that Lindsay chose. Fourth—I'm running out of reasons—" Mark paused for dramatic effect. "Fifth—I'm driving. My car, my rules?"

Lindsay cleared her throat. "Actually, it's my car," Lindsay said, smiling.

"Yes, like I said"—Mark laughed—"Lindsay's car, Lindsay's rules. Where was I?" Running out of one-liners, Mark was relieved when the waitress came back to take their orders.

"Okay, I surrender," Benny said with his hands up, laughing with everyone else.

Lindsay smiled when Nathan ordered a waffle and asked if they could put peanut butter and walnuts on it.

It had been one of their favorite breakfasts since Nathan was little. Now that he was a young man, they no longer had to split it. She opted for eggs benedict and smiled again when Mark followed suit. Benny was always going to default to bacon and eggs with hash browns and biscuits and gravy, and Arlene delicately ordered fruit and yogurt.

Lindsay was in a happy mood, and looking at her family as they left the restaurant, they all appeared to be out on a fun family weekend. They retook their positions in the Jeep, and the excursion continued toward Davenport.

"We don't want to live in town, do we, Mom?" Nathan asked innocently from the back. Lindsay noticed he was pulling another bottle of juice from the cooler, and she reached in and grabbed a tea. Offering one to Mark, he shook his head.

"Most likely not, Bud," Lindsay said. "Mark was raised by his Aunt Mavis, who used to live there. I thought we'd just take a little side trip while we're out and about." Lindsay was careful with her wording. Everything she said was true; she just omitted that she now owned it and that it was a part of the "Momopoly" game that his dad had invented. Time enough for those little details later.

They drove along for nearly an hour with easy conversation and laughter. Mark knew very well the way to his aunt's little house and made the last turn slowly. It was impossible to reach her house this way. There had been major changes made. What formerly was the street leading right up to her house was now enclosed by a 10' iron fence, with a sliding gate for a back entrance. Turning the next corner, the front entrance came into view. He drove up to the security guard on duty and rolled down the window.

"Can I help you, sir?" The guard eyed every occupant carefully, making Lindsay feel like a criminal. Mark told him they were hoping to see some vacant units. The guard pointed to a 'Visitor Parking' area as he reached on his utility belt for a walkie-talkie.

Lindsay whispered to him, "Boy, this would sure be a safe place."

Mark pulled through the opening gate and rolled up his window at the same time. They all piled out as a golf cart driven by a young lady in jeans and a University tee-shirt pulled over to them, closer to the vehicle than Lindsay felt comfortable with.

She jumped out and greeted them. "Hi, everybody! I'm Christy. What kind of unit are we looking for today?" Everyone's head turned toward Lindsay. "Ah, so you're the one making decisions today." They all laughed.

"I'm not even sure what you have available. What's the largest unit you have?" Lindsay asked.

Christy motioned toward the golf cart and Gran and the guys started arranging themselves while saving the front for Lindsay. She and Christy were talking about vacancies and floor plans. Mark and Gran took the side seats in the back; Nathan was wedged between them, and Benny sat sideways on the back rack. When they were all loaded up, Christy gently steered the cart around to the north side.

"I'll show you the Penthouse first. It's 3-2-2. Three bedrooms, two bathrooms. You'll get two parking spaces with it, one covered and one uncovered. It's on the third floor, but we do have an elevator. It's vacant but hasn't been readied yet. That means we shampoo the carpet, touch up the paint, and all that. It'll be ready for the first of the month. There's a flyer on the dash there."

Lindsay reached for the flyer. It showed several diverse types of units and the prices of each.

Christy stopped abruptly. "Here we are. Shall we take the elevator?" This time she looked at Gran, who nodded gratefully. Gran was in great shape, but she wasn't up to climbing stairs for three floors. For that matter, neither was Lindsay. Christy led the way around some lavish landscaping and called for the elevator with her key.

The building was nicely renovated so that the elevator was nearly invisible from the parking area. There was room for all of them in the elevator, although snugly, and the ride was smooth and quiet. They disembarked on the third floor from the opposite side of the entrance to a tastefully decorated lobby area with a large fish tank that immediately caught Nathan's attention.

"Look!" Nathan detoured to the tank, followed by Mark. "That's a neon tetra!"

Mark was impressed. "You're right! And there's an angel fish behind that coral." Nathan looked up at him and smiled. Mark won points with Nathan when he named yet another species. Mark chucked Nathan on the shoulder as they caught up to Lindsay and Arlene.

They all followed Christy to the far end of the common area where there was an ornate double door declaring the entrance. She pulled out another key, and opening the doors wide, stepped aside to let them all enter. Lindsay was in awe.

Upscale finishes greeted her eye in both the living room and dining room which were visible from here. A few steps toward the dining room revealed a magnificent white-on-white kitchen with a large island in the middle—granite top with a deep stainless-steel sink. Italian mahogany cabinets accented the walls all around with a built-in refrigerator. Nathan's question popped back into her head. *We don't want to live in town, do we, Mom?* She loved that she and Nathan were on the same page most of the time.

Thirty-Two

Lindsay hooked her arm through her mom's. "Well?"

"Oh, this is lovely," Gran said breathlessly, taking in the elegant wood fixtures.

"It's like a President's Palace!" Nathan said innocently.

Mark and Lindsay looked at each other. A wink accompanied Mark's smile. Nathan was right. She had forgotten about the location in Tom's game that he called The Presidential Palace. Lindsay had repeated Nathan's question over and over again in her mind to keep her interest minimal. *We don't want to live in town, do we, Mom?*

"It is, Bud," she answered. They wandered around separately until each had seen it all, then met at the front door as if on a timer.

Christy was there. "Any questions?" The only question that Lindsay thought of was an unspoken 'and this hasn't been readied yet?' She peeked at the flyer and nodded to herself. Well worth the price tag.

"Ready by the first, you said?" Lindsay reworded her question.

"Yes, ma'am, but I do have an adjoining unit that could work for such a nice big family like yours. Between the two, there would be six bedrooms, three baths, and four parking spaces."

Overhearing this, Benny looked at Lindsay and teased her. "You have a large family?" They toured the adjoining units. They were just as top-of-the-line as the first unit but adjoined by double pocket doors. When closed, they blended in beside the wood trim around the fireplace making them nearly invisible. When Christy opened them, they enlarged the living room to include a den/library area. Even more satisfactory for a 'nice big family like theirs'.

By the time they climbed back in the Jeep, even Nathan was "oohing" about living in such a mansion.

They drove out of town on the new bypass and headed northeast to Rutledge. The consensus was that if you had to live in town, La Palacia would be the perfect place to live in. Lindsay didn't think that would be the best atmosphere to rear a growing boy, but considering what she had been dealing with in the last few weeks, she was more than happy with the security systems this facility already had in place. It might be a temporary fortress for them.

As they reached the outskirts of Rutledge, Mark asked her what exit he had marked on the map to take them to Lake Juniper. She told him and then put the address in her GPS. "Sorry, I didn't think to do that sooner."

"I didn't even think of it. Can you go ahead and put in the other two, too? I thought it would be good for the others to see Happy Trails, too, don't you think?" Mark lowered his voice so the back seat couldn't hear, but the outburst of giggles and silliness made it difficult for even Lindsay to hear him.

"I don't see what it would hurt. We are out here, after all." Lindsay smiled and her thoughts returned to Pam's death. She realized that she had lost track in her mind of Lucky and his business card. "By the way, Mark, have you heard anything from Chief Marsh about Lucky? I sort of pushed him out of my mind."

"We haven't talked about it. Have you heard anything more from him?" Mark replied as he changed lanes to take the exit coming up.

"Nothing. Lucky's last message was that we would meet 'some other time and place'. I don't know if he has my phone number or not. I called from my house phone."

Mark looked thoughtful. "But he messaged you on your cell phone, right?" Mark reminded her, pulling up to the stoplight at the end of the off-ramp.

"Oh, of course, I forgot that. I called his number from the diner that day. I should give him another call. Now that I know what I know, it doesn't seem important anymore, or what he knows could confirm what we know now." Who was Lucky anyway?

She was thinking out loud, and her thoughts continued silently for the next few minutes until she heard a loud whisper from the back seat. "Mom, I need a pit stop," Nathan whispered. She turned to him and nodded, then turned to Mark.

"What say we stop at a gas station for a bathroom break?" she asked Mark.

"Your wish is my command." Mark signaled and pulled into the Pilot Truck Stop. Everyone piled out and walked around while Gran and Nathan went inside. Lindsay followed suit. When she came back outside, she spotted Benny and Mark talking with intense expressions.

"Mark, I need you to be honest with me, " Lindsay heard her brother say. "Is Lindsay in danger?"

Lindsay's heart stopped as she saw Mark's face. Was that fear in his eyes? At that moment, she could see how much he cared about her, and it made an unfamiliar feeling tighten her stomach. Was she falling for this man? Was he falling for her? This was not the time to be thinking about this. She stopped, ducking slightly behind the building before they could notice her and continued to listen.

Mark wasn't sure how to respond to Benny's question about Lindsay's safety. How could he reply honestly without betraying her confidence? But if he said nothing to her brother about this whole situation, it may raise even more red flags.

"She needs to move from the Townhouse," he began. "Chief Marsh thinks she may be in physical danger. It appears the firm put a clause in the purchase agreement. It's kind of an entanglement, because of Tom being an employee as well as a partner. The clause leaves ownership of the townhouse in question. So, the Deputy Attorney General thinks it best for her to move as soon as possible."

"Ah, so now it makes sense why we're suddenly taking

a tour of properties. But are they within her price range?" Benny's face showed concern. Mark smiled and decided not to divulge more.

"Well, maybe you should talk to her about that," Mark whispered with a smile.

Mark noticed Lindsay from the corner of his eye. How long had she been standing there? Had she heard their conversation? "You ready?" he asked, smiling at Lindsay and throwing Benny a look.

She nodded, headed to the front passenger door, and climbed in.

"Wait a minute!" Benny whispered, stepping in close, mouth hanging open. "Did Tom buy them?" Mark only smirked at Benny's mouth agape as he moved toward the driver's side, eager to end this conversation, hoping he hadn't already said too much. "I always knew he was up to no good," Benny whispered as the Jeep began to fill.

Looking in the rear-view mirror, Mark could still see signs of shock on Benny's face. Benny just shook his head, and Mark smiled again, getting a chuckle out of the whole thing. Then he looked at Lindsay's face and realized she had been watching their little exchange. Her expression appeared to be one of disappointment, but she said nothing. Mark's stomach twisted. She had heard their conversation. He hoped she realized he was trying to protect her. He would never want to hurt her. He already cared about her too much.

A few more minutes and a few more turns, and they were out of town again and on a beautiful tree-lined farm-to-market road. Gently rolling hills suddenly transformed the topography. "No wonder they call this area the hill country," Gran mentioned. "This is gorgeous."

"It is, Mom. Are you doing okay back there?" Lindsay asked.

"Yes, dear. I'm doing fine." She tapped gently on Nathan's leg, and he moved it, opening the cooler for her so she could get an iced tea. Everyone settled into the lull of the car for the next several minutes.

"In one mile, turn left." The voice of the GPS startled everyone. Everyone chuckled, but Mark noticed Lindsay only smiled and looked out her window. In a few minutes, they turned left. According to the GPS, they would arrive in 20 minutes.

What little traffic they had encountered was reduced drastically with each curve and with every hill. They passed a community college campus with a nearly empty parking lot. Just past the building, Mark saw what appeared to be an apartment complex, old but bright and cheerful as if recently painted. Lindsay leaned forward in her seat, seeming to take it all in. Why was he so aware of her?

Thirty-Three

Lindsay found herself bouncing around in the seat, looking in all directions at once. "What an interesting layout for a town!" she said, marveling at the curved roads. The conversation had picked up again, everyone making comments on different parks, buildings, and stores that they passed.

"There are certainly a lot of churches in this town," Gran commented. Mark agreed with a nod. They drove past St Mary's Catholic Church, First Baptist, and United Methodist within two blocks of each other. They counted seven churches. Lindsay knew that as the strong Christian woman she was, her mom would be pleased with the variety of churches this town had to offer. Lindsay also realized she felt the same way, more so every day.

Another announcement from the GPS: "Arriving at destination on right in 100 feet." Mark slowed down and started looking at house numbers. There were only four houses on the right, so if their friend "Gypsy" (also known as the GPS) was right; it would be the last house on the block. Everyone was suddenly quiet, taking it all in.

"Wow, we could live here?" Nathan seemed impressed, leaning over Gran to look up at the rock and log-arched entrance adorned with greenery.

The rustic sign hanging from the arch said "Lado Soleado." Lindsay's High School Spanish failed her. As they turned, they followed the River Rock lane for nearly a quarter mile and came to a stop under the pergola, supported by rock columns. Lindsay was speechless. *Wow, just wow.*

Or as Tom would have said, 'Wowzer.' Lindsay snapped her mouth shut when she realized she had been staring open-mouthed as the car rolled to a stop. Everyone was having similar reactions as they got out of the car and found themselves standing in a line, facing the magnificent front doors.

"Lindsay," Mark whispered, touching her elbow. "I didn't say anything other than tell Benny he needed to ask you. He guessed the rest." Lindsay had no chance to reply. Those grand doors opened, and a young man in a suit came out to meet them.

"Good morning! You must be the Davis party. We are so happy to welcome you. Please, come in." He motioned for them to enter, and he fell in behind them. "You're right on time. Which of you is Mrs. Davis?" Lindsay extended her hand and shook hands with him, and then introduced the rest of the Davis party. "So happy to meet all of you. Master Nathan, you might be interested in our game room just there." He motioned in the direction of the doorway to the side of the large foyer. "There are buckets just inside the doorway with tokens for your use. I will take the rest of you to the dining area." He motioned to the next doorway, about ten feet away. "He is safe. He can join you when he is ready."

At Nathan's excited hopping, Lindsay nodded. "Ten minutes and you join us, Bud."

"Yes, ma'am," he said as he was already nearly in the room. The rest of them followed the maître' d into the dining room.

"I made reservations for lunch and a tour," Mark whispered to Lindsay. "I was not aware of the formality." Lindsay smiled and raised her eyebrows. She felt they were being treated like royalty.

"Please have a seat." They were immediately greeted by a waiter who took drink orders. He gave them unique menus that were more like greeting cards, written in elegant calligraphy. Shortly afterward, the waiter brought back the drinks. The menu was also unusual in that dinners were only served family-style. After discussion, they agreed to have the blackened pork chops with rice pilaf and green beans almondine with salads. Unsure how her son would care for the heavily seasoned pork chop, Lindsay ordered a burger and fries for Nathan just as he came in.

"That sounds great, Mom," Nathan replied. "But I don't get it. There's nobody else here—no kids, either."

Mark spoke up to explain. "This is a lodge, and it is currently vacant. As I understand it, these people are the caretakers, and when they learned we were driving so far to get here, they volunteered to serve us lunch and then show us around the place." All the time he was explaining, Lindsay was looking at him, pleading with her eyes that he wouldn't say too much as he had with Benny. She was grateful that he received her message.

The meal was as delicious as the entire event was intriguing. They took their time eating, and the ever-attentive waiter appeared in more casual jeans, cowboy boots, and a worn denim jacket. "We will begin our tour whenever you are ready, folks. I'll be just outside that door past the restrooms." Lindsay could tell by the amused look on his face that he was rather enjoying the puzzled looks on theirs.

While the rest of the family was making use of the bathrooms, Benny grabbed Lindsay's elbow. "Sis, you own these properties?"

"Shh—please, Benny," she whispered. "I don't want Nathan to know yet. Looks like I do—I mean, Tom acquired them before he died—but I didn't know anything about it."

"Wow," Benny said, shaking his head.

"Mark had no right to tell you anything." She spun around and would have left to join the rest of the family when he caught her arm.

"Wait a minute, Lindsay," Benny whispered loud enough for her to hear. "I asked him if the properties we were looking at were in your price range. He said I needed to talk to you, and I guessed about Tom. I figured all along he was up to no good."

Lindsay stopped and stared at her brother, speechless. After a second, he dropped his hands from her arms, the regret in his eyes meeting the hurt in hers. Lindsay turned and went out the door. She needed to talk with Mark. She refused more tension in her life, especially with her brother. Or should she just have a family meeting and spill the truth to everyone at once?

Thirty-Four

Lindsay asked their driver about the name of this place. "I never did well in Spanish in school," she commented. "What does the entryway sign say?" The family was seated in a wagon hitched to a four-by-four with their waiter at the wheel. The wagon had seats facing out from the center.

"Of course." He smiled. "It means Sunnyside. Mr. D didn't tell you? We were so sorry to hear of his passing. We miss his routine stays with us. He used to come out about once a month and stay a couple of days." Lindsay again felt the sting of the secret Tom had kept from her. "I'm so sorry, Mrs. Davis. I never introduced myself. I am Eduardo Cruz. Folks around here just call me Eddie." He watched the recognition register on her face. "My uncle is Javier Cruz. He works with Whitley, Morris, and Cruz in Davenport."

"No need to apologize, Eddie." Lindsay crawled into the four-by-four and sat in the front seat beside him.

"And, please, call me Lindsay. You work for the firm that manages the property?"

"Yes, ma'am." He started the four-by-four and drove around the courtyard. The brick lane led away from the lodge and transitioned from brick to gravel as they headed toward the stable. "I helped Mr. D with all the properties."

Mark, who was seated directly behind Lindsay, although about two feet away from her, due to the hitch, leaned in closer to hear better.

"Do you think we could sit and talk with you a bit after the tour?" Lindsay suggested as they rolled to a stop amid a cluster of outbuildings. They all exited the side by side, Nathan rushing over to climb on the bottom rung of a wooden fence. He was greeted by three quarter horses.

"Hey, Mom, you gotta come over here!" He couldn't contain his excitement. Everyone approached Nathan and the horses gently. Lindsay thought they looked familiar.

"They are great, aren't they?" Eddie extended one hand over the fence and stroked the big bay roan's neck. "This is Tomboy, and this is Satin." He reached past Tomboy to the paint Nathan had warmed up to. "And that's—"

"Silk," Mark said as he walked around Nathan to the Palomino. Eddie nodded jovially. Lindsay's memory flooded back to their first date—the trail ride, on Silk and Satin, and the tension between them faded as she took Mark's hand.

"Yes, sir. You met her before, at Happy Trails." Eddie had come around to stand behind them. "We rotate the horses every now and then, so they all get plenty of sunshine and exercise. We just brought these two girls here and took Daisy and Dollop over there. They stay here on weekends and go back on Monday morning."

Nathan danced around in front of Lindsay. "Can we go riding, Mom? Please?" Lindsay shook her head, taking hold of his hand.

"Sorry, Bud, we don't have time today," Lindsay answered. "Besides, there aren't enough horses for all of us."

"It's been way too many years since I've been on one of those creatures," Gran said, laughing. "I'd have to pass anyway." They all chuckled with her.

Lindsay put her arm around Nathan's shoulders. "Besides, don't you want to go meet Daisy and Dollop?" This cheered him, and he jumped off the fence and ran alongside it. He was ecstatic when Tomboy trotted along with him on her side of the fence. Lindsay's eyes roamed over the field the horses occupied. Along one side were lean-to like shelters and stalls with gates on both ends, much like the ones at Happy Trails.

Eddie motioned toward one of the buildings behind them. "This is the barn. If you want to go inside, we certainly can, but it sounds like you're a bit pressed for time. Mr. D had the old structure torn down and rebuilt four years ago. Then he upgraded the shop there," he said, pointing to the next building. They followed along the corral, Tomboy and Nathan still playing games along the fence. "There are ten stalls in the barn, and there are four more horses out in the pasture," he whispered to Lindsay, so Nathan didn't hear. She smiled.

"Thank you," she whispered. "How many do you have in total?"

"*You*, Mrs. Davis—Lindsay—have 22. Right now,

there are ten here, eight at Happy Trails, and four at Old MacDonaldson's." Lindsay was becoming more and more overwhelmed. She turned, and finding Mark standing nearby, she slipped her arm through his. He automatically bent his elbow slightly to accommodate her hand and placed his left hand over hers. "Shall we move on?" Eddie resumed his tour.

"This is the haybarn, brand new roof," Eddie motioned as they passed it. "And the tool shed. Back behind the shed is the infirmary. Doc's trailer is back there, so he can stay overnight whenever he needs to." The trailer he referred to appeared to be about a 40' foot travel trailer, complete with awning and landscaping. Eddie walked back to the four-by-four as he continued. "There are 400 acres here, going clear back beyond Bear Creek. We'll go to the lakeside next, so you can see that area."

"Wow, Mom," Nathan's voice got shrill. "This place is even bigger than Alex's uncle's ranch!" Lindsay enjoyed her son's excitement, but she felt guilty. Here she was now keeping secrets from him. She would tell them all the first chance she got.

They all climbed back in, and Eddie drove back toward the lodge. "I forgot to show you the smokehouse!" he called, pointing toward a big building with an open pavilion attached. "There's a smaller one on the lakeside." Just before they got to the lodge, he took a turn onto another lane lined with trees. The shadows transformed it into semi-darkness, even in the early afternoon sun.

The passengers gazed around, awestruck. The lane opened into what appeared to be a park. Lindsay held her breath at the plush green grass, the occasional oasis of lovely flowers, and the immaculately kept bushes and trees scattered all around. Horse trails crisscrossed the area. Occasionally, an area of picnic tables and shelters butted up to the lane. They kept driving to an area that sported a driving range, putting green, tennis courts, and a large outdoor swimming pool. Lindsay noticed hitching posts dotted the area, and there was even a rock-climbing wall. Eddie turned off the engine and sat sideways in his seat.

"This is the community area," he explained. It's open to the community year-round at no cost. There's an area around this next hill that we flood every winter for ice skating. And coming up here"—he started moving again—"is the roller rink. It's closed right now. We're in the middle of renovations that Mr. D lined up before."

Lindsay nodded, trying to smile.

Eddie was quiet as they continued past the skating rink and around a big curve through a thick stand of trees. As the trees thinned, he pointed out the second smokehouse, smaller than the first and surrounded by sheltered picnic tables. Then they passed a small corral with a lean-to along one side with watering troughs sufficient for several horses.

"Folks can ride horseback from here if they want when they're camping!" He shouted back as they approached a camping area with campsite hookups. They stopped before the road met a paved street. As they turned around, Lindsay noticed the city-style green street sign. They were on the corner of Nathan Avenue and Lindsay Lane. She felt the prick of tears at the back of her eyes. It touched her heart that Tom thought of so many ways to honor her and their son. She smiled at the thought that he would always be in her life, even if she moved forward with someone new... She snapped to attention and looked at Nathan to see if he saw the sign. It was obvious he hadn't, but Gran's facial expression told Lindsay that she had seen it and caught the significance of the street names.

Thirty-Five

Lindsay spoke just loud enough for Nathan to hear her. "Nathan, did you see the names of the streets?" Eddie slowed and made a wide U-turn to enable Nathan to take a second look.

"Mom? That's our names." His mouth stayed open. She didn't correct his grammar.

"Your Dad named these streets after us," she answered simply. She winked and smiled, expecting him to bring the subject up later.

Eddie picked up his speed and drove them back the way they had come but took a side path just after the trailer area. After a few long curves, he slowed down as they came into view of the glistening lake. One side appeared pure and untainted by the human hand. The other side held two fishing piers, complete with extended decks, and along the far side, an area was roped off for swimming. As they continued rolling along, the lake appeared and disappeared, and finally, they were at lake level. It seemed to go on forever.

"Is all of this mi— part of Sunnyside?" Lindsay asked wide-eyed, looking around to see if anyone noticed her near slip.

"Yes, ma'am, right up to this fence line we're coming up on," Eddie answered. "The lake, of course, is state property, but the adjoining property is yours on three sides. There are about 250 acres on this side. There's an aerial map in the lodge office; we'll stop there when we get back if you like."

They turned left and followed the white wooden fence line for several minutes before turning left again into another thicket of trees. The next turn a few minutes later revealed the lodge in the distance. The rest of the ride was accomplished in silent amazement.

When they got back to the lodge, Eddie took Lindsay and Mark to the office to show them on the map, where he had taken them on the tour. Lindsay was glad she hadn't seen the aerial map before the tour. It made much more sense to her now. She was able to put everything into perspective. Eddie had not taken them to the undeveloped area. On the map, it looked to be about the same size as the lakeside, but thick with trees. Only one long road appeared winding through the whole area.

When she turned around from examining the map, Eddie and Mark had moved across the room, and were talking with Nathan. All of their faces were illuminated. As the four of them approached, she could hear why. They were talking horses, Eddie filling Nathan in on the rotation schedules, and which horses didn't get rotated, the "old folks," as Eddie called them, and what it meant to put them out to pasture. Nathan's face saddened a bit as he turned around, but lit up again when he saw the horses coming toward them. Yes, she had to tell Nathan what was going on.

"Ready to continue on foot? You haven't seen the living quarters yet." Eddie motioned to the elevator in the corner.

Eddie took them to the third floor first, and the doors opened to reveal the most magnificent ballroom Lindsay had ever seen. Tables and seating were arranged behind a railing on a raised platform around three walls. As they stepped in, they could see a stage area behind them to the right, running all the way across the fourth wall of the room. Eddie reached behind her and flipped the switches to light the entire room.

Although wall-to-wall windows surrounded the glistening wood dance floor, the heavy drapes blocked out any hint of sunlight. Eddie turned the lights back off and hit another switch. The blinds opened, splashing the entire room with afternoon sunlight. Another switch and the windows were partially tinted. Lindsay laughed and turned to see the others beaming smiles as well.

"Yeah," Eddie said. "Mr. D loved his projects! He left us a list a mile long!" His smile dimmed. "There are restrooms on both sides." Lindsay saw the neon signs above the doors. 'And the bar is in the back." Eddie pointed straight ahead. "Mr. D didn't drink, so it's stocked with pop, lemonade, sweet tea, and such—some juices, oh, and Mike's hard lemonade—in all flavors." He smiled sheepishly. " I guess for those who drink."

Lindsay and Mark walked to one side to take in the view. Nathan had taken off his shoes and came sliding up beside them sock-footed. "This is so cool, Mom. Can we come here for vacations sometime?"

Lindsay smiled at him. "I think that would be a great idea, Bud!"

"There are stairs here if you'd rather take them down to the second level." Eddie offered. Gran nodded to Lindsay, and the decision was made.

This viewpoint only added to the feeling Lindsay had that she was in a 5-star hotel. Even the stairs wore a wide wooden base along the carpeted floors. Eddie led the way, with Gran right behind him, and then came Nathan, Benny, Lindsay, and Mark. Eddie opened the door with a key and held it open for the rest of them.

High-end finishes greeted them here as lavishly as downstairs. On one side, warm, inviting oversized chairs were scattered around a fireplace, a fire built in it, ready for a match. They wandered further in and Lindsay soaked in the luxurious elegance. An ivory chess set rested on a gleaming table with ornately carved legs. The shelf above it held other board games, within arm's reach.

The group toured the next room, the kitchen-dining room, opening to another smaller more casual family area. Then they walked down a short hall, past a restroom and two bedrooms, each with its own adjoining restroom. Then the double doors opened to a lovely master suite, donning the same windows as the ballroom above her. This was all way too fancy for her. But Nathan was right. What a place for a vacation!

As they came back down the hall, the other side of the entryway held more offices, smaller than the one downstairs, and a room with a pool table, table tennis, and old-style pinball machines along one wall. As Nathan ran in, he found another bucket with tokens near them.

"Go ahead," Lindsay said to his unasked questions.

"We'll be out here. Eddie, do you have time for a talk?" She led the way to the dining room table and sat down. Eddie and Mark joined her. Benny and Gran snuggled down in the oversized chairs, talking softly.

"Of course, ma'am." They sat in silence for several minutes. Lindsay took a deep breath and exhaled.

"Eddie, my husband didn't—I was not aware of this place nor of any of the properties you take care of. I'm learning that he amassed quite an empire. That's why we are touring them today. We are currently living in the townhouse in—"

"Yes, ma'am. That's one property I haven't helped with. That and the house on Jefferson." Eddie interjected. Mom's house.

"I have a decision to make, Eddie. We need to move out of the townhouse, and I was hoping one of the properties would work for us, but everything we've seen is a bit—"

"Fancy? Over-the-top? Mr. D said you would say that." Eddie laughed. "He was working on the Homestead when he—anyway, he was building it just for you, he said."

Nathan burst into the room. "Mom," he whispered close to her. "I'm thirsty. Can I go back to the party room and get a drink?" Eddie overheard.

"You don't have to," Eddie said, smiling. "There are always a few drinks in the fridge here in the kitchen."

"I'm thirsty, too. Let's see what they've got." Lindsay put her arm around Nathan's shoulders, and they went to investigate. One shelf held sweet tea—her drink of choice. The other held lemonade, apple juice and orange juice, the third held orange soda, and root beer—Dad's Old-

Fashioned Root Beer. Tom was crazy about root beer floats. On a whim, she opened the freezer, and as she suspected, found vanilla ice cream.

Seeing her face, Eddie smiled. "Would you like a root beer float? Mr. D often wanted a root beer float; we keep it stocked, even after—"

"Sure!" said Nathan, excitedly. Lindsay asked everyone, and Gran and Mark accepted her offer. She and Benny settled for drinks, Benny having an orange pop and she, falling into her norm, grabbed a sweet tea. When everyone was settled at the table, she and Eddie found chairs in the living room and continued their conversation.

"The Homestead is complete now, exactly to Mr. D's specifications. He was very detailed in how he wanted it finished out, right down to the furniture. Come in here, there's a map in the office." He stood and turned toward the office. Lindsay caught Mark's eye and motioned him to follow as he was placing his glass in the sink. He walked in behind them and closed the door noiselessly, joining her at the map that took up most of the wall.

Eddie pointed to a small yellow triangle on the map. "We're here," he said, dragging his finger along the road. "If you go out the front entrance, where you came in, and turn right to the main road, here, then turn right again, you'll be on the main highway. Stay on that road and you'll pass Happy Trails on the right. Exactly 6.8 miles past that entrance, you'll see a little sign on the fence post on the right that says *Home Sweet Home*. But, you gotta watch closely, or you'll miss it. I don't really think you'll have any trouble finding it, but if you come to Old MacDonaldson's Farm, you've gone too far."

Eddie walked over to the desk and reached above the lamp to a cabinet that Lindsay hadn't noticed in her preliminary perusal. He opened the cabinet and drew out three keys. One by one he handed them to Lindsay. "This one is to the house. This one is to the garage and this one is to the shed out back. Like I say, you can't miss it." He smiled.

"You've been so helpful, Eddie," Lindsay said and shook his hand. He handed her a piece of paper. When she looked at it, she noted his name and phone number. "Thank you so much."

"My pleasure, ma'am. You call me when you're ready to move, and you'll have all the help you need. Ma might be there at the Homestead. She's been taking really good care of it for ya. She was partial to Mr. D, so she kinda went overboard taking care of that place, knowing he built it for you."

After the snacks were finished, they loaded up the Jeep and drove down the road, following Eddie's directions. Lindsay heard Benny unbuckle his seatbelt, and turned toward the back seat as he scooted to the front of his seat, resting his arms on the back of Mark's seat.

"Hey, Sis, I'm sorry about earlier." She noticed that Nathan and Gran were oblivious to their conversation, discussing the pamphlets they had picked up in the showroom. "Tom really bought all these properties?" he asked quietly.

"He did, Benny," she whispered. "But I didn't know about any of them until recently. And they don't know anything about it." Lindsay motioned to Nathan and her mom. "Mom doesn't know about the house being ransacked, either and I don't want her to."

"Sure, Sis. Not a word." He zipped his mouth. "But how?"

"I'm not sure, but Tom bought a lot of properties, rented out some, and left some vacant," she said. "That's what this tour is about. We're looking for a place to move into. We're leaving the townhouse. There are three more properties up the road."

Mark spoke up. "Happy Trails is the stables that you saw on the way to Rutledge."

Lindsay continued. "And Old MacDonaldson's Farm. Mark and I thought there were only those two besides the ones that we've already seen today, but Eddie told me about another one that Tom called The Homestead. He said that Tom built it specifically with us in mind because he knew the others would be too fancy for us." Lindsay smiled and turned back to the front, pensive. She closed her eyes to fend back the tears. Melancholia threatened.

Mark asked the group, "Happy Trails first or Homestead?"

"I so want to see the Homestead, but we get to Happy Trails first, and Nathan really wants to see that, so let's go there first." Lindsay smiled, anticipating Nathan's reaction.

"Happy Trails!" Nathan shouted, and he started singing the old Roy Rogers and Dale Evans' song that his dad had only partly taught him. Everyone sang along. When they ran out of the words they knew, Lindsay laughed even more. It certainly wouldn't break her heart if Happy Trails was Nathan's choice. She was raised in such a peaceful lifestyle that she didn't appreciate until she was grown. She wouldn't mind at all returning to it.

Thirty-Six

Just as Lindsay was nearly dozing herself, she felt the car slowing down. "We should be coming up on Happy Trails pretty quick," Mark said. A few miles down the road, they saw the worn-out fencing with the brightly painted sign welcoming them to Happy Trails. As Mark made the turn, those in the the back seat sat up straining their necks to see better.

Lindsay wiped the tears from her eyes as they approached the familiar buildings. She remembered the ticket stand that had formerly been a tool shed and smiled. As they were unloading, Lindsay warned Nathan. "This is going to be a quick peek, Bud. So don't run off. We'll stay just long enough to meet Dollop and Daisy." He grinned and ran to the fence line where he could see several horses grazing.

Joey came out of the house and smiled. "Hello again. Sorry, we're not riding today, but you can surely look around. Eddie called and told me you'd be by." As they met in the middle of the flower-speckled yard, he reached out, and they shook hands. "I'm sorry, I didn't realize who you were when you were here last."

Lindsay smiled. "No problem, Joey. I didn't realize you ran this place!" He showed them through the yard, pointing to the barn, the shop, and other outbuildings. Nathan wandered over to the fence where several horses scrambled for his attention. He extended one arm over the fence, nuzzling a paint's nose, his other hand combing a smaller horse's mane. As Joey led them to the fence where Nathan was loving on the horses, he stroked Buck's blaze.

"We saw Silk and Satin at the lake, and Eddie was telling me that Dollop and Daisy were over here. Great names!" Lindsay shared. They all agreed. "Nathan was bound and determined to meet them."

Joey whistled a few times, and all the horses came loping to the chutes. It always took Lindsay's breath away to see horses lope or gallop. Such majesty and grace. As the horses each walked through the chutes, he closed all the front gates.

"You know Buck—he's a sorrel gelding. He and I think alike." He opened the gate and Buck walked through. "This one is Daisy. She looks like a swirl cake my ma used to make. Her pasture mate here is Dollop." He opened the gates and let them go through. Dollop was snow white with a pink nose and blue eyes. "This is Domingo; he's a pretty laid-back fella. Loves kids." He winked at Nathan. Joey opened the gates and let Domingo and the next horse walk through.

"Josie?" Lindsay gasped. The horse of her childhood recognized her immediately, coming quickly to her side and nuzzling under Lindsay's left arm, where she used to always carry her treats. "Oh my Gosh! It's Josie, and she knows me!" Lindsay looked at her mother, who had tears running down her face to match Lindsay's. "She's got to be 20 years old by now. Mom, look, it's Josie!" Gran nodded, remembering.

"Vet figured 22, but she's still fit as a fiddle," Joey said, laughing with Lindsay. "And she's had a good life, so she could live ten more years if we're lucky."

Lindsay turned and hugged Nathan as he approached. "Josie used to be my horse, Bud, when I was a kid."

"Maybe we need to move here, Mom, so you can be near her again." Nathan's tenderness had always been a joy to her heart. She mussed up his hair, but with his hair cut short, he didn't mind anymore. He laughed with her.

Joey motioned for them to walk toward the house. Awkwardly, he said, "I live here now, but this is your property, Mrs. Davis, so I'll find somewhere else, if—"

She lowered her voice when she answered him. "Oh, no, Joey. This is your home. Whatever arrangements you had with my husband; you have with me." Lindsay sensed his relief. "And call me Lindsay, please. We don't need to invade your privacy by touring it." Lindsay turned around, looking for Nathan and Gran, grateful to see them out of earshot, but she realized she would have to bring them up to speed. Everyone in the properties they were visiting knew the whole story.

They followed him to the old farmhouse that showed signs of recent improvements and paint. "I would prefer you to come in. I hope you'll appreciate what we've done." They mounted the steps, the porch creaking as they walked across to the painted white screen door. The interior door was standing open, so they went on in. "This is my mom." He gestured toward the kitchen where a woman drying her hands was coming toward them. By the time she reached them, Gran was the last to come in the door.

"Edie!" Gran's mouth dropped and became a smile as she crossed the room and hugged the woman.

"Arlene Burke?" The two women hugged while the others looked at each other smiling. "Oh Arlene, I didn't know where you moved after Albert died! What a joy it is to see you again!"

"You look wonderful, my dear friend." Gran's face lit up. "It has been so long. How are you?"

"Oh, please, sit and have coffee with me." Edie turned and began making coffee, Gran nodding as she leaned against the counter, and they picked up their conversation.

The two women sat at the table having coffee and catching up over old times while the rest of them followed Joey through the house. This was the original old farmhouse that had been beautifully restored. Lindsay was overwhelmed with melancholia as she passed what had been Pam's bedroom when they were kids. Joey guided them down the back stairs. It led to the mudroom and back porch, which opened up to the same pasture the horses were in today.

"That's about it, Lindsay. I sure am sorry about Mr. D. After you left last time, I looked up the scrapbook. I remembered he was killed at the same time Pam was. They never did figure out what happened. Don't know what she was even doing over there," Joey said with deep sadness in his voice. "Excuse me." He teared up and turned away, walking back to the front of the house. Lindsay felt her throat close, so she walked with him, squeezing his arm, and smiled sadly.

By the time the group walked around to the front of the house, Arlene and Edie were standing on one side of the front porch facing west. "In the winter when the trees are all bare, you can just see the house there." Edie pointed in the distance, and Mom turned to look. "They finished it up, oh, six or seven months ago. It's quite a place! Mr. D called it the Homestead from the moment he cleared the land. Maria comes by for coffee sometimes when she goes over there, and she brings homemade tortillas! They are so good." Both women were cheerful as they came down the steps. Edie looked at Lindsay.

"You, my dear, have grown to be a lovely young lady. I can still remember you and Pam—inseparable as kids!" Edie's smile was bittersweet.

"Yes, ma'am. Thank you. It's so good to see you again. I was so sorry to hear about Pam."

"Thank you, dear," Edie said sadly.

Lindsay looked at her mom. "Ready to go, Mom?"

"Of course, dear. We do have other places to see, don't we?"

She hugged Edie again as they loaded into the Jeep. Lindsay's thoughts consumed her as they left the driveway. *The Homestead.* Why would he have called it that? Tom wasn't raised around here. This was *her* 'old stomping grounds.' They had met at college.

She had always assumed he had come from an unhappy childhood. He had never talked much about his life before they met. Maybe he felt it would make up for her homestead. She had told him how sad it was for her to have to leave the ranch after her dad died. Knowing Tom, it was a combination of those two heartbreaks and a plan to keep Nathan from living with the same wounds. And who knows, Lindsay thought, there may be answers amid the answers they were already discovering.

Thirty-Seven

Mark made a note of the odometer. They rode in silence for a few minutes when he announced, "Okay, we're at 6.4 miles. Look for a small sign on the fence post on the right." When the odometer said 6.6, he slowed the Jeep down, his left hand riding the signal lever. Lindsay discreetly pointed to the sign, and he signaled his turn.

"There it is, Mom. Home sweet home." Lindsay felt like she wasn't just talking about the road they had just been on. She felt like she was home. The lane along the road was gravel, so Mark didn't regain speed after he made the turn. They followed the recently graded road for several miles before they came to a long curve.

When they started into the curve, the road changed to chip seal and was suddenly lined with white fences and delightful landscaping features. A stump with colorful planters on it, a ladder standing against a tree, with vines pouring from the pots on the rungs, a boulder with desert plants protruding from the cracks. Everywhere she looked, there was beauty to catch one's eye. Another curve and the house came into view. For some reason, she immediately felt at home. Tall chain-link fencing surrounded a simple two-story house, white brick with gray streaks through the bricks. The gate was standing open as if they were expected. Lindsay smiled. In her mind, she knew they were. Eddie was her first guess.

They drove through the gate and parked facing a lovely little courtyard that looked peaceful and inviting. Nathan excitedly pointed to the picnic table and basketball court beyond. Lindsay smiled. It all looked very familiar. Still, no one spoke as they walked up the sidewalk to the front door.

Lindsay pulled out the keys and rang the doorbell, just in case Maria was still there. When there was no answer, she used her key. She wasn't surprised that it worked smoothly. The door swung open, and she froze. She couldn't take a step forward. At her hesitation, Mark stepped off the sidewalk onto the grass and passed Gran and Nathan to reach her.

"Lindsay? You okay?" She turned to face him with tears streaming down her face. She took his hand, and they went inside slowly. As he stepped in behind her, he understood. The entire entryway was a replica of her current townhouse, right down to the color scheme.

Everyone followed, and one by one, their eyes widened as they recognized everything. The same desk, the same sofa and chairs. They just didn't reflect the recent rearranging made after the townhouse had been ransacked. The same coffee and end tables. She went into the kitchen and wasn't surprised when even the paper towel holder was the same style as the one she had on her townhouse counter. Lindsay was forcing her lungs to inhale and exhale normally.

She sat down at the same kitchen table she had at home. "We don't have to look any further," Lindsay whispered. How strange this all felt. Then she saw the note hanging on the bulletin board by the back door, held by a pushpin.

Mrs. Davis, I left the gate open for you, so you could come right in. Mr. D told us you would come one day if he was not able to bring you himself. I am so sorry I could not stay to greet you. There are taco fixings in the fridge, the meat is in the electric skillet, and the tortillas are on the rack in the pantry. They are homemade. I hope you enjoy them. When you are ready to leave, please push the code (777 and the pound key) to close the gate. But there is room for everyone to stay the night if you would like to. I am so sorry we lost Mr. D, and I am sorry for your loss. Welcome home, dear.

—Maria Cruz

Lindsay smiled through her tears. "Anyone hungry for tacos?" She felt like she had eaten enough today to last her through the weekend, but the very thought of homemade tortillas made her mouth water. She looked at her phone and saw that it was 5:45. Close enough for supper. Gran came in beside her and put her arm around her waist.

"You okay, sweetie?" At her smile and nod, she went on. "You gonna tell an old lady what the heck is going on?"

"I'm sorry, Mom, for keeping secrets. I just wanted to learn it all for myself before I told you and Nathan." Gran found a tissue on the counter, right where she expected the box to be, and passed one to her daughter. "I still don't know much, but all the properties we saw today?" At Mom's nod toward Nathan coming in, Lindsay stopped.

As the two women set the table and brought out the food, the sense of déjà vu could not be ignored. "Mom, it's such a long story, and I don't even know all of it yet. But I'll tell you what I do know. First, with every day, it becomes more obvious to me how very much we were all loved by Tom and what he sacrificed to be sure we were taken care of. Tom owned every property that we have looked at today. Now, of course, it looks like they all belong to me."

Nathan came back in and grabbed a handful of black olives off the tray in the middle of the table. "Mom, my room is just like home! This is so cool! But weird, too!" Just as quickly, he escaped back into the living room.

Mom sat down and let Lindsay finish. "He—I also own property in Washington state, a casino in South Dakota, your house, and the townhouse. The only problem is that there is a clause in the deed to the townhouse that I don't want to deal with, so we're looking around at these properties to see which one we want to move into. And I want you with us, Mom, and Benny, too, if he'll come." Lindsay talked fast, in hopes of getting it all out before Nathan came back in. Instead, Benny joined them.

"If I'll come where?" Benny asked. Instead of answering his question, Lindsay blew through her mouth in exasperation. "Come and eat!" she called, and Mark and Nathan arrived instantly. "Who wants to say grace?"

Benny spoke quickly. *Lord, I don't know what you got going on, but if it's in your will, we're in. I thank you for protecting us, for providing for us, and for lovin' us, and I sure thank you for these tacos. Amen.*

"Help yourselves, everyone," Lindsay said. "But I need to talk to you, so listen while you make your tacos." Gran was helping Nathan avoid soiling the pale-yellow linen tablecloth. "Tom had a game that he was creating before he passed away. It was kinda like Monopoly, Nathan told me, only it was with real properties. Nathan's dad called it 'Momopoly' and told him it was a game we couldn't play until later." She scooped some diced tomatoes on top of her tacos, buying some time while she chose her words. No one interrupted. She added the sour cream and taco sauce and sat back to take a bite before she continued. "Mm-mm," she said, planning her words.

Nathan answered, "Mm-hmm." Everyone chuckled, trying to keep food in their mouths. She swallowed and continued.

"The names of the properties in Momopoly were the President's Palace—and the first property we saw this morning was named La Palacia, which means Palace, and do you remember what you said, Nathan, when you saw that gorgeous place?" Lindsay asked, taking another bite of her taco.

"Sure, I said it looked like a President's Palace." He beamed as he took another huge bite of taco, juice escaping down his chin.

"Then we went to the place on the lake, remember?" Lindsay continued. "The huge place. The sign on the front said Lado Soleado. Anyone know what that means?"

Benny answered, "Sunnyside."

Nathan jumped up. "Sunny Side Up!" He roared and sat back down.

"Yep," Lindsay agreed. "In Momopoly—in Tom's game—it was called Sunny Side Up. Another name in his game was "Happy Trails," she continued. "And that's where we met Joey and Edie, and Daisy and Dollop."

"But that was the old Donaldson Farm," Gran interjected.

"Right, but we got confused because the last place on Mark's map for today, another place in Tom's game, was called 'Old MacDonaldson's Farm.' We haven't been there yet, but while we were at Sunnyside, Eddie told us about a property we didn't know about, called the Homestead, that wasn't on our list. That's where we are now."

Gran picked up the story. "I think it's wonderful that since you want to move from the townhouse anyway, you have all these choices!"

Nathan downed his chocolate milk and set his glass down with a clunk. "Hey, Mom, if we move here, we won't have to bring our furniture! Everything's already here. That's just weird, Mom." He sat down and finished the goodies that fell from his taco onto his plate.

"He's right," Mark said. "It is weird. But kinda cool... I think." He looked at Lindsay with a big question mark on his face.

"I'm not sure yet, either." She scooted her chair back and started gathering plates, rinsing them, and putting them in the dishwasher. A brand new one, but the same model as the one in the townhouse.

"Let me finish this, dear. You go upstairs and check it out."

Lindsay hugged her mom and walked toward the stairs. She took a stabilizing breath before she took the stairs slowly. The guest room was easy. She had always kept it simple and gender-neutral, so there was no emotional stress here.

She went into Nathan's room next. The scratch on his bookshelf from his failed attempt to climb it wasn't there. That's what felt weird to her. Everything else was the same, except the drawers were empty. The bottles of shampoo and body wash were in place in the bathroom. The towels were hanging just so. Lindsay reminisced. It was perfect—that was a problem! Nathan's bathroom was never perfect.

She stepped into the hall and hesitated. This was eerie. She felt like she had slipped into a fantasy world. Tom had built it, especially for her—for her and Nathan—to be safe. *Lord, I need you to go in there with me,* Lindsay prayed. *This is all getting to me. I know Tom was trying to make us feel at home, and I'm glad that Nathan is okay with it, but I'm struggling here. Please help me.*

Thirty-Eight

Lindsay hesitantly opened the door to the same bedroom she had at home, but it was all different! This room was done in pastels—pinks and aqua and yellows and greens and light blue! She loved light blue! Tom knew she had wanted to remodel their room, but they hadn't chosen colors yet.

The paint samples were spread out on her bed the night she got the call about his ... wreck. The walls here were painted soft eggshell, and he had installed the chair rail that she had requested. "Oh, Tom." She whispered, letting the tears flow again. It was apparent in this kind gesture that he did love her. But it was like he was overcompensating. Like he knew he was going to leave them.

The furniture was the same. The chaise lounge was the same as hers but with upholstery in a beautiful pastel plaid, with solid pillows and throws. The bed was adorned as if it belonged to a princess. It even had four posters, which hers at home did not. She was touched that he had gone so far to make her feel like a princess. It was so like Tom.

A French provincial trunk made for seating sat proudly at the foot of her bed. There was a bookshelf made of dark glowing wood, sitting where her door led to Tom's man cave in her townhouse. She walked behind her chaise and ran her hand along the shelves of the bookshelf. Smooth as silk, rich and glistening. The wood matched the nightstands on both sides of her bed.

On the bookcase, she reached to the top shelf where her eyes rested on all her favorites—*Anne of Green Gables, Little Women, Gone With the Wind*. She pulled one out and heard a click. She reached into the space left by the book and let her hand fall against the wood. Her fingers fell against what felt like a metal clasp. When she pushed it toward the back of the shelf nothing happened, but when she brought it toward her, the shelf moved, just slightly, toward her. She backed up and grasped the side of the bookcase, drawing it gently toward her. It was, indeed, a hidden door.

She looked at the other side of the shelf and found the hinges. On the wall that supported the bookshelf, there was a latch release instead of a doorknob. She found the light switch inside and turned it on. There was no trunk, only a desk and a recliner, neither of which were matches of the ones at home. Simple office furniture, but the gun safe was up here. It should have been in the garage. Lindsay sat in *Tom's recliner* and closed her eyes.

Oh, Lord, this man knew me so well. How could he ever be replaced? She thought of Mark, downstairs hanging out with Nathan, and smiled. He could never replace Tom, but having him there helped ease the ache all of this was rekindling. Lord, this is just too wild. I don't know how to deal with it, but I put my trust in you.

She took a quick peek into her bathroom, beautiful baby blue with white trim. Different—beautifully different from her townhouse bathroom—yet so comfortable, and it felt like home... like a homestead. Now she understood.

She glanced out the window and saw the sun dropping into a majestic pillow of oranges and pinks. She ran down the stairs and grabbed Mom by the hand as she was giving the counter a last wipe. "You gotta come and see. This is so magnificent." Lindsay felt as giddy as a schoolgirl.

They didn't run, but they did take the stairs quickly. The guys were right behind them, everyone laughing at Lindsay's excitement. She plopped on the bed as her mother took in the difference. "Aw, Lindsay, it's you! It's lovely," her mom said, smiling.

Lindsay heard the paper as she lay her head on the pillow. She looked under it, but nothing. Then she felt the paper inside the pillow sham. She reached in and pulled out a pink card. Opening it gently, she recognized Tom's writing instantly.

My darling, Lindsay. I hope you feel like a princess. If Eddie carried out my instructions, you should. I love you more than life itself. Always have, always will. Again, I am so sorry for the danger I have put you in. I am especially sorry for burdening Nat with some of the details. I felt I needed to make connections and really didn't know how else to do it. I am so very sorry. I hope some of what I have left you is good and fun and exciting to make up for some of the dangerous negative issues you are going to have to deal with.

To make it easier for you, I changed the combination of the new safe — so here is the same as there. Enjoy your shampoo. Love you to the moon. ~ Tom

Without a word, Lindsay put the card back in its envelope and slipped into her bathroom. There were two bottles on the shelf in the shower—the one she used to use and the one she had changed to just before the wreck. She picked up both and looked at the bottles. There, on the bottom of her current shampoo, was a small price tag sticker. The price was $214.95. Pricey shampoo. Lindsay shook her head. And then she realized: the combination to both gun safes was their anniversary—Valentine's Day—2/14/95.

Nathan and Benny came in, and Mark poked his head around the door. "Aw, Mom," Nathan said. "It's so girly!" Everyone laughed. Nathan ducked between the men and went into his room and came back out, nodding approvingly. "I'm just glad Dad didn't do that to my room!"

Joining in the laughter, she said, "We need to get going. You guys go load up, and I'll be right there." As they left, she opened the bookshelf door and went back into the hidden office. Opening the safe as quickly as she could, she yanked it open. There was one leather portfolio on the shelf, tied with straps. She grabbed it, closed the safe, closed the hidden door, and ran down the stairs. She locked the door of her new home and stepped out into the early evening breeze.

She hopped in the front passenger seat of the Jeep, clutching the leather pouch, and they slowly drove to the security keypad. Mark punched in the code, and after they rolled through the gate, it started to close. They stopped on the outside, and he watched it close completely before he pulled back out onto the road.

"I have the combination to the gun safe in the garage back home. Here we go again?" She smiled at Mark. He returned her smile and kept his eyes on her a beat too long. Her eyes danced and she could feel an inward glow. The radio wasn't on, but her spirit was keeping time to some music from somewhere. She caught Mark looking at her, and she smiled even bigger. In the dim light, she could still see the entrance to the Old MacDonaldson's Farm. She pointed to it and he signaled. "Mark, this is—"

Gran's voice squeaked from the back seat. "Lindsay, this is our farm! There's your swing!" Tears and laughter filled the Jeep. Even Benny was dabbing at his eyes. It felt like it took forever to navigate the long winding gravel road, but finally, the house came into view. Lindsay heard her mother's breath quicken. The house was exactly as Lindsay remembered it, except with fresh paint, shutters had been replaced and the porch steps had been straightened. They all piled out as a Hispanic woman came running out of the house, all smiles.

"Oh, I am so glad you stopped! I was just sure I would not get to see you! Mrs. Davis, I am Maria. It is so good to meet you finally!" Before she knew it, Lindsay found herself in a bear hug from this petite but hefty woman. "Oh, forgive me. Mr. D talked so much about you I just feel like I have loved you forever."

"Thank you, Maria, that is so kind. Please call me Lindsay." She introduced everyone to Eddie's mother. "And thank you so much for the taco supper! It was such an unexpected treat and so-o-o good!"

Nathan even chimed in his approval.

"I am so glad you liked them! Come in please and have dessert." The thought of any more food did not interest Lindsay, but they all walked into a bright warm kitchen that smelled of cinnamon. "Do you like snickerdoodles?"

Immediately, Nathan was over the moon in love with this woman. "Sure do!"

"Well, these aren't snickerdoodles; they are a Mexican treat that tastes a little bit like them." Nathan bit into the crispy rolled-up pastry. "They are called churros."

"Hmm." Lindsay caught up to him in time to hear his approval of the dessert.

"Hey, Bud. You started without me?" She bit into one of the delightful sugary sticks that looked to her a little bit like a cactus. "Hmm-mmm is right! Oh, Maria!" They talked about Mexican cooking while the rest of the bunch savored their first experience with churros.

"It is getting late, though. We need to get with it and get out of your hair!" Lindsay said cheerfully. Maria started walking around the house, tour group in tow, talking about different things that had been done to restore the house. To Lindsay, it looked pristine. Even Gran was impressed. The integrity and personality of her home had been honored beautifully. As they reached the back door, Maria shifted her focus.

"Let's slip back outside before we lose the last of the daylight."

They stepped out onto the back deck to see party lanterns hanging around the fence keeping the livestock out of the back yard. There was a string of smaller lights about ten feet off the ground following the fence line to the barn.

Lindsay stepped off the deck and walked toward the

gate to the pasture, feeling like she had stepped back in time. She sensed her father standing right beside her. She heard hooves behind her and turned to see a horse that looked a lot like—

"Spook?" The gray gelding her father rode with her when she was on Josie was standing three feet away from her. She reached out as she stepped closer, and he lowered his head, maneuvering it, so her hands were between his ears. "Oh my gosh, you *are* Spook!" Tom had listened when she shared her memories of the farm. She turned to find her mother beside her, tears rolling down her face. "Oh, Mom, I'm so sorry, we need to go."

"Oh, no, dear. I'm fine, I'm just swept away with all these memories—it has been such a long time. My emotions have been all over the map today. I'm sure yours have as well." They walked arm in arm back to the porch. "This house has been restored to perfection."

The rest of the house tour was the emotional part for Lindsay even more than unexpectedly meeting Spook. What had been her bedroom was a guest room, nicely done in taupe and blue. Benny scoffed that his room had been turned into an upstairs den. He said it took on a stuffy air, too polished.

They had added a bathroom so that Mom and Dad's room was now a master suite that could shine with the best of them. Back downstairs, Nathan was curled up in a rocking chair with a fluffy gray cat purring loudly on his lap. "Hi, Mom, this is Malachi. He's coming home with us."

"Oh, he is, is he?" she teased. "We'd better figure out where home is before we start adding to our little family! Come on, Bud, we need to head home."

The Jeep was particularly quiet on this last leg of their adventure. Lindsay wondered if everyone was just worn out as she was or if they were contemplating the day. There was a lot to contemplate, that's for sure. Her thoughts were dancing around in her head, and she couldn't latch on to any one of them. She leaned her head back and turned sideways to look at the man driving. How very thankful she was for him setting up this trip for her. She and Tom had driven thousands of miles just like this, him driving her Jeep.

As she relaxed, she allowed herself to remember. In her mind she felt clear— file the memories of Tom in the safe and go forward with Mark. In the shadows, as she blinked, she clearly saw the new man in her life driving her home— wherever that could be.

Thirty-Nine

The light-sensitive streetlights came on as they drove into the parking lot of her townhouse. Everyone scattered quickly, making plans to meet at church the next day. Lindsay wasn't sure they would make it for Sunday School, but church was a go.

Lindsay slipped her hand into Mark's as they walked to his truck. "That was quite a day," Mark said.

"That's a definite understatement," Lindsay replied. As they reached his truck, he turned to face her, taking both her hands in his. "Mark, I can't tell you what it has meant to me having you in on all of this. But even more so, just to have you in my life —"

His lips closed on hers for only a second, but she had no idea what else to say.

"Sleep well, milady." He slipped his arms around her for a quick hug and left without another word. Lindsay stood there and watched him leave. When she realized the deputy still on guard in the corner had witnessed the tender moment, she felt her cheeks warm. Spinning in embarrassment, she walked into the house.

She rushed Nathan into the shower, and she went into her bedroom. It was a disappointment after seeing her dream bedroom at the Homestead. Lindsay plopped in the middle of her bed and pulled out the leather pouch. Then she realized she now had the gun-safe combination, so she slid her feet into her slippers and trotted down to the garage. The safe didn't open until the third time. It was a bit stiffer to open than the new one, and it opened with a groan. Lindsay squinted her eyes but couldn't see a thing. Frustrated, she went back to the door and turned on the second set of lights to see the contents of the safe.

Inside the safe was a package wrapped as if for a party, and a leather portfolio like the one on her bed. That was it. Nothing marked "Level 4," or IMPORTANT, or anything like that. She took the contents with her and closed the safe, turning out the lights before heading inside and back upstairs. She laid the leather pouches side by side.

She threw back the covers and walked barefoot to the chaise, picking up the package as she sat down. The card was to her, just her name, nothing more. Should she open it? The paper didn't suggest a specific holiday. It didn't say happy birthday. It didn't have Happy Anniversary written on it anywhere, and it wasn't Christmas wrap.

Slowly, she pulled one end of the ribbon, letting it fall from the package. She peeled a piece of tape away from the seam and let the wrapping paper fall. A plain white box— no hint here of what it might have been. She opened the box and could see it was a snow globe, nestled in Styrofoam especially formed for the base of the snow globe. Tipping the box, she let the snow globe fall gently into her hand. When she tipped it back up the snow inside fell to the bottom to reveal a figurine. At first, Lindsay thought it was a copy of the topper they had had on their wedding cake, but at closer inspection, her breath caught. It was them.

It was a picture of Tom and Lindsay, made into a 3-D figure. They were standing on what appeared to be the top tier of a wedding cake, with gold script: Happy 13th Anniversary. As she turned it around, she saw the tiny print: *Linds, I love you more than life itself, Tom.* Her breath caught in her throat. Tom had been killed just three weeks before their anniversary. A tear slipped down her cheek. This was a bittersweet finish to a bittersweet day. She hugged the snow globe close. She would trade everything she saw today to have Tom back. *Aw, Tom, I miss you so much. I miss what we had. I miss the times we had as a family. Thank you for remembering the anniversary we were never able to share. This going forward isn't going to be easy.*

Lindsay slapped the alarm clock, not realizing she had been asleep. It was going to be a long day. She slipped into the shower before going downstairs for coffee. She steered her brain back into focus mode as she stepped out. She donned her robe and wrapped the towel around her hair. It was 7:00 when she went in to check on Nathan. He awoke as she sat on the edge of his bed. "Morning, Bud," she whispered. "Are you ready to rise and shine for Jesus today?"

"Sure," he moaned sarcastically as he pulled the blanket over his head. Then suddenly, he snapped it back down and opened his eyes wide. "Mom, did yesterday really happen, or was it a dream?"

She smiled. "That was no dream, Kiddo. That was a real day that God gave us, and He outdid Himself with blessings, didn't He?" She stood. "I'm going to go fix breakfast—waffles or biscuits and gravy?"

"Hmm. Surprise me." He smiled. They were two of his favorites, so it was always a hard choice. But she felt a bittersweet sting at the phrase his dad used frequently. Once she made sure Nathan was, in fact, getting out of bed, she went downstairs and put biscuits in the oven.

She put the coffee on and came back upstairs and went into her room just as Nathan called out from his room. "Mom, do you want me to wear anything special?"

"Nope. Take your pick. If the shirts are hanging in your closet, they'll fit you." She had boxed up some of the shirts he had outgrown when she did the laundry the night the house was trashed. She slipped into a pair of khaki linen pants and the cream sweater she had rejected not too long ago. It wasn't so warm yet that the sweater would be too much. She put her earrings on and her necklace and then went back downstairs.

She poured some bacon grease from the jar into the skillet and started the gravy. She pulled the biscuits out of the oven, and stirred the skillet, adding the milk and turning it down. Nathan came in and poured orange juice for himself.

"Wow, look at you, Bud. You did a nice job. I like that shirt." She hugged him and turned again to stir the gravy.

"Aw, Mom. It's just a blue shirt. It's nothin' special."

She knew she had embarrassed him. When was she going to learn to play it cool? He just looked so much like his dad, especially when the blue picked up the color in his eyes.

"You want to grab the butter?" She picked up a plate, cut open a biscuit, and put it on the table at the same time he sat down with the butter. She poured the gravy into the boat and set it in front of him. "Let's pray." She said grace and poured the gravy over his buttered biscuits. "Save me one. I'll be down in a second."

She ran upstairs and put her makeup on, pulling her hair out of the towel. It was nearly already dry, so she put it in a French braid down her back. Slipping on tan heels, she grabbed her Bible and Sunday School quarterly and went downstairs. She poured her coffee, grabbing the cream as she sat down in her chair. She split a biscuit, buttered it, and poured the gravy over it.

"Hmm," she said.

"Hmm-mmm," Nathan answered in kind. They ate in silence, and Nathan went through their routine of clearing the table and leaving the dishes in the sink.

A glance at the clock showed it was 8:30. Maybe they would make Sunday School after all. "Run up and brush your teeth. Grab your Bible and Sunday School book. We need to leave pretty quick." She finished the last bite of her biscuits, picked up her plate, and dropped it in the sink. She poured a coffee-to-go and splashed some cream into it. She went to the front closet and pulled on a light jacket as Nathan was coming down the stairs. She ran her hand over his short hair and smiled.

"Do you like your hair short?" she asked as they walked out to the car.

"Sure; I can wash it with the washcloth, and it's dry before I even get out of the shower!" She laughed. His reasoning was perfect. They got in the Jeep and drove out of the parking lot, waving to Deputy Stevens on the way.

The Sunday School discussion was inspirational. So much so that lively conversations were still quite animated as the attendees were visiting with others during the fellowship. Nathan caught up with her and chatted excitedly about the Jonah lesson. "Mrs. Mitchell says maybe you should teach Sunday School sometime."

Lindsay blushed. She had the definite idea that Nathan had brandished the ideas she had shared with him to Mrs. Mitchell's despair.

She and Mrs. Mitchell had never been more than acquaintances, but she distinctly felt that was more by Mrs. Mitchell's choice than by accident. Lindsay's mother joined her, and Nathan shared his Sunday School teacher's remarks with her.

"My goodness, Lindsay, what did you tell him?" Gran smiled.

"Mom! I didn't say anything that most Bible students don't know. Am I not supposed to help my son understand the Bible? I just can't imagine how Nathan said it to her that would have prompted such a statement!"

"My dear, I'm not sure about that, and I'm not sure she is a Bible student. She was rather roped into the position," she whispered. "But it brings up an interesting idea. You could be a Sunday School teacher. You know the Bible well."

Lindsay hadn't thought of serving her church in that way. She stepped up when special needs came up, she was on the Fellowship Committee, and she took her turn at being a greeter.

"Hmm, if I weren't working full time, maybe." She considered it. "Oh, but Mom, we are moving, so the timing isn't good at all. We're getting ready to start a whole new life somewhere else. But it does sound like a challenge I would like to do—after we get settled."

"Of course, you're right, sweetie. That sounds like a wonderful idea."

The lights flickered, signaling service was about to start. They turned to go into the sanctuary just as Ben walked in with Melody at his side. He extended his arm to escort Arlene. As his sister, she could occasionally see through his façade. Oh, she understood it too well. She had used it herself. In her most despondent times, after Tom's death, she could remember forcing herself to put on the lighthearted act. She had heard it said, "Fake it till you make it." She wasn't sure that was quite the truth, but she didn't want to let the depression win, either. She was a fighter. She remembered fairly early in whatever crisis she faced that she was a child of God, and He was her strength.

But Benny? Lindsay was so hoping that Benny was staying with his counseling with Mark. Benny had been through two deployments and both times had come back more broken than before. Oh, the wound in his back healed well enough, and the pain was severe only during weather changes. Emotional wounds don't heal as easily. Considering the loss of his platoon buddies, not to mention all that he had seen, Lindsay couldn't imagine him ever being the Benny she grew up with. Then with the divorce as well, she knew he had a hard path in front of him.

The worship team was singing the opening song as they found their seats. Mark slipped in beside them just as the opening prayer was finishing up. Lindsay forced away her worries about Benny and tried to pay attention to the announcements. But having Mark sit beside her was a bit of a distraction.

Pastor Billings preached from Psalm 46:10—*Be still and know that I am God.* Lindsay felt he was looking at her every time he repeated the verse. She'd heard a hundred messages on the verse before, but every time, more was revealed. Pastor Billings was teaching on the importance of learning how to still one's heart, to be able to hear God's heart.

Lindsay had often thought of John, the disciple. He was the youngest of the disciples, and he called himself "the one Jesus loved". She had imagined that as a young man, during the last supper, he laid his head upon Jesus' chest, and that way he could feel His heartbeat even better than hearing it.

After the congregation had been dismissed, Lindsay's thoughts jumped back to Mrs. Mitchell, and she decided to go have a quick word with her. Lindsay saw her talking with some of her mother's friends. As she approached, Mrs. Mitchell stepped away from the other women and faced her, rather nervously, Lindsay thought.

"Good morning, Mrs. Mitchell." Lindsay smiled. She waited until she got closer before she said anything else.

"Oh, hello, Lindsay," she said, spreading her arms wide for a hug. "I'm so glad you came over. I wanted to talk to you about something Nathan said this morning."

"Oh, I hope he didn't—"

"No, no. He was great." She chuckled. "The whole class got a much better understanding of why Jonah wasn't digested!" She laughed again and placed her hand on Lindsay's arm. "He is a very bright young man. I told him I would love for you to teach class sometime if you'd like to."

"Ah." Lindsay acquiesced. "That's not quite the way he put it. I thought I had offended you! I wanted to come over and apologize."

"Not at all. No apology is necessary unless you say no!" Mrs. Mitchell's jovial personality was contagious.

"Well, I will certainly pray about it. I'm afraid the timing isn't quite right, but thank you."

As they were departing the church, Mark invited Lindsay out to dinner. She declined, inviting him, instead, to join them at the townhouse for the dinner she already had in the works. She told him about finding the leather portfolios and thought he would want to help her explore them afterward. He was all in for the next chapter in her adventure.

Forty

Lindsay's original townhouse was bubbling with laughter as Gran delighted in having both of her kids and both of her grandchildren with her for Sunday dinner. Lindsay seasoned the salmon and put it in the oven, then stirred some veggies into the rice already cooking in the cooker. She spun around and pulled the salad out of the fridge and retrieved the bread from the pantry. After setting the table, Arlene got the tea pitcher and the butter out of the fridge as the timer went off, announcing the salmon was done.

Gran seated Benny at the head of the table, with Melody on one side of him and Nathan on the other side. Gran was next to Melody, Lindsay next to Nathan, and Mark between her and her mom, facing Benny. As the laughter and chatter quieted, Lindsay asked Benny to say grace.

Benny nodded and stood silently for a bit before he began.

Dear Lord, thank you for my family gathered around

me, and my friend, Mark. I ask you to forgive me for walking away from you in the first place. I went through some rotten stuff, and I thought I could do it without You. I'd rather have You with me, Lord, if you'll have me back. I'll never make the mistake again of thinking I can live without You.

As he sat down, he chuckled and stood again and quickly but reverently blessed the food. After the amens, they all laughed, and Arlene cried, and Lindsay rejoiced and commented that God was probably chuckling, too. Mark jumped up from the table and slapped him on the back, which prompted hugs all around.

The salmon was done beautifully, with rice pilaf, glazed carrots, and pistachio jello salad. Even the kids decided they liked salmon. But the high point of the meal was the prayer. Nathan's voice boomed above the celebration. "I never heard of anyone saying a prayer of salvation for grace!" That just started everyone laughing again, to the point where they practically had cold salmon for dinner!

As everyone finished their meals, Lindsay's mom ran them all out of the kitchen. She insisted she could take care of the cleanup herself since Lindsay had done most of the cooking. Benny and the kids went out back, taking advantage of the swings in the courtyard. Mark sat in the living room, and Lindsay came down with the leather pouches, placing them in front of him on the coffee table.

Sliding the lighter-colored one in front of him, she said, "This one is Level 4—it was in the gun safe here in the garage. Chief Marsh doesn't know about this one." She opened it and carefully slid the rolled-up papers out onto the table. There were four rolls of paper, tied with thin red cords, like scrolls. Lindsay looked at Mark with a puzzled look on her face. She hadn't reconciled with her own decision to not share it with the chief of police. Mark didn't question it. They each took one and gently slipped the cord off, unrolling the papers and spreading them out flat on the table, holding them flat with their coffee cups.

They both focused on the legal-size paper in front of Mark, studying it quietly for a few minutes. Lindsay could see her name and the name of Mt. Zion Home for the Deaf. Mark spoke intensely. "Lindsay, this looks like a property assignment, but it's incomplete. I don't know why Tom didn't finish it himself, but it's in your name. It assigns title from you to a home for the deaf in Washington. I'd have to compare what we've already seen, but I'm guessing it might be the Heavenly Acres property out there." Mark flipped through the remaining pages and then slid the document face down to the edge of the coffee table. He picked up a book from the end table and placed it on top to further flatten the document.

"This one is similar," Lindsay began. "It assigns property in South Dakota— Pine Ridge School for Native Americans." Lindsay passed the paperwork over to Mark and gingerly unrolled another scroll. "And this one is the same thing, only to Riding for Dreams, but it's property in Washington, too." She passed it to Mark and opened the last document. "We might need to get out to Washington and see exactly what these are."

"This one's different," Lindsay said, studying the document. "It looks the same, but there's a big blank space on this one where those all have the property information." She handed it to Mark, and as he looked at it, he smiled.

"It looks like a template, Lindsay." He flattened the documents and placed them all under the book. "I guess it's in case you want to do a similar deal with any of the other properties. You just fill in the blank with the property you want to give and who you want to give them to. Or he intended to do it again."

"My goodness!" Lindsay exclaimed. "When did he have time to do all this? When Eddie said he made his periodic visits at Sunnyside, I assumed Tom went out there for weekends now and then. He did go on an occasional business trip. But these are in South Dakota and Washington. He would have to have flown out there." Lindsay huffed with frustration. "We could have done some of this together." She blinked back the tears and looked at Mark for answers she knew he didn't have either.

"A lot of this could have been done online," Mark replied. "Or by hiring management companies as he did here, but I can't imagine he would have done it all without ever viewing the property in person."

Lindsay picked up the pouch and smoothed flat the worn scarred leather. "This pouch isn't empty," she said as she slid her hand slowly into it. She pulled out a folded crumpled piece of paper. She smoothed it out as she laid it on the table. Another yellow-lined note from Tom. This was a list of the properties, some of which had check marks beside them.

Mark leaned close to her to see, and she turned the paper more toward him. "The properties that have the checkmarks are these three." He tapped the book being used as the paperweight. "But there's another one listed in Washington." He leaned back and smiled, raising his eyebrows. "This just keeps getting more and more intriguing. It looks to me like he was checking each one off as he finished the assignment."

Lindsay inhaled deeply and leaned back into the couch. "Well, shall we?" She reached for the other pouch, handing it to him. "You do the honors." She smiled as she shook her head. Mark tipped the contents of the pouch into his hand. Yellow-lined papers were typed and folded as if ready for envelopes and small sticky notes overflowed onto the table. They sorted them out together, Lindsay reaching for the yellow sheets first. Folded inside was a copy of the first note they had discovered. She skimmed it and put it aside with a slight smile. The next page was nearly a full hand-written page:

I have decided to take some steps that will hopefully leave Lindsay in a better position to deal with all of this. The tax attorney tells me that giving some of these properties away will reduce her tax burden tremendously. If I know my Linds, it will relieve her emotional burden as well. The hard part is second-guessing which she will want to keep. The school in Washington is self-sustaining, other than keeping taxes paid, and the property manager takes care of that. If I can get the assignments done so all she has to do is sign them and get them back to JB Bower, that will simplify everything. Then she can sell whichever one she wants and make amends for some of the horrors my family caused. Oh, God, please strengthen her to be able to clean up this mess. If I can't be with her, Lord, please send someone to be beside her who can help her understand it all. Give her the mercy and grace to forgive me for never having the guts to tell her myself.

"I think you're right, Mark," Lindsay said. "He knew how out of my league this would be. This note explains it.

He was simplifying my life." Lindsay stood and with her coffee cup, walked quietly into the kitchen. Arlene was just finishing up everything. She couldn't absorb the part about his family. *What is going on, Lord? How horrible could his family have been? Give me the strength to finish this, to even continue reading his notes.*

She slipped her cup into the sink and looked out the window facing the courtyard. Benny and the kids were still there. Now they were shooting hoops. Her mom came beside her for a second and slipped her arm around Lindsay's waist. They stood there for several minutes, no need for words, Lindsay feeling like she was soaking up her mother's peace and strength.

Arlene went back to wiping the counter one more time, and Lindsay felt Mark's presence behind her. "Lindsay, I finished reading some of the papers," Mark said. "More information about his birth family. It's making a lot more sense now." She turned to face him.

"About his birth family?" she asked, afraid of the answer. He nodded.

"Yeah. Let's go for a walk." Mark reached for her hand.

Forty-One

Mark put his coffee cup in the sink and followed Lindsay out the back door. They turned away from the recreation area and strolled down the winding concrete path. Quiet for several minutes, content with the companionship, Lindsay thought about Tom's note. They had both been into journaling before they met, so she didn't find it unusual that Tom would write his thoughts to God. His written prayer included a request that God had already answered. Mark had been beside her since the onset of this journey. She was so grateful.

They walked on a bit and came to a seating area with potted flowers. It had been way too long since Lindsay had gone for walks here. She and Tom had created a routine of doing this nearly every evening after supper. Sometimes Nathan would join them, but most of the time they listened to his basketball bouncing on the concrete or against the backboard. She could hear it now, but it was Mark beside her instead of Tom, and it felt good.

Lindsay walked to a stone bench and sat down. "Okay, spill it," Lindsay said nervously as she turned toward him. He sat down on the other end of the bench and settled himself so that he was facing her squarely. "He never talked about family," Lindsay whispered. Mark took a deep breath and gave her a crooked smile. Watching her closely, he began.

"Hold onto your boots. This gets rather heavy, Lindsay. Your husband's birth family appears to have been part of the Italian mafia." He paused until she started breathing again. "At least that's as close as I can figure. His family name was De'avistelli, and many of them are still alive—at least they were when Tom was. One of those notes is a list of people who the family swindled out of their properties. As close as I can tell, it even looks like a couple of them were won in crooked poker games." He paused again, watching Lindsay's face regain its color.

"There's a letter in here from a woman—it looks like she was Tom's grandmother. She is pleading with him to come back into the family and 'all will be forgiven'. It sounds like they're the ones who needed forgiveness from him. I would think these papers are enough to put his family away forever, but that's not what Tom wanted. Although the family thought it was, and they may still think that. There's a copy of a letter that he wrote to them that spells it out: If they attempted to find him, or you, he was going to go to the authorities and tell them everything he knew. It looks like it was written in late 1989." He stood and faced her.

"Lindsay, he was so young, and taking on such evil power." He shook his head briefly and gazed out over the path. "The paperwork shows a legal name change in 1990 from Domingo Excelsior De'avistelli to Thomas Nathaniel Davis." He nearly paced in front of the bench where she sat but stopped to face her.

"Wow," she whispered. "We met in 1991 at school. No wonder he didn't tell me anything about his family. He spoke like they were all dead." Lindsay followed his gaze back to the bridge they had crossed. "And no one came to our wedding."

"I'm sure he did it to protect anyone that would come into his life after that." Mark went on seriously. "There is a copy of a letter from Tom to this woman apologizing for what he was about to do. It was dated right before the name change request was granted. In that letter, he told her not to attempt to find him, that he had learned from his family very well how to cover his tracks so that they would never be able to find him."

Mark sat facing her with both hands on his knees. He moved his elbows to his knees, leaning forward just enough to take her hands in his. "Do you want to hear more, or do you want a break?"

"I think I'm okay," Lindsay whispered, strengthened by the warmth of his hands. "I never would have dreamed he came from a family like that. He's so kind and generous and considerate—always thinking of other peoples' feelings, even people he didn't know. I mean he was. I remember one time in the bank when a customer in line in front of us was outwardly belligerent to the teller. When Tom stepped up to the counter, he apologized to her for the man's rudeness."

"I can see him doing that, just from what I'm learning about him." He paused. "There is a folder of old newspaper clippings in there also. They're all showing bankruptcies, deaths in families, or crimes that were never solved. They are taped onto pages with his notes on them. Some of them indicate that his family was responsible. Others have questions that he wrote, suspicions that he couldn't prove yet, but he felt his family was the culprit in those events, too. Then, there's a list of those people who suffered at their hands intentionally." He stood and pulled her up with him before he continued.

"Lindsay, the bottom line is this. It looks like Tom tracked the activities of his family so that he could make amends to the victims if he could. There is a monetary evaluation penciled in beside the name of each victim. His estimated total comes to $27,000,000. Tom's tally of assets that he had accumulated so far was $15,000,000." He paused again. "'Course it isn't dated, so we don't know when he came up with those figures."

Lindsay's mouth dropped. Her eyes opened wide. Suddenly, she smiled. "Of course! Mark! That's why he was amassing this fortune! It did not make any sense until now. Tom is not a greedy man—I mean he wasn't a greedy man." She turned and walked away a few steps, then spun around and faced him again.

"Oh my gosh, Mark, of course. It all makes sense now. He wanted to protect himself so his birth family couldn't find him, and of course to protect us, so they couldn't find Nathan and me, either. He needed the money to create new identities—new lives for all of us, to relocate us, but even more to pay these people back."

"As I said, Lindsay, I wish I had known the man. I think you are exactly right," Mark whispered. She nodded and turned away from him. She stood listening to the bouncing basketball in the distance, the rippling of the creek. She heard the laughter and happy voices, the birds chirping in the trees. Her husband had been ready to give up everything to make right what his family had done wrong. He had truly made the ultimate sacrifice. She had to continue Tom's passion. Somehow, she had to finish this for him. She knew she wasn't equipped to do that alone, and she was so grateful for Mark's presence in her life.

"Mark, you have been an answer to prayer in more ways than one." She smiled at him as they turned together and walked toward the bridge. "First, you helped me get through that first day when you told me about Tom's death, then you helped me through Sarah, helping me through the next year or so, learning to be me again, without him. Then, helping Benny—that has already shown huge results—"

"Stop. I know where you're going with this," Mark said. Lindsay thought he was blushing. "I'm just a man doing what I can to live right, help folks out, and do what God tells me to do."

Lindsay leaned on the bridge railing, facing him. "I know you are. That's all any of us can do, but some folks are just better at it than others. I just—I want you to know that I think you are the answer to Tom's written prayer. I think he would think so, too."

"I really wish I had known him." Mark's eyes were full of emotions. Some Lindsay could read, others she could not.

"He would have liked you." Lindsay looked down at the colorful koi fish swimming in the little pond beneath the bridge. "I think you and Tom could have been good friends, talking about these transactions over a game of golf." They stood without talking for a few minutes, then she took Mark's hand and began walking down the other side of the bridge. As they walked, she felt the depth of his care, yet she also felt his fear. She understood both. She wasn't sure if she was ready to take things to the next level with Mark, but they had become closer in just over a week than she thought possible.

Forty-Two

As Lindsay and Mark came to where the trail widened, Lindsay felt totally comfortable with him. Feeling assured that Tom had "prayed him in" to her life put her at ease. Maybe she was ready to move forward after all. *It feels right, with Mark, anyway. But what was he feeling? What would she do without him, right now? Thank you, Lord. Please guide us. Father in heaven, I need you. Help me to go forward. Help me to continue what Tom started here. Protect us from his family, and show me, step by step, how to move forward.*

"Mark, knowing I don't know what is ahead, are you interested in going with me through to the end of this? I don't know what more it—" She turned to face him, stopped mid-sentence, and felt her face flush. What was that look in Mark's eyes? It was as though he was seeing an angel. "What are you thinking?" she asked.

"You're just so—I don't know—you're always ready to do whatever you feel God is calling you to do." His voice was full of admiration. "I love that about you."

Lindsay looked away, her cheeks growing hotter. She didn't know what to say, so she cleared her throat and continued with the previous conversation. "Since new information appears with every piece of paper, I can't tell you how much more we might find. But I can tell you I can't do it by myself. I can't think of anyone else I would want beside me, right in the middle of this mess." She laughed nervously. "After hearing what you just described; I can't go forward without doing everything I can do to make Tom's plan happen. Besides, I believe God would want me to." Another nervous laugh.

He joined her. "I can't imagine letting you go further into this adventure alone. Nor can I even begin to fathom allowing you to continue without me! I'm in it too deep to back out now!" Mark smiled as he said the words, but he knew the truth. It was his heart as well as his curiosity that was in too deep. "And I think you're right. I'd be honored to come alongside you and work with you to see to it that God's will be done, wherever that may lead us." He stretched out his arms and she stepped forward into them. For a moment, she listened to his heart, letting his arms around her comfort her. Then she broke away from him nervously. He caught her hand as they started walking back toward the house.

"There is also a contact list that Tom made, that has his accountants, lawyers, and the management companies —Eddie and his mother are on there, and David Harrell, so I think you have some homework to do before we go to Washington." He turned to watch her expression.

"*I* have homework to do?" she teased. "You just said we are in this together, and you're already backing out? And who says we're going to Washington anyway?" she asked, intentionally allowing her voice to become intense, but now, she lowered it to a low chuckle. "And besides, I can't go next week anyway."

Laughing, they increased their pace, both realizing they had a mission in front of them. It would take both of them doing their homework to complete the huge task that Tom had only brought to its early levels. Wheels were turning in her mind as she thought of the next step. They needed to update Chief Marsh, the Attorney General's office, and the FBI. How much should she tell her mom, Benny, and Nathan? She hated keeping secrets, but would they be in more danger if they knew the whole story? Did they need to know the whole story?

"I want to see the list of his attorneys, Mark. I need to get the full picture."

Mark nodded. "You're right, of course. And there are more papers in that pouch, that I didn't look at very closely, yet. There are also some envelopes that he mailed to himself. I don't know what those are. People used to do that and leave them sealed when they didn't go through attorneys to write their wills. I don't think we should open those without someone being witness to it—like Chief Marsh or one of the attorneys." He could tell she was only half-listening. "Are you sure you don't want to go to Washington with me next week?" He laughed as her face showed a combination of excitement and fear. "I would be honored, my lady, to accompany you, whenever you decide to go."

Lindsay and Mark continued on the trail the way they had come, which brought them alongside the basketball court where the kids were playing. As they approached, Melody stole the ball from Nathan.

"Way to go, Mel!" Lindsay cheered.

"Not fair, Mom." Nathan scolded. "You're supposed to be on my side!"

"What's the score?" Lindsay asked.

Melody answered. "Daddy has H-O, I have H-O-R, and Nat has H-O-R-S." She ran over to Lindsay and jumped into her arms.

"I'm so proud of you! You're doing great!" Lindsay twirled her niece around and stood her back on her feet, holding her a second to be sure she wasn't dizzy. Turning to the rest of the players, she called, "It's about time to come in, guys and girls!"

Benny looked at his watch. "Yep, I need to get you home before too long, Munchkin." She raised her arms, and he caught them, swinging her up onto his shoulders. "You won, Nat. We forfeit." Nathan made the sound of the crowd roaring as he caught up to the group advancing toward the door.

"Hey, Gran." Nathan was still hyped when he dribbled the ball into the kitchen. As soon as he caught Lindsay's look of disapproval, he caught the ball and rolled it into the garage.

"So, I assume you won?" Gran held up her hand and Nathan graciously contributed his half of the high-five. "So that means you're getting the first dessert." Lindsay had pulled the ice cream bars out of the freezer and was already passing them out, so she snatched Benny's back, so she could give the first one to Nathan.

"Sorry, bro. The winner must be rewarded. Besides, he has to finish and get on his homework." She watched Nathan's face fall.

"Aw, Mom. It's only 5:00!" Nathan tossed his wrapper to the trash, barely hitting his target.

"Yes, it is, and there is a movie coming on tonight that you wanted to see, remember? No homework now, no movie later," Lindsay said, closing the freezer door.

"Oh, that's right! I almost forgot." He, Benny, and Mark were off into the living room, deeply discussing the advantages of watching movies at home as opposed to going to the theater. The women sat at the kitchen table, finishing their ice cream. Nathan threw his stick in the trash and turned to hit the books.

"So, Mom, what do you think? Where would you move if you were making the decision?" Lindsay plucked a napkin out of the holder on the table and dabbed at the ice cream running down Melody's arm.

"Such a hard call, sweetie! You've got some magnificent options." Arlene was watching Melody lovingly. "I'd have to start eliminating properties one by one. Process of elimination." She smiled at Lindsay.

"Good idea. I don't think I could ever relax in the one in Davenport." She paused. "And Sunnyside is way too fancy, too! Although I agree with Nathan; it would be a great place to vacation! Shall we plan for next summer?"

"Absolutely, and that's a good start. But the rest of them, wow. That's going to be a hard choice."

Lindsay nodded. "You are so right. I'm not sure how I'd feel about living back on the farm we had when Daddy was alive. I think that would be extremely hard, don't you?" Lindsay finished off her ice cream, threw the stick in the trash, and grabbed a clean washcloth.

"Yeah. I get that." Arlene wrinkled her forehead in thought. "But I think that will pass after a while. I mean, you're always going to have those déjà vu moments, but for the most part, I think you'd be okay."

"I might be okay, but how would *you* feel?" Lindsay washed Mel's face and hands and ran the washcloth up her arms where the ice cream had run.

Mel giggled. "That tickles, Auntie Lindsay!" She hopped out of the chair and went running into the living room just as Benny was coming out. He caught her mid-collision to keep her from crashing to the floor.

"Hey, Sis, we gotta go. Go give hugs, Mel," Benny said as he set her back down. Hugs and kisses were lavishly shared all around, and Benny and his fireball daughter were out the front door. Suddenly, the house was too quiet. Gran decided to head home too and walked out with Benny and her granddaughter, so Lindsay never got an answer to her question. She felt it was enough to have planted the seed in Arlene's mind. She'll be thinking about it. Nathan brought his backpack down and spread books out on the counter.

"Wow, Bud." Lindsay raised her eyebrows. "How much homework do you have?"

"I have a spelling test tomorrow, and some reading in history." He was hedging, and Lindsay was afraid he would be up late with homework, let alone not getting to watch the movie. "I need to finish my English paper. I already started it in class, and I have a page of math problems."

"Well, hop to it, Bud. I guess we should have checked on how much homework you had before the game of HORSE! We're going to be right in here, so if you need help, sing out." Mark was already in the living room, and he stood as she came into the room. She smiled and sat down on the sofa. She hadn't noticed his manners before. "If Nathan finishes in time, we are watching a movie tonight. I'm not sure that it's going to be possible, but you are certainly welcome to stay. We usually have popcorn and fruit for supper on Sunday nights, so if I can tempt you with that meager fare—"

"Oh, I'm in!" Mark laughed. "Nathan was giving me a preview of this movie. Sounds right up my alley."

"Great!" She smiled. Lindsay's mind took off for a moment. She envisioned the three of them, her in the middle, snuggled on the couch, watching TV. "So, do you want to go through more of the contents of the pouch, or do you want to watch the movie, or just talk?"

Forty-Three

Lindsay set a tray on the coffee table with glasses and a pitcher of sweet tea.

"Hmm." Mark rubbed his chin. "Do you think we have anything to talk about besides your adventure?" he teased her. He was enjoying the various facial expressions she could display.

"Maybe we can come up with something while Nathan is finishing his homework." She smiled. They sat together on the couch.

"What would you like to talk about?" Mark asked with a teasing look on his face.

Why was he smiling so? Lindsay could feel the corners of her mouth tip up. "Well, I have one question for you." Lindsay chose the ornery route in answer to his question. "When are you going to start going to Sunday School?" He hung his head in mock shame, still wearing his silly smile.

"When are you coming to Washington with me?" He didn't wait for her answer. "Sorry, I didn't mean it like that." Mark continued as her expression changed yet again, accompanied by a blush. He shifted his weight to face her sitting beside him. "I just think you need to go see your holdings before you assign them or decide what to do with them. It looks to me like Tom got you started, but the final decisions are up to you. And here we are right back on the same topic." They both laughed.

"You haven't really told me much about yourself," Lindsay hinted.

"Sure, I have," Mark hedged. "What would you like to know? I don't care much for talking about myself." He smiled.

"I never would have guessed that," Lindsay joked sarcastically. "It's been like pulling teeth to get you to tell me about yourself!" Lindsay shifted in her seat, "I don't know, anything important, I want to know about you."

Mark nodded, "Okay, well you know I moved in with my Aunt Mavis to finish High School when my folks died."

Lindsay nodded, "Yeah, that much you already told me, and you went to college in Springfield, and I know my counselor, Sarah, was your classmate. Is that what prepared you to be a chaplain?"

"Partly. It all started when I was in the military, so when I came back and went to college, it was supposed to be just to finish up, but it took two years. Then I came back here about six years ago and started the Counseling Center."

"Never been married?" She came right out and asked.

"Nope." He didn't act offended by her question. "I had a girlfriend in high school that I thought was the one, but she found somebody else while I was deployed." He looked down at his hands like he was distracting himself from the painful memory. "After that, I pretty much threw myself into my studies, and then my work. I've always known I wanted a family someday. I just figured God would let me know when it was time to get serious about it." Red tinged Mark's cheeks. Was he embarrassed to share his heart with her?

"Thank you for telling me that," Lindsay said gently to help put him at ease. "It can't have been easy. How long were you in the service?"

"Eight years. I feel like I grew up there," Mark replied, "and I sure learned a lot about people, what makes them tick, and how people deal with life."

"And death," Lindsay finished sadly.

"Yes, but dealing with everything—disappointments and stress and life changes. Some people even have difficulty dealing with too much good news as well as bad news. Some people go into horrible depression when good things happen in their lives because they think they don't deserve it."

Lindsay nodded, somehow able to understand. "A month ago, I wouldn't have imagined that could be true, but after learning about what Tom did to set me up for life, I can believe it." Lindsay was pensive. "I did nothing to earn all the fortune that Tom worked to build. I am kind of relieved, now, that I don't view it as my fortune. I've just been entrusted with it all, so I can make things right for the people who his family hurt."

"One of the most exciting parts of my job is helping people get to the point where they understand that God wants to give people things they don't deserve." Mark realized he hadn't talked this much about himself since

Aunt Mavis passed away. She had been his biggest cheerleader and was forever encouraging him to reach for the stars every time he felt like giving up. "Did your aunt pass away while you were in the service?"

"No, it was right after I opened my practice. She was a wonderful lady." He smiled to himself. "It was pretty hard at first because she and my mom were twins."

"A bittersweet memory?" Lindsay loved how his face showed his feelings.

He nodded. "I called her 'Mom' accidentally one time, and it upset me. I was angry—a teenager doesn't know how to release that anger in a healthy way, so I yelled at her. 'Why do you have to look so much like my Mom?' As soon as I said it, I was sorry. She was such a wonderful, loving woman, and so sensitive; I could tell I broke her heart. I started crying, and she just wrapped her arms around me and let me cry it out, telling me she understood. You know, it wasn't until I was in the army, it hit me that she was mourning, too. After all, my mom was her twin sister. But anyway, when I came home from school the next day, she had dyed her hair." His smile was melancholy.

"So, she didn't look so much like your mom," Lindsay filled in, smiling.

"Yup. They both had brown hair, but Aunt Mavis had hers dyed kind of a reddish blond. It was pretty, and I could relate to her better. She kept it that way for a long time. She was pretty special."

"She didn't have any children of her own?" Lindsay was intrigued.

"She had a daughter two years older than me." A

shadow fell over his face. "But Ella died in an accident while I was in the Army. Drunk driver."

"Oh, no. I'm so sorry," Lindsay said, meeting Mark's grief-stricken gaze.

Nathan came in and sat down in the chair across from them.

"Can you quiz me on my spelling?" He was upside-down in the chair, with his head hanging down off the front seat toward the floor.

"Can't quiz you without your list," Lindsay teased, holding out her empty hands. He slid out of the chair, jumped to his feet, and ran back into the kitchen for his book. "What I would give for an ounce of that boy's energy!"

She and Mark looked at each other as he returned and dropped the open book in her lap.

"Abandon." Lindsay was always impressed with Nathan's skills. He rattled it off easily. "Mysterious." Not even a hesitation. "Accomplishment." "Banquet." Doing great. "Mortgage." She thought that one would stump him, but he rattled it off flawlessly. She worked her way through his 20-word spelling list, and the only one he missed was 'benefiting' by putting two t's instead of one. *Hmm, she would have missed that one, too.*

School books were put away and the trio made their way to the kitchen to make supper. Lindsay pulled the fruit tray out of the refrigerator. Mark popped the corn and melted the butter. Nathan turned on the TV and came back into the kitchen. He was filling the bowls when the movie's theme song came on the TV.

They grabbed napkins and Mark carried the tray into the living room, placing it on the side table, beside the plates and fruit Lindsay had already carried in. They all sat on the couch, and all three sets of feet landed on the glass-top coffee table. With drinks in one hand and hands in the bowls in their laps, they laughed when they realized they were all still in sync with the first handful of popcorn. The movie began and grabbed their attention immediately. In a matter of moments, Lindsay realized she had just envisioned this scene in her mind. She felt more relaxed than she had in weeks.

Nathan was on the edge of his seat more often than he was sitting back with her. She went to the kitchen and when she returned, the "boys" had merged into her space, so she sat in the chair. It was interesting to watch them interacting as well as their reaction to her. Mark was as caught up in the movie as Nathan was. Nathan didn't act like he realized she had left and returned. But when Mark stood to go to the restroom, Nathan encouraged him to hurry, because "the good part's coming up."

The movie was a success, and the boys were excitedly chatting as the glasses and bowls were dutifully returned to the kitchen.

"Say goodnight to Mark, Nathan. You need to hop in the tub."

Nathan and Mark shook hands and then smacked each other's hands in the air. Lindsay smiled at the exchange, with satisfaction that these two were getting along nicely.

"What time do you go in tomorrow?" Mark asked as he was heading toward the door.

"I start the evening shift, so I need to leave here at about 1:45. Why do you ask?" Lindsay was hoping to go see Chief Marsh before work tomorrow.

"Well, if you're up for it, I thought I'd buy you lunch and then we could go see Chief Marsh." Mark smiled.

Lindsay returned his smile. "I was thinking about going to update him. But we could reverse that and go see him first. Will that work for you?"

"I think it will," he replied. "Shall I pick you up or do you want to meet there? I can get loose at about 10:30."

"Let's meet there. I'll call him in the morning and let him know we're coming. Do you think I need to take anything?" She valued Mark's opinion highly.

"No, it's all in the safe here," he replied. "We can tell him everything, and he can decide what he wants to have a copy of. I'll see you there at 10:30."

"I never told him about level 4," Lindsay said,

watching Mark's eyebrows raise in question. "I just wasn't sure who I could trust so I kinda just left that part out. Course, we can tell him tomorrow."

"You're a wise woman, Lindsay," Mark said. "I don't think you ever have to question when your inner spirit tells you what to do or not do." He smiled at her and squeezed her hand.

"Thanks for spending the day with us, Mark." She opened the door for him.

"Oh, thank you, Lindsay. I enjoyed every minute of it. You should be proud. Nathan is an amazing young man!"

"Thanks, Mark. I am pretty proud of him. Good night." Lindsay leaned on the door frame.

Mark leaned forward and kissed her on the cheek. "And thank you for the proof."

"Proof?" She was puzzled.

He teased. "Proof that you are indeed an amazing cook. Sleep well." He walked across the yard to his car and was quickly and quietly gone.

Lindsay stood and watched as he turned the corner and drove out of sight. Maybe it was time. Could she fall in love again? Was she already falling? Maybe it was time to let herself do that. She looked up at the sky. She wanted to take things slow, but her heart wasn't paying attention. *What do You think, Lord?*

After Mark left, Lindsay closed and locked the door, and went to the kitchen. The dishwasher was finished, so she emptied it, putting away the clean dishes and loading their glasses and popcorn bowls into it. She wiped off the tray, stored it, and turned out the lights to go upstairs.

She knocked on Nathan's door and he opened it,

already wearing his pajamas and ready for bed. "Hey, Bud. Did you have fun today?"

"Yeah, Mom. Mel is a cool kid, and Uncle Benny's just like one of my buddies." He rolled back the comforter and climbed into bed. "Want to hear my prayers?"

"I would love to." He hadn't asked her to do this in a few days. She sat on the bed beside him, feeling all warm inside that her son was growing up in the way of his father and herself.

Dear Lord, it was a good day, and I thank you for letting Mel come and shoot hoops with us, and thanks for Gran and Uncle Benny. I thank you that Mom's friend, Mark, came and had fun, too. He's a pretty cool guy. Lord, I ask you to help me remember my spelling words tomorrow and help Mom get used to workin' nights. Amen. Oh, and Lord, can you tell Mom where you want us to move, please? Thanks again, Lord. Amen.

"Amen," Lindsay agreed. "Great prayer, Bud. Don't forget you're going to Gran's after school this week, and you're going to have your homework done over there—"

"Yes, Mom, and you won't see me until around bedtime. We've been doing this for a while, ya know." He sounded so much like his dad sometimes.

"I know, Bud. I just don't like this shift. I don't get to spend any time with you. I'm just glad it's only one week a month!" She hugged him and lay down beside him on the bed. "Nathan, where would you like to move?"

"Hmm. I think I like the place that looks like home. But I like that ranch, too, with the horses and where Malachi lives, and where Miss Maria made churros!" He was getting wound, and it was too late for that.

"Okay, well, you be thinking about it and decide, and

we'll talk about it again." She slid off his bed onto her knees and whispered to him, playing with the hair damp against his forehead. "Nathan, I am so proud of you. I want you to know that I see how gentle you are with Melody and how well you take care of her. You are just an all-around good kid, and your daddy would be proud of you, too."

"Aw, Mom." He blushed.

She ruffled his hair as she got to her feet. "Well, it's true. And I love ya, Bud. To the moon—"

"And back, Mom. G'night."

She turned off his light, closed his door, and went into her room. When did the days start getting so long? She undressed and slipped into her robe, and picking up her Bible from her nightstand, went to her chaise and got comfortable. She needed to stay awake a while later tonight to get accustomed to the late hours at work tomorrow.

Dear Lord Jesus. I thank You for my son." She prayed, *"I thank You for guiding us in raising him as a child of God. I thank You for his heart—tender and loving. I thank You for giving him the ability to learn and figure things out. Lord, show me what to do from here, please. Show me where You want us to move. And show Mom if You want her to come with us, and Benny, too. It could be closer to Melody but further to his job. And Lord, help me to let You be You and keep me out of Your way. In Jesus' Name, Amen.*

Forty-Five

As Lindsay remained in prayer mode, the peace and quiet of late evening enveloped her. She opened her Bible and started reading Psalm 14:

The fool has said in his heart, "There is no God." They are corrupt, They have done abominable works, There is none who does good. The LORD looks down from heaven upon the children of men, to see if there are any who understand, who seek God. They have all turned aside, they have together become corrupt; there is none who does good, No, not one. (Psalm 14:1-3 NKJV)

How could a person think God didn't exist? Everywhere Lindsay looked, she saw the evidence of the Lord working in her life. Creation shouted His glory. It broke her heart that so many have turned away from Him, His truth. No one could be good who turned away from Him. She was so grateful that the Lord had surrounded her with people who kept her on the right path. Who strengthened her and guided her toward her faith in God.

Tears of thankfulness poured from her eyes as her heart overflowed with gratitude.

In her journal, Lindsay told God how thankful she was for Tom and his care for her even after his death. Mark came into her vision and more tears came. He had such a servant's heart. He had been able to be with her in her grief because, as she had learned today, he had walked through plenty of his own grief. She wrote about him in her journal, too.

From deep in her subconscious, Lindsay heard a dull hum. No, it was a beep. No, it was her alarm, from clear across the room! She sat up, confused as to why she was on her chaise instead of in bed. As she walked groggily to the nightstand to turn off the incessant noise, she remembered. *Sorry, I fell asleep on You, Lord. I was enjoying our conversation. But I sure needed that sleep. Thank You, Lord!*

Peace, my daughter. All is well.

Lindsay's heart was filled as she went downstairs and put the coffee on. It had been too long since she had heard the Lord's voice. She chastised herself, knowing that He wasn't the one who had become too busy in recent times to meet with her. She used to meet with Him every morning when she was on this shift, and every evening when she worked days. Now's a great time to reboot!

She went back up the stairs and slipped quietly into Nathan's room. Sitting on the edge of his bed, she whispered to him. "The Bible says in Psalm 118:24, 'This is the day the LORD has made; We will rejoice and be glad in it.' Your Momma says, 'Rise and shine, Bud.' And Jesus says in Matthew 5:16 'Let your light so shine before men, that they may see your good works and glorify your Father in heaven.' Hmm." Lindsay walked her fingers down Nathan's arm. "And if that doesn't work, there's always Mr. Dumbo here." As she reached for the stuffed elephant on his headboard, Nathan started coming to life.

"Aw. Mom, I'm too big for Mr. Dumbo." He turned toward her and gave her a smile-yawn-stretch. "What's for breakfast? I'm hungry."

"And that doesn't surprise me a bit. What sounds good? Eggs? Oatmeal? Pancakes?" She stood so he could throw his legs over the side of the bed. "I'm starting nights today, so I have a bit more time."

"Waffles?" he asked sheepishly. "With walnuts and peanut butter?"

Ah, one of his favorites, and hers too for that matter, and it had been a while since she had made them.

"You got it, Bud," Lindsay said, going to work. "But get a move on or you'll be late." She headed for the door. "Be in the kitchen in fifteen minutes or I will eat them all."

He dashed to the bathroom as she slipped out the door. Waffles would get him moving faster than anything else.

Running down the stairs into the kitchen, she reached up to the open shelf above the stove, pulled down the waffle iron, and plugged it in on the counter. Then she grabbed her cookbook and opened it to Mary Ann's Waffles. This recipe and her waffle iron was a gift from the deaconess at church not too long after they had moved into the townhouse.

"Here we go a-waffling," they had decided to call it, a play on words with the old Christmas song about "a-wassailing". Mary Ann had come to their home and made waffles for them, bringing all the ingredients with her, including the waffle iron, brand new still in the box. The waffle mix was in a canning jar, holding a cup of oatmeal, and filled with a simple boxed pancake mix. "Just add one cup of water," Mary Ann had said.

As Lindsay did just that and whisked the batter, she felt the back of her eyes sting. It hadn't been too long afterward that Mary Ann had passed. And even though Lindsay knew very well that she was joining in the singing with the angels, she still missed her. Lindsay poured the batter into the hot waffle iron, closed it, and flipped it over. As she went to the fridge to get the maple syrup, she remembered that Mary Ann had also brought with her three homemade toppings—blueberry, strawberry, and pineapple. What a treasured memory that night was. She would never make waffles again without remembering this godly servant who had made a place in her heart.

Lindsay put the syrup in the microwave to warm, plated Nathan's waffle, and started her own. She smeared peanut butter lightly over all four sections of his waffle, then sprinkled chopped walnuts over the top. She set the warm syrup on the table and prepared her waffle the same way. Glasses of milk were just being set on the table when Nathan came into the kitchen. They both sat and held hands and Nathan prayed.

Dear Lord, I thank you for a mom who knows how much I love waffles with peanut butter and walnuts. Thank you for the waffles, too. Amen.

At her shaking head and half-smile, he answered her unasked question. "Mom, I think God likes me to talk to Him like He's my friend. That's how Dad talked to Him, so I think it's okay."

"I agree," Lindsay replied. "God *is* your friend. He is your very best friend. But He is also God, so let's be sure and respect Him, too, okay?"

"Yes, ma'am. I get it. Hmm-mmm." He heaped another mouthful into his mouth, but Lindsay could see on his face that he understood her light reprimand.

"Hmm-mmm is right!" she said in agreement. For the next few minutes, they finished their breakfast in silence. She walked upstairs with him and sent him to his room to brush his teeth and grab his book bag. Then she went into her room and picked up her Bible and journal. "You want me to take you to school or do you want to walk?" Lindsay asked as they both came back down the stairs.

"I think I'll walk with Rusty. I haven't seen him since Friday! Love ya, Momma." They shared a healthy hug, and he stepped out the door. Lindsay warmed up her coffee in the microwave as she rinsed the dishes for the dishwasher. She called Chief Marsh and let him know their plans, then she wiped off the table and joined her Bible calling her from the couch. Her journal had always been a two-way communication with God. She wrote her prayer.

Oh, Lord, I'm so sorry to have kept You waiting. But I thank You for being with me all this time, through everything we have discovered in the last couple of weeks. I know I would have been a basket case if You hadn't been there with me. I thank You for bringing Mark into it. I thank You for all he did for me when Tom died, and for all he is doing for Benny, but also for bringing him here now, for me. I don't know what You have in mind for us, Lord, but I am open to Your will—I want what You want, Lord.

She waited for His answer in silence for a little while,

feeling His sweet presence permeate the room. From the depth of her spirit, she heard His comforting voice.

I hear your heart, my daughter. It is nice to be together again like this.

It is, Lord. I'm planning to do this every day this week, to restart this daily routine.

She waited again. She could sense the joy that her pledge brought to God's heart as he spoke again.

I will be here. You have been through a lot lately, and I am glad you sensed Me there with you. I have heard your panic prayers, as you call them. I hear all prayers. Thank you for letting Me lead you. I love it when you let Me be Me. I Am still I Am. Continue to be faithful in all that I have given you to do. I will never leave you.

Thank You, Lord Jesus. I do trust You to always be with me.

Lindsay closed her eyes and lay her head back on the sofa's high tufted back. She just relaxed and felt God's presence with her, basking in the love of her dearly beloved Father. No matter how long between these visits, He always welcomed her with open arms. Lindsay sat for a while, oblivious of time. It was of no concern right then. She felt the warmth of tears flowing down her face and realized she was singing.

For the first time since Tom died, she was singing. "Since I gave to Jesus my poor broken heart, He never has left me alone. Since I for the Homeland eternal did start, He never has left me alone. He never has left me alone."

She closed her journal and laid it and her Bible in the magazine rack. Feeling more peace than she had in quite some time, she got up, put her cup in the dishwasher, and went upstairs to take a shower and get ready for her meeting with Mark and Chief Marsh.

There was another song in her heart. "Jesus is the sweetest name I know. And He's just the same as His lovely Name. And that's the reason why I love Him so; Oh, Jesus is the sweetest name I know."

Lindsay was still singing when she stepped out of the shower, wrapping her hair in a towel. She went to the closet, humming now, and chose a pair of slacks and a tunic top when her cell phone rang. She answered, glancing to see a number but no name on the screen. "Hello."

"Mrs. Davis, this is Lucky. Don't hang up."

Lindsay's heart stopped. She had nearly forgotten about Lucky, and here he was, right in the middle of her joyous time with the Lord.

"If you listen to what I need to tell you, you and your son won't be in danger. But we must talk in person. Alone this time." The line went quiet, and Lindsay knew he was awaiting her answer. *Lord, I need You,* she prayed in her heart and immediately heard the quiet voice of God soothe her.

I am here, my daughter.

"Okay, when and where?" As long as Lucky didn't want to meet in the middle of nowhere, she felt ready now to talk to him without her entourage. Now it was his turn to hesitate, Lindsay noticed.

"There's a little café on 3rd and Madison. How soon can you be there?" Lindsay looked at the clock, 9:15. She had to meet Mark at Chief Marsh's office at 10:30.

"Fifteen minutes," she said with more boldness than she felt.

"Good." The call ended without another word. Lindsay hurriedly finished her makeup. She brushed her hair out and twisted it into a knot at the back of her head. She smiled inwardly as she remembered that Tom expressed amazement, every time she did her hair this way. She donned her necklace and earrings, dressed her feet, and took one last look in the full-length mirror. Satisfied, she grabbed her cell phone and purse and headed downstairs and out the door. *Lord, I am strengthened because You go with me. Help me to make wise choices and listen to You.*

Forty-Six

The café held several patrons laughing over their coffee and finishing breakfasts. Lindsay found an empty booth and sat and waited. The waitress took her order of coffee. Lindsay felt perfectly relaxed and more curious than anything. She had made it here a little quicker than she expected, so she was waiting patiently. The waitress brought her coffee, and Lindsay realized she didn't need any more caffeine, nor did she want it, but she poured the creamer into her cup anyway. She stirred her coffee, waiting—not so patiently. *Where is he?*

When her cup was nearly empty, a man stood from a table near her and walked over to her booth. He stood looking around, then spoke. "You're alone this time, Mrs. Davis?" She didn't answer, and he shifted to face her but remained standing. "I'm Gerard McKenzie, otherwise known as Lucky. Listen close, 'cause I don't have the time to repeat this."

Lindsay straightened and leaned forward, her forearms crossed on the table in front of her. Finally, he sat down across from her, eyes combing the room. "Your husband hired me six years ago. If anything ever happened to him, it was my job to keep an eye on you from a distance. You weren't ever supposed to know that I was around, but he paid me good money to be sure you never got hurt."

"Who is trying to—" Lindsay's voice failed her.

"Please. Just listen." Again he eyed the room nervously. "Your husband pulled some strings to get into the firm he worked for, and the partners weren't happy about it. Then they found out that he was gathering information on them to give to the cops. That's why he was killed. They have connections. And the partners hired some thugs. They followed him to a meeting with a woman that was helping him get the goods on them, and when they left the meeting, they killed both of them. They weren't together, but they killed both of them near the same place and at the same time. You've got to believe me, I was there, and I saw it. I had just met with him, and he went to meet her. It happened so quickly, I couldn't do a thing." Lindsay was watching his face as his eyes filled. "I'm taking a chance even being seen with you, but I had to let you know I am not a threat to you." He looked around nervously. "No, I've gotta go. I'll call you." Before Lindsay could catch her breath, he was gone again.

She looked around and could see nothing amiss anywhere. The people who were there when she walked in were pretty much the same ones that were here now. Maybe he saw something else. She paid for her coffee and walked out, looking around to see if she could see him anywhere, but Lucky was gone. *Now, what do I do? Do I tell Mark and Chief Marsh? Of course, I have to, but I don't want anyone to be in any further danger.*

As Lindsay walked back to her Jeep, she realized she was believing Lucky's story. Was that the wise thing to do? Glancing at her watch, she decided to go ahead and go to the chief's office downtown, even though she would be early. As she parked in the visitors' parking area of the City Municipal Building, she saw Mark's truck. *Good, he's here.*

She went to the left wing of the building and checked in. She hadn't sat down yet when she was called to follow the young lady behind the receptionist's desk. Chief Marsh opened his door just as she arrived, and the young lady did a graceful U-turn back to her desk. After greetings, the chief motioned her to a chair facing his desk, beside the one where Mark had been sitting. As she entered, he stood. As she sat, both men sat down.

"I have news." She started a bit nervously. Mark and the chief looked at her expectantly. She wasn't sure how to proceed other than just spit it out. "I just met with Lucky." Eyebrows raised on both men, and Mark turned in his chair to better face her. "He called me this morning and asked to meet, and I did. I didn't sense any fear, and I'm glad I went because I don't think he is a danger." Lindsay realized she was talking as fast as her heart was beating, so she took a breath and squirmed a bit in her chair before she continued.

"He told me that Tom had hired him to protect me if anything happened to him. He told me that he had witnessed the murder of Tom and Pam, and they had been killed right after they had a meeting, that Pam was helping Tom find evidence against the firm. He said that even being seen with me could be dangerous for both of us, then he kinda panicked and left." She took a breath and leaned back against the chair, blowing the air out so she could breathe better.

Mark and Chief Marsh looked at each other. "Is that everything he said?" the chief asked.

"I think so. He is protecting me." She forced herself to think. He talked so fast. "Oh, his name is McKenzie. Oh, shoot, I don't remember his first name. I'm sorry. I think that's everything."

Mark reached over and took her hand. She appreciated the strength he offered, but she was learning that she was growing in her own strength and faith. "So, Lindsay, I filled Chief Marsh in on the most recent discoveries. I hope you don't mind. I only got here just a bit before you did."

"No, that's fine; thank you, Mark. So, Chief, what do we do now?"

The chief rocked back in his wood desk chair and screwed his face up to one side, thinking.

"I'll relay this latest information to David Harrell, so he can share it with the FBI and Mrs. Coleman. I think, Lindsay, that your best move is to fly out to Washington and go to South Dakota, and look over all the properties you own. Pick one to move to and *do it. And do it now.*"

Lindsay nodded hesitantly. "But aren't they – I mean is my family in more danger with me gone?"

"I will assign deputies to run by your mother's house on a regular basis. We'll keep close tabs on them while you're gone." Chief leaned toward her. "I will investigate this Mr. Lucky McKenzie and see if I can track him by his nickname. Maybe I can determine if Lucky has been honest with you. I still believe he is connected to a casino, but as I said earlier, there wasn't one by that name. We'll keep looking into that. I don't want you to do any investigation on this end. If you back off, maybe they will think you've given up." He straightened in his chair. "You can check into the properties. Just talk to people and feel them out. Watch their reaction. Trust your gut, if something just doesn't feel right."

"Chief, I am not a spy." Lindsay declared.

"Of course, I understand." The chief reached for her arm. "But you are an intelligent and intuitive woman. Trust your instincts. Actually, it's better that you aren't a spy. Just go in the guise of inspecting your newly acquired properties. Focus on getting you, your son, your whole family, if that's what you want, to somewhere behind the front lines, to safety."

Lindsay nodded, thoughtfully. "Am I—are we—" She didn't know how to phrase her question. "Chief, I'm afraid of leaving my family here, while I go look at these properties. Do I - do we need to become different people?" Mark and the chief looked at each other.

"We've been thinking about that. At this point, I don't think so, but keep your plans under wraps for now. I think you are safe for now because they don't know what you know." He sat up in his chair with a jolt. "But please don't meet with Lucky again without giving us a heads up. It could have been dangerous, and if he thinks he is in danger of being seen with you, that means you would be, too."

"I understand. It just came up so quickly." Lindsay stood and Mark stood with her.

"Thanks, Chief. If you'll excuse us, we have a lunch date." The chief smiled and stood as they shook hands and left his office, Mark reaching for Lindsay's hand, and Lindsay accepting it quite naturally.

"Where would you like to eat?" Mark asked her as they got in his truck. "We're early, so we could run to Davenport if you want to," he asked.

"Where do you have in mind?" She smiled.

"There's a little Mexican food place where we could get in and out and have you at work twenty minutes early," Mark suggested. Lindsay looked at her watch and agreed with his assessment. The authentic restaurant had quickly become a favorite.

"Sounds good." They chatted amicably as they drove out of town. When the conversation lulled, she spoke. "So, would you be able to take a day or two off, to make a trip to Washington?" She looked over at him, sideways.

"Of course." He smiled. "You tell me when you can get off work, and I'll do what I can to make it work."

"Okay; I'll have to check with Melissa and Crystal to see when one of them can cover for me." She thought about the arrangements with Nathan as well as her job. "I'm thinking maybe Thursday and Friday this week. As much as I want to go out and see the properties, I really want to meet the people. Maybe they know something about what Tom got into!"

"That makes sense." Mark spoke thoughtfully.

"We'll need to get airline tickets and hotel rooms," Lindsay replied. "You've done more research than I have. Where is the closest airport?" They parked and went into the Mexican restaurant.

"Why don't you leave that part of it to me? SeaTac is about two hours away, but it is the closest. I'll rent a car while we're there." He smiled.

"That works for me, if your brother will let me bump his appointment to next week." Mark smiled.

Lindsay was beginning to enjoy seeing his easy smile. "Tell him I said so." Lindsay opened her menu. "I don't know why I even look at menus! I always order either enchiladas or taco salad."

"Mexican food is one of my favorites, but I don't like spicy hot." Mark perused his menu.

"Just a bit of a bite," they said simultaneously and laughed.

Lindsay continued, "I agree completely! I'd like to do the entree with beans and rice, but their servings are usually so big! Would you care to split something?"

That was the plan, and they talked casually, sharing likes and dislikes. They learned they had a lot in common. Lindsay became more and more comfortable with him. But she was still confident that he wasn't telling her his whole story. There was a gap around his military service.

She knew a lot of military folks didn't care to share, but she hoped one day he might trust her with all his story. She would never judge him. She had no right to judge anyone. Putting the menu to the side, she prayed silently that God would give them both the strength to be fully honest with each other, that they would both stand in His truth.

Lindsay and Mark finished their meal, and as he dropped her off at her car, he took her hand. "This was nice, Lindsay. Thanks for coming with me."

"Thank you, Mark. It was nice, and isn't it a great restaurant!" She felt content and was humming again as she drove to the manor. She felt successful at filing away her recent meeting with Lucky into the very back shelf of her mind.

Forty-Seven

Lindsay was still humming about her date with Mark hours later as she and Crystal were bringing the residents in for supper.

"You're in a good mood today, dear," Betty greeted her as she came into her room to take her to the dining hall. "Did you have a Sunny Sunday?"

Lindsay smiled. "I did, thank you. I spent a lovely day with my family, went for a nice long walk, and watched a movie." She picked out the happy parts of her weekend and kept Lucky filed away.

Norman was passing as she was moving Betty down the hall, and Richard, pushing Margie's wheelchair, joined them at the nurse's station. She wheeled Betty into the dining room and seated her next to Margie. The others in the parade took their places as if they were assigned. Norman, of course, sat next to Opal.

Lindsay often thought it interesting that the residents created their hierarchy. They rarely had two residents who did not get along, but little groups were formed. All these elderlies were like family.

This group was adamant that they all wanted to sit at one table. "After all," Norman said, "we're family." Mr. Foster was agreeable to their requests, so the maintenance staff had pulled three square tables together to allow room for wheelchairs as well as straight chairs for those folks using walkers, and the staff could still maneuver around the family-style setting. There was no need here for names to be taped on the edges of the tables. Everyone knew Norman was at the head and Richard at the foot. Margie and Opal were on one side, Betty and Grace on the other.

Supper encountered only one mishap when Grace spilled her green beans on Betty, which threw poor Betty into a fretful cry. Lindsay was happy that both women had nearly finished eating, so it was easier to deal with. Of course, Grace was sincerely apologetic, and Betty kept saying, "Oh, it's nothing," but Lindsay saw Betty's face begging her to help quickly, which she did. She snatched up the three loose beans that made it to Betty's lap, and tossing them on her nearly empty plate, backed Betty up and swept her away to her room for a clean blouse.

Even with the quirks that she dealt with regularly, these people had become an extension of her family. Her meeting with Lucky had prompted a new concern. She had been so adamant about keeping her family safe, but she now realized that these dear elderlies were family, too, and could be in danger just because she worked here. It would be easy enough, Lindsay thought, for anyone with evil intentions to follow her, to learn what shift she was working. *Lord, please tell me how to keep them safe.*

As soon as she had formed the prayer, Mark's words drifted through her mind. "You don't have to work another day in your life if you don't want to." Maybe that was it. She should probably turn in her resignation right away before it was too late. That would actually free her to pursue Tom's passion full-time, without shortchanging her job or her family. Oh, but she would miss them. Lindsay felt the stress leaving her. *Thank you, Lord. But I can't do it alone.*

I AM HERE, MY DAUGHTER. I WILL ALWAYS BE WITH YOU.

She had Betty re-dressed, and in the Commons well in time for the Monday movie the group always watched together. Betty motioned to Lindsay to park her near Grace. Lindsay smiled, knowing that Betty wanted to assure Grace of their continued good relationship. As the two women neared each other, both smiled, reaching for the other's hand, and holding it in silent comradeship for several minutes before they dropped hands, and prepared for the movie.

Lindsay took advantage of the movie to find Melissa and ask her if she could cover for her on Thursday and Friday. "Sure! I have to miss Wednesday for a dentist's appointment! You want to cover for me? That'll work out great." The details were worked out, and Mr. Foster approved the arrangement.

Lindsay considered giving him a heads-up on her upcoming resignation, but she hadn't prayed about it or talked to her mom or Mark. She took the time to call Mark and let him know they were good for the trip, but she didn't approach her resignation yet. The movie ended all too quickly, and the residents were tired and ready for bed when they were wheeled back to their rooms. Lindsay was next to Richard as he pushed Margie's wheelchair. "You know, Miss Lindsay, my son, Matt, will be so disappointed when he learns of your cowboy."

Lindsay could feel herself blush. "You behave, Richard. You know your son knows nothing of this arrangement you came up with!" She was hoping that would be the end of it as she pushed Betty along beside them, but dear quiet Betty picked up the conversation.

"Well, I think it's delightful, dear. You would make such a lovely couple." Margie was clapping her hands in agreement.

"You are all terrible!" Lindsay blushed. "How would you know anyway, Missy?" Lindsay kissed Margie on the cheek. "You only saw him once when he picked me up! And you're all jumping the gun. Trust me, I will let you know if there's anything to get excited about."

Betty was nearly asleep before Lindsay got her tucked in. Margie gave her no problem at all. They were both worn out. Lindsay was so glad that all her elderlies generally slept all night, and when Norman woke up, he was easily assuaged and ready to go back to bed.

Grace was a bit talkative tonight. She was still concerned about how clumsy she was with that bite of green beans that got away from her. Lindsay sat with her for a few minutes and comforted her, reminding her of what a sweetheart Betty was, accepting her apology. "You need to know, Grace, that it was Betty's idea to sit next to you during the movie. She didn't want you to think she was upset with you. So don't be upset with yourself, okay?"

"It was? You didn't just seat her by me? You know, Lindsay, we don't always get to sit where we want to sit."

Grace was looking at her square in the eye, silver hair splashing across her pillow.

"It was all her idea. But, Grace, you can always speak up and say where you want to sit. I don't want you sitting next to someone you don't want to sit by." She watched Grace's expression change and her eyes sparkle.

"Oh, I'm just talking, girlie. Don't you think a thing about it. There's no one here that I don't love like a sister or a brother, and that goes for you, too, only you're more like my granddaughter." Lindsay bent over and leaned into Grace's outstretched arms. "Good night, my dear."

"Good night, Grandma Grace." Lindsay patted her, and the expression on her face made her walk out of the room before she felt the tears slipping down her cheeks. It wasn't good to get too attached to these wonderful folks, but for Lindsay, it was way too late. These were all her grandparents.

Lindsay hadn't known her father's parents at all, and her mom's parents died two years apart. She was in her early teens, and she remembered them well, especially her grandma. Lindsay was still thinking about them as she sat taking a break in the Commons, listening to the 10:00 news. It would be so hard to leave these precious people. They had become a huge part of her life.

Hearing the sound of whimpering, she slipped quietly into Norman's room. Lindsay sat gently on the side of his bed, listening to his cries for his children. She softly ran her hand along his forearm, whispering. "Shh—they're with Jesus, Norman, happy and singing with the angels. Shh." He stopped calling their names, but he was not asleep.

"They are, aren't they, Lindsay? Jesus is there holding

them, isn't he?" He never turned to look at her. He never changed positions. As Lindsay rested her hand on his shoulder, he just relaxed, taking a deep breath.

"I believe He is, Norman." She just sat there, not sure if he was drifting back to sleep or thinking of what he wanted to say.

"We never raised our kids to know Jesus. It wasn't until we lost the girls that we figured it out. But it was too late for them. They died in the fire, and I keep dreaming they're still burning!" He sat up on the side of the bed, and she sat near him with her arms cradling him as he rocked.

"Oh, but they aren't, Norman." She tasted her salty tears. "God doesn't allow innocents in hell. They are not there! Jesus has them. He's holding them, rocking them, just like I am rocking you." *Lord God, please let him see the truth. Let him be comforted by my words to his heart.* "Norman, it is not the will of our Father in heaven that one of these little ones should perish." She sat beside him until he started to relax and dropped his arms which had raised to hold her arms tightly against his chest. As he lay back in bed, she stood and lifted the blanket over his feet, and tucked him in.

"You're right, Lindsay. I love your words," he said.

"They aren't my words, Norman. They are God's words. Go to sleep now and rest." Lindsay stood in his doorway, waiting for his breathing to settle. She realized she was humming and praying again. *Thank you, Lord, for cradling this broken-hearted father in your hands. You know his heart, Father. You have a father's heart. You can understand his loss like no one else can. Help him to sleep well and to see his daughters in the arms of Your Son.*

Forty-Eight

The rest of the night was quiet, and she was ready when her shift was over, but she kept remembering Norman's nightmares. The very thought of thinking your own child was burning in hell was terrifying. Lindsay was grateful to know that Nathan had accepted Jesus as his Savior when he was nine years old. He had signed up for church camp and then decided he didn't want to go. He and Tom had sat at the kitchen table after supper discussing the dilemma. Lindsay could still hear Tom's question as she drove home from work.

"Why did you sign up?" Tom had asked him nonchalantly. Lindsay had overheard their conversation and remembered it well. Nathan talked about hanging out around a bonfire, having weenie roasts, and roasting marshmallows for s'mores. Tom was so patient with him and so wise. He handled this in the same method, asking questions until Nathan thought of the right thing to do.

She was surprised when Nathan told Tom the story. When Nathan signed up, Rusty was going to be at his grandma's that week, but then his grandma got sick and couldn't go. So Rusty would be home alone. Tom had told him how considerate that was, but that the camp had saved a place for him and—"a place that another boy would have been able to use, except now, you have it." Then Tom had volunteered to pay for Rusty's way to camp.

Lindsay was thrilled when Nathan jumped up from the table with excitement. Tom called Rusty's father that same night, and it was all arranged. Little did they know that God had already arranged the whole camping trip. Nathan and Rusty both gave their lives to Jesus at camp that year. Tears came to Lindsay's eyes as she realized that it was just months before Tom was killed. *Lord, thank you for letting Tom have the assurance of knowing before he died that Nathan made that decision.*

Through Lindsay's tears, she saw bright lights in the rearview mirror. She ducked a bit so she could see better but realized the car was getting closer. She turned away from home and went toward town, hoping they weren't following her, but they turned also. Quickly she commanded her phone to call Chief Marsh and explained the situation.

"Lindsay, where are you right now? Look around you. Stay calm but don't stop." Chief Marsh was trying to calm her down while his own heart was racing.

"I'm not sure, Chief." She answered. Another turn, a little faster, but they were right on her tail. *Oh, Lord, what do I do?* After a breath, she realized where she was, and turned onto Main Street—the most brightly lit street in town. "Oh, I'm downtown, near the Police Station."

"Good, I'm in my office, I'll meet you in the lobby."

She hit the accelerator and pushed into the huge parking lot speckled with black and white police cars. She slammed on the brakes, and jumped out of the car. Watching where the car went, she ran up the steps and plowed into three uniformed police officers, who embraced her to keep her from falling.

"That car was chasing me! I didn't know where else to go! Chief Marsh is here, waiting for me." Her voice was trembling.

"You did right, Miss. Come on in." One of the officers led her in and the other two ran down the steps to see if they could find the car, but it had turned too quickly to see where it went.

Lindsay sat nervously looking around, hoping to see the chief. She accepted the cup of coffee the officer handed her as he sat at his desk facing her. "What can you tell me?" The chief rounded the corner and walked quickly to where she was.

"Oh, Chief! I was on my way home from work. Suddenly, I realized he was behind me with his brights on. And he got closer and then I turned, hoping he wasn't following me, but he was. And I called you. And he skidded around behind me, so when I realized how close I was to here, I just turned." Lindsay stopped. After she took several deep breaths, she answered the chief's questions.

"Did you know the car? Was it a man?" The officer wrote notes but never looked up, as Chief Marsh asked the questions.

"I think it was a man, yes—the shadow had short hair like a man—light hair, either gray or blonde," Lindsay took another shaky breath. "I didn't recognize the car, but it looked like a big Suburban—dark color."

As the two officers returned, they stopped at the desk where Lindsay was sitting with Chief Marsh.

"I'm sorry, miss, we weren't able to see the vehicle." Chief Marsh asked one of the officers to follow her home, to make her feel safer. Then he addressed the officer at the desk.

"Corporal, pass the word that Mrs. Davis is to be looked after any time she calls or comes in. She has a legitimate reason to be concerned." Chief shook her hand as he was giving instructions and walked to the door with her and her escort. She felt safe for tonight, but what about tomorrow?

Her alarm went off way too early, and she felt like she hadn't slept at all. Lindsay went downstairs, made the coffee, and came back upstairs, meeting Nathan on the stairs. "Hey, Bud." She wrapped him in her arms and sat on the steps, holding him tight. "Why are you up so early?"

"I dunno," he said, sleepily.

"Come on, let's get you back to bed and you can get another hour's sleep." She tucked him back in and laid down beside him, quietly singing "Amazing Grace". Lindsay needed the warmth of her son next to her for a few minutes. It didn't take long for Nathan's breathing to become steady and even. She slipped off his bed and took a quick shower, donning jeans and a tee shirt. She went downstairs and made

French toast while she was drinking her coffee, letting Nathan sleep as long as possible. She crept back upstairs, tiptoed into his room, and slipped back onto the bed carefully and started singing. It didn't take long for him to roll over, pretending to be asleep, and throw his arm around her neck.

"Oh, 'scuse me, ma'am. I thought you were my Dumbo." He giggled.

"Likely story! You just wanted to steal a hug from me!" She hugged him firmly, squeezing him tight as he giggled more. "Up and at 'em, kiddo. Your French toast awaits you! Hop in the shower. I laid your clothes out here for you."

She left the room when he got out of bed and stumbled toward the bathroom. He was up too late last night, and it was her fault. She called Mom on her way back to the kitchen and arranged for him to stay with her tonight. She told Mom about the Washington trip, and she agreed to cover that as well.

She had plated the French toast and was pouring his milk as Nathan came in and sat down at the table. She poured her coffee and joined him, holding out her hands. He put his in hers and began to pray.

Lord, thank you for this French toast that smells so good. Thank you for my mom and my gran. Help us through this day. Amen.

She took a sip of her coffee, before cutting into her breakfast, so he beat her to the first "Hmm," She smiled as she put the sweet cinnamon pastry in her mouth.

"Hmm-mmm." The taste reminded her of the churros that Maria had made for them. "Hey, Bud. I'm going to work a double tomorrow, so I think tonight you can stay over with Gran and then go to school, okay? That way you'll get a good night's sleep."

"That's great, Mom. Uncle Benny's going to be there tomorrow night for supper, too." He was bubbling over with being able to shoot hoops, "so Benny doesn't get bored while he's there."

Lindsay laughed. "But you'll be staying a little more than that."

Nathan looked up, stuffing another forkful in his mouth. "What's up?"

"You know the properties we looked at Saturday?" At his nod, she continued. "Well, there are some more properties across the United States, so Mark and I are going to fly out to the West Coast and look at them. I don't think they are places we would want to live, but I need to go see them to decide whether to sell them or not. So you'll stay with Gran tomorrow night and Thursday, and I should be home on Friday."

"Cool! Take pictures. I wanna see it, okay? It'll be great, Momma. Gran's kinda lonely sometimes." His tender heart always caught her off guard.

"Ride or walk to school?" she asked him.

"Yeah, you're all dressed. I'll ride today," he answered with a mouthful of cinnamon and syrup.

"Okay, I'll take some extra clothes over to Gran's before I go to work today. Anything special you want?" She wondered if he would want his elephant.

"No, I don't think so. Clothes are clothes, Mom." He gave her that look that reminded her how grown-up he was becoming. It felt like just last week he was upset because his favorite shirt was still in the laundry the day after he last wore it.

She dropped him at school, received his hug while they were still in the car, and drove back home. She went about her normal duties, cleaning the kitchen, throwing in a load of laundry, and going upstairs to pack him a duffel bag. As an afterthought, she stuffed Mr. Dumbo in one end of the duffel bag, then slipped his Sunday School quarterly in the side pocket and drove over to Arlene's house. She wasn't looking forward to at least part of this conversation.

Forty-Nine

Having coffee with Mom was always one of the things Lindsay enjoyed the most. Rather than rush off, she took her time. They laughed about silly things and cried about memories that had been rekindled at the ranch on Saturday. But the cloud over her was her recent conversation with Lucky.

"I'm excited about the trip to Washington," Lindsay told her mom, refilling Arlene's cup. "The place is called Heavenly Acres, and it looks like a pretty big place; at least in my imagination it is!" Lindsay laughed. "But there is another piece of property out there, too, so we're going to see them both."

"It sounds like it is appropriately named," Arlene replied. "You said they have horses?"

"It does, but I don't know if they're theirs, or if they belong to the ranch or to Riding for Dreams," Lindsay replied.

"What is Riding for Dreams anyway?" Arlene asked.

"Well, I don't know too much about it, but they reach

out to help at-risk kids through horses," Lindsay explained.

"Sounds like a great organization," Arlene replied. "You used to spend a lot of hours on your horse, especially when you had a rough day at school."

"Yeah, Josie." They sat quietly, just remembering. Then Lindsay whispered, "Mom, I hope you know that Mark and I—"

"You don't have to say another word, dear. I understand. Mark has been so helpful, and you're just friends." She repeated the words Lindsay had said only a few weeks ago.

"We-l-l," The pitch of Lindsay's voice raised as they both smiled. "Mom, can I ask you something?"

"Sure, sweetie." Arlene looked into her daughter's beautiful blue eyes.

Lindsay took a deep breath and blew it away before she continued. "When Dad died... how did you—you know. How did you decide it was time to— How did you move on emotionally? And how did you—"

"Decide to date again?" Mom winked as she smiled.

"Yeah, I guess." She suddenly felt shy and giddy—that would have been her mother's word—but it fit. "Because, you know, I don't want to do anything that affects my baby boy negatively."

Her mom offered another cup, which Lindsay declined. "You know I like Mark, and I think he's good for both you and Nathan."

Lindsay felt herself blush. "He is pretty great, and he is —it's just—I kinda feel like I may not be ready to just move on." Lindsay was so glad she was able to spend time this morning with her precious mother.

"I know you, sweet girl," Arlene began. "Come over here, so I can pray for you." Lindsay took her mother's extended hands as she sat beside her. "When your dad died, it was difficult to face life alone. I lost my husband, my best friend, and my spiritual covering. But God leads us if we're paying attention. For me, I felt that it was okay for me to go forward. In fact, in recent months, I've felt free to maybe find someone else myself. I just haven't found him yet. But I believe I will know him when I see him."

"Oh, Mom, I'm so glad." Lindsay squeezed Arlene's hands.

"But the point is, my darling girl," Arlene whispered, "it's okay for you to be open to someone new. If you feel it here." Arlene touched her heart. "And if you know that God puts that feeling there."

Lindsay could hardly speak.

"Mom," Lindsay whispered. "There is one more thing we need to talk about before we pray." Lindsay cleared her throat, watching her mom's gentle eyes resting on hers. "I, um, I haven't been totally honest with you about our current situation."

"Oh?" Arlene said nothing more.

"Well, not exactly hiding." Lindsay was struggling with how to tell her mother how serious the situation was. "You know we're in a bit of danger, and that's why we're looking at moving, but—"

"Lindsay, dear, what on earth is going on?" Arlene leaned forward, elbows on the table.

"Well, that's just it, Mom." Lindsay took a deep breath. "We don't really know what's going on. But we do know that Tom lost his life pursuing something, and I feel like I have to follow it through to its end. I also know that by doing that, I'm putting my family in danger." Lindsay saw her mom look down and fold her hands, patiently giving her daughter the space she needed. "Mom, I'm scared that the people in the nursing home are in danger just because I work there."

"Oh, dear!" Arlene's eyebrows went up as she sat taller. "Of course, they could be! I understand now why— oh my poor dear, what are you thinking?"

"Well, last night, a car followed me, and drove kind of recklessly, so I turned off quickly and went to the police station. But the car got away. "Please pray, Mom," Lindsay looked at her own folded hands. "I think the Lord is freeing me from work. I mean with everything I'm learning about what Tom set up, I don't financially need to work. And as much as I love the Manor, I wouldn't be able to live with myself if anything happened to any of them because I work there. And I don't know who it was, so they could find out where we live." "

"Of course not." Arlene unfolded her hands and reached once again for her daughter's hands. "We definitely need to pray, don't we, sweetie?"

Lindsay's throat closed, but she nodded.

Dear Lord, God, we are so grateful for all Your blessings, for who You are in our lives, Lindsay's mom prayed. Hearing her mom's words made it all okay. She heard that sweet voice again. *I thank You, Lord, that You have known Lindsay since before she was born and that she has known You nearly that long. I thank You most, Lord Jesus, that she hears Your voice and is obedient to You. I ask that You continue to speak loudly and clearly to her regarding Mark and that she continues to follow You as You lead her. I believe, Lord God, that Mark is Your choice for my precious girl, but if he is not, I ask also that You speak quickly before her heart gets any more attached than it already is. Let them hear You and obey, keeping pace with You. Let them not lag behind, nor get ahead of You. We thank You, Lord God, for the compassion You placed in Lindsay's heart. We give You thanks for the ease with which Lindsay cares for others. We are grateful that it also leads her to pour herself deeply where You place her. That's what makes it difficult for my dear girl to say goodbye when You ask her to move on to Your next challenge. We trust You, Lord. Speak. We ask You to keep all those elderlies safe for her, and her and her family as well. Your servants are listening. Thank You for hearing my prayer, O Lord God. Amen.*

Arlene sniffed and reached for the nearby tissue as she patted Lindsay on the knee. "You go take care of business and get to know each other a bit better. Find out everything you can about these places and people. Pray together. I'll be praying for you both, and Nathan and I won't miss you at all," she teased.

"Sure, Mom, forget all about me when you've got Nat and Benny here." She teased back. "I hope you have a good time with the guys. How is Benny doing?"

"Lindsay, I think he's doing very well." Arlene's voice remained tender. "He calls me a lot, and he's talking to Janet more. She's being nicer to him and he's being nicer to her. He says he will always have PTSD, but he's hoping to keep it under control without the alcohol. Mark's counseling has helped him so much!" Her mother's face glowed with excitement at the thought of having her son back.

Lindsay knew it wasn't that easy, but between God answering their fervent prayers and Mark doing everything possible on his end, maybe it would be a possibility down the road. Living with PTSD couldn't be easy.

"Well, I'd better get going, I've got clothes in the washer, and I need to get myself ready for work and this trip." She stood and hugged her mom. "It's so nice to have you so close, Mom. By the way, have you thought any more about moving with us?"

"I've done better than that, I've been praying about it, and I'm thinking it could just work out. We'll talk about it when you get back. I do love being close to you, too." She gave her another squeeze, and Lindsay walked toward the door.

"Love you, Mom." Lindsay said.

Her mother laughed. "To the moon—"

"And back," Lindsay finished, smiling. Arlene stood and quietly laid her hand on Lindsay's shoulder, squeezing it as she released her hand and walked away.

Lindsay stood thoughtfully. Lucky had told her she and her family wouldn't be in danger if she did what he told her to do. But who was Lucky? Could she trust him?

After the car followed her, Lindsay decided she would call Chief Marsh. She wasn't about to go to Washington without him taking some extra care of her family and the elderlies. Even not being sure about Lucky, she was ready to move; the question was where? When? It wouldn't hurt to start downsizing and pack some of the things she knew they would keep, no matter where they moved. So where? The Homestead? Maybe, but that was a little weird, with it being a replica of everything here at the townhouse. Or the Presidential Palace? Nathan would never be comfortable in a place like that—way too fancy. Maybe they could spend the summer there and decide on a permanent place later.

As much as Lindsay loved her townhouse, she knew. It was time to move on—without Tom. To move forward with Mark. Where would they be the safest? Would they be safe anywhere? *And for what dangers do I need to be on the lookout?*

What's Next?

The End

Want to read more of the adventures of Lindsay and her
loved ones?
Watch for Book 2 in the Momopoly series.

About the Author

In her hunger for God's truth, Dr. Hutchins is continually seeking God's heart for the wisdom He wants to impart to His Church today. She conveys that wisdom through speaking at women's groups and conferences and holding weekly online Bible Studies. Karen married her husband, Hutch, in 2003, and they have been active in ministry, both jointly and individually, ever since. She joined Christian Motorcyclists Association (CMA) in 2003 and enjoys riding her Harley both for ministry and for fun.

She has authored several books: *The Truth About Angels; Does God Really Still Speak?; No Strings Attached; The Unconditional Love of the Savior, Breakfast With the King, and Protective Custody; Miracles Can Happen When God Has You Right Where He Wants You.*

At First Baptist Church in Lisbon, ND, Karen has led worship, served as church clerk, performed administrative duties, and assisted her husband in his duties as lead pastor. She also facilitated a weekly Bible Study at the Villa Assisted Living Facility in Forman, ND and LAP (Ladies at the Parsonage) Study in Lisbon. She served as North Dakota State Chaplain for the American Legion for four years, which she had to relinquish with her recent retirement.

Her move in 2023, to the beautiful Ozarks of Missouri has opened a new adventure for Hutch and herself, enabling more time to facilitate her Monday Night Live Bible Studies on Facebook as well as spending time with her husband, her horse Amigo, and her Dachshund-Chihuahua mix, Abi. Karen's son, Jason Breshears, lives in the Houston area with his wife, Jennifer, and their daughters, Hannah Breshears and Hayley Sauceda, Hayley's husband Matthew, and her great-granddaughter.

www.ingramcontent.com/pod-product-compliance
Lightning Source LLC
Chambersburg PA
CBHW032121050726

47591CB00010B/1209